FINDING HOME

BRIDGET E. BAKER

For Whitney
I am just as happy today as I was on our wedding day that we chose to find a home with one another. <3

FOREWORD

This book was a tricky one to write because I decided (for better or worse) to use a real country for Cole and Paisley's home. That means that I spent hours researching the House Law and the Liechtenstein law. (I even read the Constitution—twice!) I did not want to write about the actual Princely family, but I wanted to use the real history.

That resulted in a sort of mish-mash of odd characters loosely based on real people, and also a bunch of characters who are entirely and utterly fictitious. For instance, Cole and Paisley's father is entirely fictitious, as is Cole. Cole's father's brothers who are mentioned are also not real. However, I did draw on some family elements to come up with the dynasts.

So—if you're reading something about their past, it's probably spot on. (Or as spot on as an American who has only been to Vaduz once in her life can get!) If, however, you are reading about the present, assume it's utterly fiction. I hope this enriches the experience instead of confusing you! Liechtenstein is a fascinating country and I had a wonderful time when we visited.

1

BETH

I botched my very first haircut.

Badly.

Luckily, the college student whose hair I was cutting liked that the sides of her bob were uneven—she asked me to make the difference even more dramatic, and I dyed her hair a deep ebony for free. I still recall the sound of her combat boots clomping against the Aveda Institute's wooden floors as she strutted out. But now, six years later, my hands don't shake, my heart doesn't race, and my breath doesn't hitch when a new client with ultra thick hair down to her bum asks, "Can you do a long feathered bob?"

I'm at least as comfortable now with a pair of scissors in my hand as I am without.

"Do you have an interest in donating to Locks of Love?" I ask.

She sighs. "I wish, but I went gray super early, and I color my own hair."

"That's too bad," I say. "Because you have a lot of hair." Now that she mentions it, I can feel the color in her hair. I must have been distracted, to have missed it before.

"I have too much hair," she says. "And I'm sick of getting headaches from all the weight."

"We can take care of that." I pump the seat up repeatedly. Being abnormally tall in my profession is a little obnoxious, but my boss, Persephone, ordered me a special, high lift chair, and that has helped my back tremendously. Watching all her deep brown hair falling to the floor in sheets when I start snipping is a high that's hard to replicate.

"What prompted the change?" I expect one of the standard responses: new job, new baby, new relationship, or the most common of all, divorce.

"Nothing, really," she says softly. "I just woke up this morning and realized that I've been in a rut. Same job, same boyfriend, same apartment. It's time for a change. Does that sound crazy?"

"Do you like your job?" I ask.

She shrugs. "I don't *not* like it."

"What about the boyfriend?"

"Same." She laughs half-heartedly. "This sounds really depressing. But maybe I'll start by changing my hair and go from there."

"Not a bad plan," I say, ignoring the buzz coming from the phone in my pocket. Probably a telemarketer.

Snip, snip, even, feather. My hands fly across Virginia's hair, almost without thinking. Thick hair in cute, short styles is all about layers, layers, layers. By the time I finish and spread a little more smoothly on the edges, my spirits are lifted. She looks transformationally different. Younger, stronger, more energetic. I spin the chair around.

I expect her to grin from ear to ear. I expect her to gush. I did an amazing job, and she looks adorable. She should be delighted.

Her face falls. "What if Steve hates it? Oh no, oh no!"

She begins to breathe in quick, shallow breaths. "What have I done?"

My phone rings in my pocket. Again. I ignore it. "I'm so sorry to hear that you don't like it."

She shakes her head. "It's not your fault. But, oh, what was I thinking?"

"Sometimes it's a shock at first, but it might grow on you."

Her eyes widen and then pool with tears.

Good grief. "I'm so sorry that you hate it."

She wipes at her eyes. "No, please, it's not your fault. You did a beautiful thing. It really does look exactly like the picture I showed you. Thank you." She chokes and drops her face into her hands.

My phone rings again. Geez. I sneak a look at it while she's sobbing. Unknown number. Well, it's not like I can take the call right now. Hopefully they'll leave me a message. I pat Virginia's back and murmur that things will get better. I'm not quite sure how, but a moment later she's hugging me.

This is a strange job sometimes.

My last client is right on time—an uptight businessman who usually makes me nuts. But after the mess from earlier, Mr. Predictable is a real relief. I trim a quarter inch off his hair like I do every ten days without fail. He tips me exactly twelve percent, and I'm finally done for the day. I hang up my apron and disinfect my clippers and my scissors and wave to my boss on the way out. "Night, Persephone," I say.

"Goodnight, Beth! I forgot to tell you that I can't make it tonight, but I bet you have a big turnout."

She almost always comes to see me perform on Thursdays. "No problem! See you tomorrow." I unlock my Civic with the press of a button and pull my phone out of my pocket to see who called.

"Beth!"

The sound of my name makes me jump, and I very nearly drop my phone in the gutter. I look up and meet my brother's bright blue eyes. "Uh, hey Rob. You startled me."

"Sorry," he says. "But I have some news, and Brekka and I leave tomorrow for a week in Colorado."

"Is she skiing again?"

Rob laughs. "It's May." His tone implies that should mean something to me.

"Uh, okay."

"The slopes all closed a few weeks ago," he says.

"Right," I say. "I mean, that makes sense." I think of Colorado as the land of mountains and snow, but I suppose even there snow melts eventually.

"Do you mind if I sit in your car for a minute?" Rob mops his forehead with his sleeve. "A little air conditioning might be nice."

I roll my eyes. "Sure, whatever, that's fine, but I've got like five minutes, tops."

Rob circles around and opens the passenger door. He slides into the seat, shifting a box of Kleenex and a few empty protein shake containers without comment. "Are you headed to Parker's tonight?"

I nod.

"How's that going?"

"Well, I'd love to chat with you about it, or maybe have you and Brekka in for a dinner—I get half off on two separate meals every time I play—but if I don't leave soon, I might be late. I'm too new at this to be late. We really need to get together soon, but for now, maybe just tell me what's up."

He smiles broadly and bites his lip. "Well, I have good news and bad news. Which do you want first?"

Ugh. "Start with the bad, I guess."

"You know that Brekka was prepared to compete in the Special Olympics next year. . ."

Oh, no. "What's wrong?" I ask. "Why can't she compete?"

Rob smiles so wide that I can practically see his tonsils. "Well, they won't let you compete if you're pregnant or if you recently had a newborn."

"Huh?" Had a newborn? Wait. They got married in February, and now it's May. My hands begin to shake like I'm using discount hair dye. "Are you kidding me right now?"

He shakes his head. "Not a joke, a honeymoon baby."

And then I'm crying, and so is Rob, and I'm leaning across the center console of the car to hug him, and I'm screaming, and I'm a total mess. "Oh my gosh, Rob!" I shriek. "This is just the best news in the whole entire world." I can't stop shrieking.

"I had to tell you in person," Rob says. "I knew you would be the most fun person we told."

"I just. . ." I can't think of the right words. "Oh my goodness, Rob, a BABY! This will be the most adorable child of all time, and don't take this the wrong way, but let's hope that baby gets Brekka's brains."

Rob laughs out loud, his belly laugh shaking the car. "That's exactly what I said."

"Do you know whether it's a boy or a girl yet?" I ask.

Rob smirks.

"You totally do! You have to tell me."

"My beautiful wife wants a huge party with a big surprise gender reveal after the formal twenty-week ultrasound, once we know things are all on track."

"Oh, come on. You can't *not* tell me now that you know." My mouth drops open. "Wait, how far along is she? Don't you have to be four months to know the gender? Or is it five?"

Rob laughs. "We're eighteen weeks, but Brekka's high risk due to her lack of mobility, so they did a blood test at ten weeks."

High risk. A chill runs up my spine.

Rob covers my hand with his. "It's going to be fine, Beth, I swear. Don't fret. Brekka and her mom are anxious enough for everyone, believe me."

I bet they are. "You'll be in my prayers morning, noon, and night."

Rob squeezes my hand and then releases it. "You need to get going. I don't want to get you fired, but I wanted to see all that unbridled glee. Brekka did, too, but she had to tell Trig before we left. She's in charge of some kind of graduation speech in Colorado again, and then she has a bunch of client meetings across the east coast next week."

"Thank you for telling me," I say. "And I could not possibly be more excited for you. But get on that gender reveal party. I have some adorable baby blankets to knit."

"It will happen soon." Rob's right eyebrow rises. "Wait, you knit?"

I laugh. "Not even a little bit, but how hard can it be?"

He grimaces.

"Oh please. If I can't figure it out, that's what Etsy's for."

He laughs this time. "Alright, well, drive safely to your fancy restaurant, and have fun." He leans over and kisses my forehead, and then he climbs out of the car.

I can't suppress my smile as I pull out and drive away. My brother is having a baby! I wonder whether he or she will have Brekka's flashing golden eyes, or Rob's deep blue ones. One thing is sure. It won't have my squinty ones. No one in the family does—or my unruly curls, or my pasty pale skin. Because we aren't really related, not genetically, anyway.

Not that it matters. I'll love that baby exactly the same, no matter what.

My phone buzzes again, and I wonder whether it was Rob calling me earlier. Maybe he forgot to tell me something and he's calling me again. Or maybe he's rethinking the gender surprise thing. I never touch my phone while I'm driving, but it syncs with my Bluetooth, so with the press of a button, I answer the call.

"Hello?" I ask, expecting Rob's baritone.

"Hello," a smooth soprano voice says. A woman's voice, and definitely not Brekka's.

"Uh," I say, "I answered in my car, so I can't see who's calling. Who is this?"

"Is this Elizabeth Graham?" The woman has a stiff accent, Germanic maybe.

"Yes, this is Beth," I say. "Who are you?"

She clears her throat, but it's not gruff, and it's not choppy. Somehow, it's elegant. Who clears their throat elegantly? "My name is Henrietta Gauvón." The name is familiar, but I can't quite place why.

"Uh, okay," I say. "Well, I'm actually not looking to renew my warranty right now."

"Excuse me?" she asks.

"Why are you calling?" I ask. "Because if you're trying to sell me something—"

"Actually, this is a strange circumstance," she says. "And my English is not the very best of speaking. I don't use it enough to make it really good."

Henrietta Gauvón. I think about the name—and wonder whether it's a name from the musical world. Then it hits me—she's a singer! Very famous in Europe, but not so much in the United States.

"I don't have any trouble understanding you," I say. But why would a European singer call me?

"I was hoping you might have time to meet with me,"

she says. "You see, twenty-five years ago, I gave birth to a child. I gave that child up for adoption."

I yank my car over to the side of the road and slam it into park. My fingers tremble. "You did?"

"It was a closed adoption, so I was unable to find you for ah, much, no, many years."

I close my eyes and lean my forehead against the steering wheel.

"Are you there?" she asks.

"I am," I say. "I am here."

"Are you in Atlanta? That's what my studier of people tells me."

"Your investigator?" I ask.

"Yes," she says. "I am sorry. Do you maybe speak German?"

I nod my head, but of course she can't see me. "I do. My mom and dad made me take it for all four years of high school, but if I'm being honest, I'm not very good. Your English is probably way better than my pathetic German."

"It was my one requirement for the adoption," she says. "I wanted us to be able to talk if we ever meet. But then, I worried, and I tried to learn the English too."

My heart swells until I worry it might burst. How can this be happening? I've been dreaming of this moment for at least twenty years.

"I'm only in Atlanta for the night," she says, "but I would like much to meet you."

"Can you come to a restaurant tonight?" I ask. "I'm working, but I'd love to see you. And I get a discount, so you would get a discount on your meal."

"It would be my great pleasure," she says. "Are you waitress?"

This time, I'm the one clearing my throat. "Uh, no. I'm actually a pianist."

"Ah, you play the piano?" she asks.

"Right, yes I do," I say. "At a place called Parker's on Ponce. It's in downtown Decatur, which is north of Atlanta. I can text you the address."

"Is where?"

"It's north of Atlanta, like above it, on the top side." What's the word in German for north? I can't recall.

"I am already in the top side of Atlanta," she says. "So it's easy for me to get to you."

"Perfect," I say. "When you arrive, tell the host that you're there with Beth Graham and they'll seat you close and make sure you get the discount."

"I'll be wearing a red dress," she says. "I can't wait to hear you play." Then she hangs up.

I breathe in and out several times before I put my car back into drive and pull back onto the road. I'm going to meet my mother, my real mother. I wonder what she'll look like. Will she have freckles? Or smooth, pale skin? Will her eyes be brown like mine? Or lighter? I'm still trying to imagine the face that would match her smooth, refined voice when I pull into a spot around back. I have three minutes to get inside.

I flip the visor down and smooth my hair back. No time to do more than apply some lip gloss and straighten my boring white shirt. I wish I could wear something dramatic, like a bright blouse, or a jaw-dropping evening gown. Oh, well. I glance every which way when I arrive, wondering whether she's already here. Could she be? But everywhere I look, there are pairs of people.

Unless. Could she be here with my father? My heart stutters at the thought. It's stupid, of course. If she and my dad were together, she'd have kept me, surely. And probably mentioned that she was with someone on the phone.

But why is she here? Work? Pleasure? Just to see me? My mouth goes dry at that thought. Could she have flown here from Europe to meet me?

Focus, Beth. You have a set to play. I wave at the manager, Stephanie, and sit on my stool. Tonight, for the first time, she wants me to start taking requests. It's not as hard as it sounds, since she has limited the requests to a few hundred super popular songs, and they have sheet music for all of them. Plus, people aren't as critical of flubs when you're playing something they requested instead of a prepared piece. In fact, most of the restaurant patrons are just amazed that I can play at all.

None of them know I almost went to Juilliard, before I screwed it up.

They have no expectations of me, so they aren't disappointed either. I pull out the songs Stephanie wants me to start with—classical pieces so that the guests can focus on their dinner conversation. I don't start playing the fun songs until after eight, and requests don't begin until nine. I fumble a bit on the first few songs, distracted every time someone new walks in, but eventually I lose myself in the music. Which is good—I can't be bumbling around in front of my mother, the famous singer.

When I take my break at eight, I check with Peter, the host for tonight. "Has anyone said they were here for me?"

He shakes his head. "You're expecting someone?"

A frog in my throat keeps me from explaining. I nod. "Henrietta is her name."

"Cool," he says. "I'll save a table close to the piano."

"Thanks." I spend the rest of the break googling my mom. She's a lot more famous than I realized. She started with opera and only branched out into pop music about a decade ago. She's worth quite a bit of money, and she's about to go back on tour for her new album, Sagenhaft. It won't be released here for another eleven days, so I can't listen to any of the songs yet.

But when I listen to one of her other albums, I realize why I recognized her name—she always has a pianist accompanying her. I've even played some of her songs. I had one piano teacher who adored her music. I scroll frenetically through one interview after another. In one, she mentions falling in love with the depth of the piano when she sang opera. I'm scanning through an interview about her new album when Stephanie taps my shoulder.

"Sorry," I say. "I'm about to start again."

"Peter wanted me to tell you that your friend came," she says. "And I have to say, she's really stunning. Who is she, and is she single?"

I almost laugh. My boss likes my *mom*? "Um, I don't think she's gay." Although, I guess you never know.

"Pity." Stephanie walks away.

My eyes sweep the area until they stop on a tall, thin woman with long, wavy curls that fall halfway down her back. Which is much more dramatic because her fire engine red sheath dress is backless. And unlike me, her skin is nearly bronze. But when she meets my eyes and smiles, her dark brown eyes crinkle up just like mine.

She lifts her hand at me, and I reach for the piano keys. And I play like I've never played before—smoother, more easily, as if her presence somehow boosts my natural ability. Somehow she focuses me on what I could always do.

When Stephanie announces that we're open for requests, I'm not even nervous. That means I only have another hour to play before I can talk to my real mother, face to face, for the first time in my life. My fingers fly over the keys, note perfect. And when I finish "Piano Man," for the *second* time, and I realize it's four minutes after ten, I stand up and curtsy. "Thank you for being such a gracious audience tonight."

For the first time since I began playing here, nearly every guest claps. They clap and clap. Just when I'm worried they're going to demand an encore, from a stupid background piano gig, the applause tapers off.

Thank goodness.

I sling my bag over my shoulders and walk the fifteen feet that separate me from Henrietta. "Hi," I say, suddenly unaccountably shy.

"That was beautiful performance," she says. "Please, sit. I order food for you, too. Your very nice boss told me you are finished at ten."

I glance at the plate on the table—filet with a béarnaise sauce. My very favorite, and somehow she just *knew*. "That's the best thing on the menu," I say. "Thank you so much."

She grins, displaying beautiful, pearly white teeth. "I don't eat meat, but your boss tells me is your favorite thing."

Wow, she's vegetarian? She must really care about animals. I feel a little guilty eating the filet in front of her, but not too guilty. After all, I don't want to waste it. "Well, thank you."

I sit across from her and realize that since she's not eating, I look and sound like a slobbery bull in a china shop. "Uh, did you already eat?"

Henrietta smiles. "I don't eat a lot."

Of course she doesn't. She looks like she weighs under a hundred pounds. Holy wow. I must have a good twenty-five pounds on her at least. "Oh. Well, that's impressive. I eat all the time."

"You look very active. I'm sure that's perfect."

"Thanks," I say. "So what did you think? It was a little stressful, knowing that my famous musician bio-mom was watching me play."

"Your playing is absolutely stunning," she says. "I was very impressed. I wish I could play half so well."

Heat rises in my cheeks. "That means a lot coming from you. But of course, I can't sing anywhere near as well as you can. I mean, no one really can."

She turns her hundred-watt smile on me, and my heart soars. "I am so happy I took the chance to meet you. I was nervous to call, and I hope your parents will not be upset."

"Please." I shake my head. "I'm an adult. Besides, they're really supportive. I'm sure they won't care."

She lifts her eyebrows. "I requested to talk to you several times over the years, but they always declined. I finally hired a professional to search for you."

Her words hit me like a punch to the gut, but I can't tell her that. Not here, not now. I blink a few times. "Um, well, they're pretty protective, but I'm sure they'll be happy we've met. You know, since I'm twenty-five years old. Besides, it's not like you need their permission anymore."

"I am happy to see how musical you are. Do your parents play or sing?"

I shake my head. "I'm the only musician in the family. Both my parents are practically tone deaf."

She frowns. "That's too bad. Do they still support you?"

"Of course they do, all the time. With all of it."

"Good. Many people do not understand the life or heart of an artist."

My heart lurches a bit. "They don't always get it, but my mom likes to sew and that's similar." Sort of.

"Sew?"

"She takes fabric and makes it into clothing."

Henrietta's mouth turns down slightly, her lips compressing.

"But tell me about you! Your new album! Your tour, all of it. You're so fascinating."

She talks about her inspiration for her new songs, the irritating woman at her record label, her amazing manager. I barely blink, and I realize Parker's is closing.

"I am so glad you called me," I say.

Henrietta sighs. "Me as well. I only wish we had more time."

I nod my head vigorously. "Me too. Can you extend your stay at all?"

"Unfortunately, I can't. My tour starts soon, and I'm only traveling because. . . for a press engagement. I had a layover here when I heard that you were living here. I extended the layover, but I must leave tomorrow at the latest."

"I read about that online," I say.

"Ah," she says. "Well, my manager told me yesterday that my pianist is pregnant and quite ill. He's working to find a replacement, but. . . after hearing you tonight, perhaps you would like to take the position. Would you be interested in joining me on tour?"

The pianist for my internationally acclaimed mother? Going on a European tour that runs all summer? Uh, yes. A million times yes.

The ramifications of such a decision crowd around me —my chair at the salon, Brekka's high-risk pregnancy, the part-time gig here that I only recently landed. I'd have to give up my chair, I'd lose my spot here, but. . .

Going on tour with a real celebrity, who also happens to be my *mother*. It's a once in a lifetime opportunity, and I already blew one of those. Most people don't get a second one.

"I would love to," I say. "Yes."

2

COLE

The castle in which I live is not a home, not for me.

Unlike my brother Noel, I'm no prince. My mom married the Hereditary Prince of Liechtenstein, Hans-Michael, when I was only three years old. I started calling him Dad almost immediately, but that didn't make it true. My father was from Belgium, and my mom didn't cry at his funeral for very good reasons.

We were both better off without him.

Mom's second marriage improved our lives in every single way, but it also threw my life down a different path. I've spent the past thirty years pretending to be someone I'm not, and in the last few years, the disconnect between my daily life and the reality of my future has only deepened. As Dad's eyesight worsened, more and more of his tasks fell to me. I met with the Foundation, directing distributions and investments. I appointed judges. I reviewed new laws with the Landtag, and reviewed their enforcement with the National Committee. I approved budgets and refused outrageous requests.

But I am still not a Prince of Liechtenstein.

I'm the Marquis of Béthune of Belgium, son of Gerard, the last Marquis of Béthune. I may not remember Gerard, but that's my legacy. No matter how many years I live in this palace, or serve the local people, I'll never be a prince. I'll never be a member of the Princely House of Liechtenstein.

Which is why I'm telling Mom and Dad tonight that I'm moving to one of my father's residences—a townhome in Antwerp. From there I'll work at a new position I've found at a bank, Argenta, and I'll monitor my family estate. The fancy house where I actually belong—the Château Solvay in Walloon Brabant, Belgium. Mom, especially, is not going to be pleased. She always insists that where we are, the royal palace in Vaduz, is my home. *Your home is at my side,* she says every time I bring it up. But she won't be here forever, and I'm far too old to follow my mother around.

If I'm being honest, I've been too old for quite some time.

The last decade was hard on my family—one hit after another. My little brother Noel died ten years ago, and our world crumbled. Shortly after that, my little sister Holly fled the wreckage, leaving me to hold things together while Mom and Dad slowly recovered. I had recently graduated from college, and I should've been headed to New York City to work for Chase Bank, but I returned home instead. It made sense for me to step in to help. After all, I was older, wiser, and more equipped to pick up Mom and Dad's slack than my eighteen-year-old sister.

I let Holly run and hide without resenting her departure.

The banking scandal hit, and I weathered it. When Dad's health deteriorated, first his eyesight and then his heart, I finally begged Holly to come back. But in the last year, I've realized that while she might have run away initially, Holly stopped running and put down roots for herself in Atlanta. She grew and stretched. She's happy. Watching my sister seize her life, find her joy, and blossom, well, it made me happy, but it also made me sad. It threw the differences between our lives into sharp relief.

I'm still treading water alone.

And no matter what I do, how hard I train, how much work I accomplish, if I continue, the end result is that I will drown here. I have no future where I am. The Princely House of Liechtenstein is a patrilineal dynasty, so I can't ever take over for Dad and neither can Holly. We'll be ousted from this palace the second he dies. Mom and Dad have done an amazing job of pretending it's not true, but it doesn't change the facts.

My sister and her husband James flew in today for one of their biannual visits, so Mom and Dad should be in an excellent mood. My timing in announcing my impending departure couldn't be more perfect. Now that my dad can't drive, he had his car titled in Holly's name. Their flight was delayed, but Lars dropped the car off at the airport earlier so it was ready when they arrived, even an hour and a half late. I stand by Mom and watch as Dad's Mercedes AMG pulls around the bend and rolls through the gate. It would have been just as easy to pick them up, but I think Mom likes the idea of Holly having her own car here, as if it might make her more likely to stay.

Holly waves at the guards as James maneuvers the car around the bend and into the garage. My sweet little sister has always effortlessly charmed everyone around her. No matter how angry I would become that she had left me to handle everything, as soon as she smiled her lopsided grin and stretched her arms out toward me, my anger evaporated.

Mom, Dad, and I race from the parlor window, through the entry hall, and around the corner into the garage, crowding onto the top step in the garage as they pull in. I let Mom and Dad bask in Holly for a moment before grabbing her by the shoulders and pulling her tightly against my chest. "Welcome home."

Judging from her squeak, I might have squeezed her a little too tightly.

"It's great to be here." Holly trots through the door into the coatroom and then walks past it into the main hallway.

Lars grabs Holly's suitcase to haul it upstairs. He reaches for the handle of James' too, but James steps away from him, yanking his bag away as if to protect it.

I love Americans. "He's just going to carry it upstairs for you," I explain.

"I can do that myself," James says. "I don't want to impose."

"It's kind of his job," Mom says. "You wouldn't want to put him out of work, would you?"

James' eyes widen, and he releases his black roller bag. Lars takes it gratefully and disappears.

Mom walks toward the sitting room, and we all follow.

"I'm so happy to be here in the spring this year," Holly says.

Liechtenstein in the spring truly is breathtaking.

"Atlanta's already muggy—in May," James says. "It makes the Brazilian rainforests seem arid."

Holly rolls her eyes. "We have been missing New York pretty hard core lately."

"Hard what?" my mom asks.

"It means he has been wishing he was in New York," Dad says, beaming with pride that he's able to interpret American for my mostly English-fluent mother.

Mom frowns. "Oh. Are you considering moving back?"

James wraps an arm around my sister's shoulders. "Nope. We're happy with Atlanta, even if we don't both love the humidity. People matter more than the climate, after all."

Mom's eyebrows rise at the perceived slight. After all, Holly's family is here, not in Atlanta, but Dad takes her hand in his and Mom's shoulders relax a hair. "Well, you're just in time for dinner. I'm glad your flight wasn't delayed. You know how slimy the asparagus gets when it sits under a warmer."

Oh good, we've devolved to discussing food and the weather. Holly's visit is supposed to make my announcement easier, not harder. "How has married life been?" I ask, trying to steer us back on track.

"They've been married for nearly six months," Dad says. "I should hope they're settling in at this point."

Holly shoots me a relieved look. "We're figuring it out," she says. "I survived another tax season, and James has set up an office in Atlanta and moved most of his management team out here. He only spends about a week every month in the New York office, and another week traveling to various locations. Otherwise, he's home with me."

Dad smiles. "Is the Vaduz office opening next?"

"Well," James says, "I haven't—"

"He's kidding," I say.

James exhales heavily. "Oh. Right." He forces a laugh.

I almost feel sorry for him. Our family isn't exactly easygoing or simple. He definitely has his hands full.

"Let's eat," Mom says. "And then we can hammer out the details of an itinerary for your visit."

"I need a minute," Holly says.

"Of course," Mom says. "Let's convene in the dining room in five minutes, then."

James and Holly head upstairs. I dart up after them and grab Holly's arm before she ducks into her room.

"Is everything okay?" she asks.

James turns back, his eyebrows raised.

She waves him inside. "I'll be right in."

"I needed to talk to you for a second," I say.

"It's nothing epic, right?" She hops from one foot to the other. "Because that was a long flight, and I really need to pee."

Pee? I laugh. She's more American every day. "I just wanted to warn you. I'm planning to tell Dad and Mom that I'm taking a job for Argenta and moving to Antwerp. I didn't want to broadside you—but it seems like even now that you're married, you have no intention of returning home."

She shakes her head.

"I figure Dad may as well start transitioning things to Uncle Franz."

"Sounds smart to me," she says. "Although the idea of transitioning because Dad won't be alive much longer is super depressing."

"It's less about that," I say, "and more that he can't possibly complete the tasks required of the Prince without me here to do them."

Holly's eyes widen. "Oh, Cole, you've put your life on hold long enough."

"I'll come back to manage the Distribution," he says. "And of course you and I will jointly own Berg Telecom. That won't change. You'll inherit half of Dad's share and I'll inherit half, so you'll own sixty-five percent to my thirty-five."

"Cole, I don't care about any of that."

Don't I know it.

Her face falls. "I didn't mean it like that. I want to help out more, and I'm delighted we'll be doing this together. I'm just saying that we may as well own it fifty-fifty."

"You gave your entire trust to save it." I swallow. A trust that held twice what mine did, thanks to Noel leaving everything he owned to her. Because he loved her so much more than me. Which makes sense. They were full siblings. "You should own more."

Holly laughs. "Oh, Cole. Neither of us needs money."

"You're right. It's not about that." And honestly, she should probably inherit the entire thing. It has always been run by the Prince of Liechtenstein.

"Look, I appreciate the heads up," Holly says. "And of course I'll support your decision, but I can't imagine Mom and Dad could be anything but positive. I mean, you've given the last decade to them when you could have left and pursued your own life right away. It was practically saintly, but they can't expect you to hover at Dad's side forever, not when he can't even make you Regent." Holly grunts. "For the record, I think that's garbage. Why can't an adopted child be Dad's heir? Does he love you less? Certainly not."

"Those rules are way beyond our reach." And whether Dad wanted to adopt me or not, no papers can change my blood—and I'm not really part of the Princely family. I've always known that. It's time for me to make a real home for myself, one where I belong. I head back downstairs.

"That was more than five minutes," Mom says when James and Holly finally reach the dining room.

"I'm afraid that's my fault," James says. "I had a conference call I forgot about, and it took me a little longer to excuse myself than I expected."

"Well, I had cook make a new batch of asparagus," Mom says. "So don't worry."

James' mouth falls open slightly.

"We take our asparagus seriously around here," I say. "And right now the white asparagus is in season—and that's practically a national delicacy. You almost can't eat dinner here without it during the three weeks or so it's available."

Holly laughs. "I've never once seen that in the United States. Did you know that?"

Dad snorts. "I'm not surprised. I hear all they eat are hamburgers and french fries."

"We offer a little more variety than that," James says. "But I am eager to sample this magical white asparagus."

It tastes almost the same as the green kind, in my opinion, but I don't bother mentioning that. Especially while Mom, Dad, and Holly are going on and on about how it's not at all the same. Before I know it, dinner's over. Mom's waving Mirdza in with the cheesecake.

"Holly told us that this is your favorite." Mom beams at James.

"Oh," he says. "You shouldn't have. I'm trying to watch the sweets."

"You have no idea how hard it is to maintain a six-pack, Mom," I say.

Mom rolls her eyes. "Oh, please. He's young. He can eat a slice of cake once in a while."

"I don't turn down cheesecake." He picks up his fork with relish.

This is probably the best opening I'm going to get. I open my mouth, but before I say a word, Mom says, "Perhaps we can take a little time now to discuss our plans. I never heard whether you wanted to go for a ride."

"Horseback," Holly says.

"Right," Mom says. "There's no more beautiful way to see the scenery around here, and you used to love riding out on Traveler. Remember?"

Holly smiles.

"We'd better not this time," James says.

"Oh?" I ask. "Not a fan of horses?" I hate them, myself. They're always looking for ways to kick or bite or poop. Unpredictable and smelly. A bicycle serves the same purpose with a great deal less effort, expense, and danger.

"It's not that," James says.

Holly puts a hand on his arm and murmurs something, but James doesn't seem to notice.

"We've got some amazing news, and we wanted you to be the first to hear." James' eyes light up and he wraps an arm around Holly's shoulder. "Do you want to tell them?" He looks down at her.

Holly's eyes dart to mine, apologetic, chagrined. "Uh, no, you go ahead."

"We're expecting a baby." James squeezes Holly's shoulders. "So we'll have to take a rain check on anything super bouncy on this trip."

Mom leaps from her chair, her hands clapping, her eyes bright. "That's the best news ever!"

So much for calmly discussing my new job. Which I'm supposed to be starting in less than three weeks. I sigh.

"We are very excited," Holly says. "But you know, I heard that Cole—"

I shake my head.

"We actually have some news too," Dad says.

Mom's eyes widen, and she turns to face him. "We do?"

Dad licks his lips. "Well, maybe it's more my news. I've been talking to Horatio, and we've worked up a plan. But before I can talk about that, I need to know something from Holly."

Holly's eyebrows draw together. "Huh?"

"Do you have any interest at all in ruling in my place some day?"

The joy melts from my sweet little sister's face. "I don't want you to take this the wrong way, Dad, but no. Not even a teensy tiny bit."

Dad bobs his head. "I suspected that, and so Horatio and I have worked up some documents." He stands up and walks out of the room.

"Umm," Holly says. "What in the world is going on?"

Mom shrugs.

Dad walks back inside, and sets a sheath of papers on the table, next to his cheesecake. "These are two rather long documents. The first is a petition of adoption, which I'm actually authorized to sign myself, but I drew them up to have the chief magistrate sign. And the second is a call for an amendment to the Princely Family of Liechtenstein's House Law."

I blink.

"I don't understand," Mom says.

"Cole has been my son for almost thirty-one years, since the very day I married you, Serena. I've always seen him as my own boy, no matter what the law said."

Tears well in Mom's eyes.

My heart stutters in my chest.

"I think it's high time we at least attempt to change the law so it reflects the reality of our family."

Mom shakes her head sadly. "They'll never approve this."

Dad smiles. "When has the Princely family ever turned and run from a fight?"

"Uh, well, two world wars come to mind," Holly says.

Dad scowls. "Our entire family was essentially bankrupt after those wars, and Grandfather created a formidable economic empire. And I've—"

"Even if that's true, this particular fight is *with* the Princely family you're so eager to defend," Holly says. "So our general stubborn and intractable natures work against us."

"Every single one of our dynasts would lay down his life—"

"Calm down," Holly practically shouts. "I was mostly kidding. And of course, if this is what Cole wants, I'll strap on my armor and attack whatever you want me to attack." She leans toward me, her eyes intent on mine. "But I think Cole might have other plans in mind."

"You'd be risking your father's lands and title," Mom says. "If you let Dad adopt you formally, your claim to Gerard's property will evaporate. Karl will take it all."

My cousin. He's not a bad guy—if someone is going to benefit from a tremendous windfall, it may as well be him.

"I seem to be the only person here who isn't sure quite what's going on," James says.

Holly takes her husband's hand. "I'm not one hundred percent sure either, but I think that Dad's offering to formally adopt Cole and make him the Regent, preparatory to becoming the new prince. Is that right?"

"But why is that a risk?" James asks.

"Dad hasn't ever adopted Cole," Mom says, "because of the laws of primogeniture. Cole would lose his inheritance from his father, which is substantial, and still be unable to rule here in Liechtenstein. Currently, the House Law makes no allowances for adoptive children."

"It's high time the family votes to change that law," Dad says.

"They never will," Mom says.

"Well, I think they might," Dad says. "I don't think Franz has any interest in politics, and Josef's too busy with his microscopes and research to want to rule."

"Neither of them has ever lived here either. Even so, it's a pretty big gamble," Holly says.

"There are more than fifty dynasts, in any case," Mom says. "The odds of all of them being fine with Cole shifting them back in line. . ."

"If you're worried, we'll try to change the law *before* we finalize the adoption," Dad says.

"It lowers the stakes," Mom says. "It might make it less likely that we'll win. But Cole will still have Gerard's title to fall back on."

"What exactly would it take to change the House Law?" Holly asks.

Dad looks at his hands. "A two-thirds majority would need to approve the change."

Holly whistles.

Dad nods. "It's a lot, I know."

"Have two-thirds of our family's males ever agreed on anything?" Holly mutters.

"I haven't heard much from Cole," James says. "What do you think about all of this?"

I lean back in my chair. I spent decades wishing Dad would go to bat for me. I used to dream that one day, the stars would shift in the sky, and somehow, I would be worthy to take over for him. But that dream died—and I've already buried it. It hurt quite a lot when I did, and I don't want to go through it all again.

"I meant to tell you this before Holly's news and Dad's surprise, but I've taken a job in Antwerp working for Argenta. I start in three weeks. So while I appreciate your very noble intentions." I shake my head. "I don't think this plan has the slightest chance of working." If it had, we'd have taken steps to do this ten years ago when Dad was strong enough for some kind of pitched family battle.

"Are you sure, son?" The intense look, the sorrow in my Dad's eyes, shakes my resolve, but not for long.

I've always known he loved me. That doesn't mean that I really belong here, governing his country. "I'm sure. I think you should call Uncle Franz and start working out the details of transitioning the rule to him."

It's time for me to move on with my life. My real life.

3

BETH

When I finally made it home last night, Mom had been asleep for a while. But I know she'll be awake and waiting with a smile when I get downstairs this morning.

I requested to talk to you several times over the years, but they always declined.

Henrietta's words have echoed through my brain on a never-ending loop since she spoke them last night. She reached out, several times. My parents never told me, and they refused contact.

Why?

I alternate between fury and sorrow. I've always been the lone musician in the family—the only one who had any musical interest. In spite of having no musical talent themselves, they've supported me from start to finish. Mom put me in private lessons, attended every single recital, and they even bought me a baby grand and plonked it down in the middle of the house. They've also never complained about the never-ending practicing, even though it must get annoying.

If they don't quite understand my obsession, well, they have always encouraged it in spite of that.

Could Henrietta be lying? I can't think of a single reason she would do that, other than perhaps guilt? Could she have felt bad about never reaching out to me? Could she have regretted the closed adoption, but never have done anything to change it?

Only one way to know.

I square my shoulders and march down the curved staircase, passing my Fazioli as I reach the first floor.

"Good morning, darling," Mom says.

"Hey." I grab a bowl from the cabinet, a spoon from the drawer, and a box of Life cereal from the pantry.

Mom grabs the milk carton. "Did you happen to see Rob yesterday before he left?"

I suppress a grin. "Rob? Why would I have seen him?"

Mom's shoulders droop.

"I'm kidding. He grabbed me right as I got off work."

Her eyes light up.

"Best news of the year, easily. I can hardly believe it." I take a bite, the cereal sloshing around in my mouth. "But that punk won't tell me the gender, which is just mean. Did he tell you?"

"They're refusing to reveal it to anyone until they can do a big production. When I was having children, the gender reveal came at birth."

I sit down, still shoveling cereal.

"How did Parker's go last night?"

I shrug. "It was fine."

"So the new requests thing didn't turn out to be hard?" Mom offers me a cup of coffee.

I take it with a smile. "Actually, I played better than I've ever played."

"Hey, that's awesome," she says. "So it upped your game. It's great to hear that you were nervous for nothing."

"I think it may have been because of my nerves that I did so well. Or maybe not, I'm not sure."

"When are you back?" She sits down near the window. "Dad and I didn't want to stress you out, but we'd like to go and hear you the next time you're there."

"So, that's kind of up in the air," I say.

"What?" Mom leaps to her feet. "I thought you said it went great. Those idiots didn't decide to stop the piano music, did they?"

"No, but I might have a better opportunity." I bite my lip.

"Well, that's wonderful to hear." Mom perches on the edge of her chair, her eyes intent. "Did someone hear you play last night and offer you a job?"

I set my coffee mug and my cereal bowl down and sit. "I got a call yesterday, just as I was leaving Zena, actually."

"Okay." Mom's brow furrows. "From?"

Anger ripples through me—that she has kept my mother from me all this time. That Henrietta had to track me down with a private investigator. "My mom." I cross my arms under my chest.

Mom's mouth drops open, and she stares at me blankly. "Your who?" Her bright blue eyes widen.

My heart constricts. That was mean. Whatever my mom did, she doesn't deserve that. She's been the best mom anyone could have wanted. She was there for me, every day. I wish I could snatch those two words back, unsay them somehow. "A woman named Henrietta Gauvón called me. She claims to be my birth mother."

Mom swallows, hard. "She is your birth mother."

For some reason, I expected her to argue with me.

"What did she want?" Mom presses.

The anger returns, burning inside my chest. "Why do you assume she wanted something?"

Mom shrugs.

"Why?"

Mom looks at her hands, folded in her lap.

"Mom." I lean toward her. "What's the deal?" I wasn't going to tell her what Henrietta said, but the words bubble out uncontrolled. "She's famous, and she doesn't *need* anything from me. But she did try to reach out to me several times, and you blocked her attempts."

"We did what we thought best," Mom says softly, still not meeting my eyes.

"So it's true."

"Adoptions are complicated," Mom says. "And your father wasn't as keen on the idea, not back then, but I knew it was right. I knew you were our baby."

"I don't get it," I say. "I always figured you sort of filled out paperwork, and then someone called, and you went and got me."

"We should probably have told you more," Mom says. "But it felt like it didn't matter. It felt. . . irrelevant, once I had you in my arms."

"Why did she give me up?" I ask.

"That's something you'll have to ask her," Mom says. "I don't know that for sure, but I can speculate. She was a performer, even then."

"Were you guys even looking to adopt?" I ask.

"We were," Mom says. "We had filled out paperwork here, and we had a completed home study, but the circumstances of your family were complicated. Your father was a rather prominent professor."

I lift one eyebrow. "Huh?"

"Henrietta was one of his students," Mom says. "And I assume she had opportunities to pursue that a baby would interrupt. Your father had no interest in pursuing a relationship with her—there was quite an age difference."

I don't want to hear anymore, and I'm desperate to find out everything. "He's American, my birth father?"

Mom nods. "But he passed away, Beth. Nine years ago."

"So, how in the world did you get me?" I ask.

"His wife wanted a child." Mom frowns. "She convinced Henrietta that they would care for you together. They wanted a fresh start, where everyone wouldn't remember that she hadn't been pregnant, so they moved to Atlanta. They didn't stay here long."

"Why not?"

"When your biological father brought you home." Mom shakes her head. "His wife couldn't do it. Henrietta had already severed her parental rights, and you were a US citizen. Your father passed you off to a social worker, and she had a horrible car accident, with you in the car. You were alright, thankfully, but she came to our dealership to buy a replacement."

"Are you kidding me right now?"

Mom shakes her head. "Your father may have given her an amazing deal on a car so that she'd put in a good word for us."

"You *bought* me with a free car?"

A tear rolls down Mom's cheek. "I was handling the books at the time, or trying. I held you while your dad helped the woman find a car. By the time she chose one, I was already in love with you." Tears stream freely down her face now. "Your huge brown eyes and your chubby cheeks. You hiccupped when you cried too hard, which is exactly what you were doing when I picked you up the first time— bawling uncontrollably."

My eyes well up, too.

"You never cried when I was holding you, not that first day, and not for months after. My other three children, the ones I created inside my body, they squalled when they were tired, when they were hungry, when their tummies hurt. For no reason at all, sometimes, but not you, not once. I knew it that day, and I've known it every day since: you're *my* daughter."

I swipe at the tears on my face. "But you kept her from me, and it wasn't her fault. How could you do that?"

Mom grabs a napkin and blows her nose. "She chose the closed adoption—she wanted no contact after your father took the baby. But." Mom inhales and exhales. "She did contact us twice much later."

"When?"

"The first time you were twelve, and we thought you were too young. Middle school was a struggle for you. We told her we would pass along her desire to meet you, when you were older." Mom wipes her eyes. "And then she reached out again when you were a senior in high school."

"I was fine then," I say.

"You had huge decisions to make," Mom says. "You were already confused. We didn't want to make that worse."

Juilliard. That was my huge decision. "You didn't want me to go."

Mom shakes her head. "We wanted you to decide for yourself."

"You were relieved when it all fell apart," I say. "I knew it then, but I still don't understand why."

Mom finally meets my eyes. "Your biological father was a professor at Juilliard. He taught Henrietta there."

"You didn't want me to find out," I say.

Mom turns away, looking out the window. "I wanted you to be happy—I wanted you to go if that was what you wanted, but I also didn't want you hurt. I didn't want to lose you, so yes, I was relieved when you didn't go."

"So I stayed here. I still live at home, seven years after graduating high school, like a loser."

Mom touches my hand. "You're happy, you're healthy, and you're safe. You're not a loser."

I yank away, flames of fury clawing their way out. "You lied to me."

She opens her mouth, but I'm not done.

"Henrietta hired a private investigator and found me herself. And last night, after hearing me play, she offered me a job as her pianist on tour. In Europe. I leave in three days."

Mom blinks furiously. "Three days? You can't go, not that fast."

I stand up, my cereal soggy, my coffee untouched. "Actually, Mom, this time I *can*. This time I'm an adult, and I finally have all the information, and I'm flying to Europe."

"You don't even know her," Mom says.

"Whose fault is that?"

Mom's quick inhalation pricks at my conscience, but it's not enough to douse my anger. Not by a long shot.

"I should probably start packing." I jog up the stairs, but once I reach my room, I collapse on my bed and sob into my pillow.

I thought telling my boss I needed to leave would be hard, but after talking to Mom, it's a breeze.

"So you'll be back when?" Persephone pulls out her calendar.

"The tour is over at the end of September," I say. "I know that's bad timing."

"You'll miss summer highlights and trims, and back to school." She taps the calendar. "But if you're willing to pull extra days around the holidays, I'll have a chair for you when you come back."

I hug her.

"Will you be coming back?" She lifts her eyebrows. "Because I heard you play at the holiday party last year. They might not let you."

"You were really drunk." I laugh. "I'm a pianist, not a

rock star. The pianist's job is to support the singer—not a hard task, honestly. Trust me, I'll be back."

She smiles. "Alright, well, don't be a stranger. Text me and let me know that nothing has changed from time to time."

I nod. "Thank you so much—I totally will."

After taking care of all my clients for the day, I spend two hours on the phone shifting the next month's worth of appointments to my closest work friends, Belinda and Daniela. I'm surprised by how supportive and excited my clients are—I might even get a few back when I return. I have a full day tomorrow, but luckily I already had Sunday off. I wish Rob was in town, but at least I heard his news in person before he left. And it's not as if I could do anything to help them between now and September.

HOW ARE THESE TIMES FOR FLIGHTS? Henrietta texts, with several screenshots—Atlanta to Frankfurt.

Frankfurt. Frankfurt! I'm going to Germany! I can hardly believe it.

ALL FINE, I text back. DON'T CARE WHICH ONE.

MY MANAGER WILL EMAIL YOU. LET HIM KNOW WHICH ONE YOU WANT, AND HE'LL BOOK IT. I CAN'T WAIT TO SEE YOU. HAPPY YOU'RE COMING.

I'm dreading going home, but Christine and Jennifer texted to tell me they're coming over for dinner. Besides, I can't hide from Mom and Dad forever. I run a few errands on the way home, but they only delay the inevitable. I park in my garage spot and close my eyes just inside the door. *You can do this, Beth. Be strong.*

I open the door, prepared for Mom and Dad to have recruited the twins for a full court press—to keep me here.

A banner stretches across the entire dining room. GOOD LUCK IN EUROPE, BETH!! The bouquet of flowers in the center of the table is surrounded with wrapped gifts.

Mom's eyes are uncertain when they find mine. "We're all excited. We wanted to wish you well."

"And I've been texting Kate and Lauren to set something up for tomorrow," Christine says. "And Rob is so sorry he can't be here to see you off."

My eyes scan the room for Dad. As usual, he's hiding behind Mom. But when I look in his direction, he tilts his head. "We're proud of you, peach. You're going to knock their pretentious little silk scarves right off."

The next two days pass in a blur. Jennifer and Christine insist on taking me shopping. Every meal is an opportunity to say goodbye to someone. Lunch with Belinda and Daniela. Dinner with Kate and Lauren and my other friends from high school. My family and friends act as if I'm dying, not traveling to Europe for a few months.

Of course, no one else I know has ever gone on tour. They probably don't know how to react. I spend most of the extra seconds I can scrape together reviewing the music Henrietta sent and brushing up on my very rusty German.

Mom insists on driving me to the airport, even though my flight leaves at six a.m., which means I need to be there at four. "You know they speak a lot of things other than German over there."

My eyes are stinging and my head feels fuzzy, which might not be helping me retain the words I'm reviewing. "I know that. I mean, duh. But I think that if I can offer to speak in English and German, hopefully I'll be able to muddle my way through Italy, France, and Spain without looking like such a tourist."

"There's nothing wrong with being American," Mom says. "Don't forget that. You shouldn't spend all your time apologizing for who you are—a beautiful Georgia peach."

I don't laugh. "I won't forget, Mom." I couldn't if I

wanted to—she literally got me a shirt with a peach on it, the word "Georgia" written across it. She put it in my suitcase this morning so I didn't have a chance to leave it behind.

Mom hugs me for so long when she drops me off that I worry I'll miss my flight. But eventually she lets go, and I step back. I ignore the pangs of guilt about leaving everyone, and march to the counter to check my bags. Mom texts me four times before I reach the gate, but I arrive in time. I'm doing it. Once I'm waiting to board, I pull out the books Brekka gave me last month. Some author that Mary and Paisley and now Brekka all love. She writes romance, but that's not really my thing.

But a book about superhuman royals who fight to the death to secretly rule half the world? That I can get into. I finish the first book just as the flight attendants announce we're landing in Amsterdam shortly. The second book gets me through the long layover and quick flight to Frankfurt. I'm debating whether to start the third when we prepare to land.

My heart hammers in my chest when I deboard, and my palms begin to sweat when I collect my luggage. I'm about to see her again—Henrietta. I wonder whether I'll be staying with her, or in a hotel. The tour starts in three days —I hope she's happy with my playing. I've been over and over the songs for the new album, but she has hundreds of old songs. I'll need a list so I can be ready for those, too.

I scan the crowd of people beyond baggage claim—and can't find her. Maybe she's running late, no big deal. Or maybe she didn't park, and I should meet her outside. I whip out my phone and take it off airplane mode to let her know I'm here.

But I have a series of texts from a number I don't recognize.

HENRIETTA HAD ME ORDER YOU A CAR

SERVICE. IT SHOULD BE WAITING WHEN YOU ARRIVE.

No explanation of who is texting me.

CALL ME WHEN YOU ARRIVE SO IF SHE ASKS, I CAN CONFIRM YOU'VE ARRIVED.

Still no name, no greeting.

ARE YOU HERE YET?

At least he's texting in English. I text back. WHO IS THIS? THIS IS ELIZABETH GRAHAM, AND I HAVE LANDED IN FRANKFURT AND I HAVE MY BAGS.

MY NAME IS UWE BECKER. I'M HENRIETTA'S MANAGER—I EMAILED YOU EARLIER.

Not quite the welcome I imagined, but I can work with it. Henrietta's probably already asleep, since it's past midnight here. That's reasonable. I scan the signs until I see my name. Or at least, I assume Berta Gram is me. I wave and the man's eyes light up.

Time to test my German. It's harder to understand him than I expected, but I'm able to confirm that he is waiting for me, and he has instructions to take me to a local hotel —which I'm surprised to find is a Hampton.

"We have these in America," I tell the desk clerk in what I think is passable German.

He nods brusquely.

Ah, well, it's late. I'm sure everyone will be much friendlier in the morning. And if the hotel's restaurant is already closed and I'm starving, at least I have crackers from the plane and a smooshed granola bar. I lug my bags to my room and collapse on the bed. Between the early wakeup and the late night, I have no problem going to sleep, even though it's barely eight p.m. back home.

The growling of my stomach and the sunlight slanting across my face conspire to wake me. . . I look at my watch. It's two in the morning back home. So that's. . . I do the math. Eight a.m. My eyes are stinging and a dull ache throbs at the base of my skull, but I'm here. I'm really in Germany.

I sit up and throw off the covers. By the time I've showered, my eyes are clear enough to face my phone and the dozen or so text messages waiting for me.

DID YOU MAKE IT? Mom asks.

ARE YOU IN GERMANY YET? Dad asks.

WIE WAR IHR FLUG? Rob took German in high school too, and I love that he's trying so hard.

I reply to him first. IT WAS FINE. HOPE YOU AND BREKKA AND BABY GIRL ARE ALRIGHT. I can't quite keep from fishing a little bit. Then I tell Mom and Dad in a joint text, HERE AND SAFE AND DOING FINE. FELL ASLEEP BEFORE. SORRY.

A flurry of texts from Henrietta make me feel better about her lack of interest last night.

ARE YOU HERE?

DID YOU GET TO THE HOTEL?

UWE MESSAGED YOU, RIGHT?

CALL ME WHEN YOU WAKE UP.

The timestamps show that she was clearly not asleep when I arrived, but anything could have been occupying her time, so it's not fair for me to be upset she didn't pick me up herself. At least she didn't have me hail my own cab. After all, I'm only a pianist. It's not like I'm a truly critical component of her tour, and that has to be her focus right now.

Maybe she wants to get breakfast. Instead of texting her back, I call. Seems simpler.

"Beth?"

"Good morning," I say. "I'm in Frankfurt! I can hardly believe it."

"I've had better mornings."

"Uh, is everything okay?" I ask. "I can call later if you're busy."

"Is fine," she says. "But I have some hard news."

Hard news? Does she mean bad news? "What's wrong?"

"It's a long story, but we have to shift the German dates to the end of the tour. Fans are not pleased, but there's a plumbing pipe that is not working."

"It's busted or something?" I ask.

"It floods the venue," she says. "Is a nightmare."

"At least that gives me more time to review your old songs." Thinking positive helps me through most things.

"You aren't prepared now?" Her tone is sharp.

"No, I mean yes, I am prepared. I could play your new songs in my sleep, I promise. But you have so many songs from prior albums. I was hoping you might be able to narrow some of those down a bit, you know, a list of the forty or fifty you usually play at concerts."

"Yes, yes, Uwe should have sent a playlist. Set list? I am not sure of the right word. But, yes. That is easy solution."

"Oh, great," I say. "But I really am so sorry about this delay. Is there anything I can do to help?"

"Nothing," she says. "I'm stuck trying to make furious fans happy about the schedule change and paying for everyone to sit around and do nothing for the next twelve days."

Great. I've been here twelve hours, and I'm already a drain. "You don't need to pay for me," I say. "I'll check out some sights I've been dying to see." Alone. While living off of the nine hundred dollars in my checking account.

"Are you sure?" she asks.

"Completely sure," I say. "Don't worry about me. Just let me know when you need me and where to be. I'll make sure I get that set list from Uwe, and you can forget about me until it's time to perform." Surely I can practice on. . . do hostels have pianos?

The second she hangs up, a knot forms in my stomach. This is a disaster. I should call Mom and Dad, but I know exactly what they'll tell me—to come home. Breakfast. I need breakfast. Then I'll feel better, and I'll work out a plan. I can totally survive twelve days on nine hundred dollars. Plus, I have a credit card. I think I've got a limit of a couple thousand dollars, which should be more than enough to float me. I could kiss my VISA card right now.

The strain in my shoulders relaxes. I shower and blow-dry my hair, and then I pull my flat iron out of my bag. I plug in the adapter I grabbed at the airport shop and turn on my flat iron. I apply my makeup while I wait for it to heat up. I'm brushing on a second coat of brand new mascara when I smell something strange.

My flat iron is smoking.

When I pick it up, the plates on the inside that flatten my hair collapse downward onto the counter. Oh my gosh, what has happened? My hands shake as I google flat irons in Germany. . . and realize that I'm a moron. I used an adapter when I needed a converter. My hair is a frizzy, puffy mess. I hated my hair until I went to school and learned how to tame it.

For a moment, I hate Germany, and I hate this trip, and I hate Henrietta.

Which is ridiculous, of course. It's a minor setback. Once it has cooled slightly, I toss my melted flat iron into the trash and pull my hair into a ponytail. On the third time around my hair, the ponytail holder snaps, and in spite of ten minutes of rummaging around, I can't find another one. No problem. I'll find somewhere to buy hair ties and a new flat iron too—right after I find a place to eat. The smell of coffee and croissants and sausage hits me as soon as the elevator doors open. My stomach rumbles as I take a seat, a little uncomfortable about being all alone. My German is nearly perfect when I order a full breakfast: sausage, eggs, toast, and coffee.

It tastes even better than it smells, and I bolt it. Finally things are looking up—until the waiter returns with an uncomfortable look on his face. "Your card has been declined," he says.

I frown. "That can't be right," I say. "Can you try it again?"

He lowers his voice. "I've already tried it three times."

Three times? "Can I pay in US dollars?" I ask sheepishly.

He shakes his head. "But the front desk can exchange them for you for a small fee."

I call Visa while I'm waiting in line to talk to the front desk. "How may I help you?" the representative asks.

"I'm in Germany for the first time," I say.

"Wonderful," the woman says. "I hope you're having a great trip."

"Actually, you guys declined my card."

"Ah, let me see what I can do about that," she says.

I provide her with all my information and wait while she clicks and clicks. "Ah, yes, we've detected some fraudulent activity. You didn't try to purchase a new tailgate smoker in Austin, Texas last night, did you?"

"Of course not," I say. "I'm not even in Texas."

"Online purchases can be made from anywhere," she says.

I sigh. "You're correct. I did not make that purchase in person or online. So clearly I need you to decline that attempt and then turn my card back on."

"I'm very sorry," she says. "We can't do that, but we will gladly send you a replacement card. It will arrive in eight to ten business days."

"I'm in *Germany*," I say.

"Well, we can send it to your hotel there. What's the address?"

I have no idea. I'm guessing I can't afford to stay at this

place, especially now that I have no way to pay them. "Uh. I'll call you back."

I hang up, and by the time I reach the clerk, big, embarrassing tears are rolling down my face. I shake my head when she asks if I'm alright. I plonk the two hundred and forty-seven dollars from my wallet on the counter and wait for her to change it into two hundred euros. My breakfast costs nearly twenty euros, and I can't seem to stop crying as I shell them over.

When my phone rings, I almost ignore it. I glance at the screen, prepared to shut it off. After all, who would be calling me other than Henrietta, and I can't very well talk to her while I'm bawling. But it's not Henrietta.

It's Paisley. Sweet, kind, always happy Paisley, who came to dozens of my recitals over the years with Rob. She always bounds up to me with a smile on her face and hugs me. She has gone rollerblading with me in the park. She's like a bonus big sister for someone who doesn't really even need one.

And it hits me like a lightning strike: *she's a European princess.* I inhale deeply to try and stem the sobbing and hit talk. "Paisley?"

"Are you in Germany right now?" she asks.

"I am," I say.

"How delightful."

"It's not delightful! It's awful." I completely fall apart, hiccups and all, just like when I was a newborn, apparently. No more capable at twenty-five than when I wore diapers.

"Oh no," Paisley says. "What's wrong? I was going to see what your travel plans were, and whether you'd have time to meet in Munich or somewhere. Are you alright? It sounds like you're having a rough trip."

I'm not sure how much of what I say makes sense, but Paisley never stops me, listening patiently as I explain all of it. She giggles about the flat iron, but I don't fault her for that.

"It's your lucky day," Paisley says. "Because I know just the place you can stay until the tour resumes, and it won't cost you a dime."

"Where?" I ask.

"With my family, here at our palace in Vaduz, of course," Paisley says.

My eyes well up with tears again. "I wouldn't want to impose like that."

"Oh please. It would be so much fun for me to host you here. Trust me. And as a special bonus," she says, "in case I wasn't already up for friend of the year, I can even provide you a ride."

"I can't possibly impose like that." Everyone says that the public transportation in Europe is tremendous. I'm sure I can find a train, or something. "Honestly. I bet I figure out—"

"With less than two hundred euros?" Paisley tuts. "My brother's driving that direction anyway. I'll just have him pick you up. Trust me, it's no trouble."

Finally something is going right. "Thank you so much, Pais. Really."

❧ 4 ❧
COLE

"**A**re you kidding me right now?" I ask. "I'm nowhere near Frankfurt."

"Cole," Holly says. "Where's your sense of chivalry? You can drive right by it, if you just drive through Cologne and Stuttgart instead of Luxembourg."

"That adds an hour, plus I'd have to drive into Frankfurt."

"I'm pregnant," she says.

I roll my eyes. "Which has nothing at all to do with this situation."

"You left during my visit and drove all the way out to Antwerp just to get away from Dad. If this gets you away for another hour or two, well, you're welcome."

"I wasn't trying to escape. I needed to check out the townhouse and sign some forms for my new job." I tap at my GPS, inputting the hotel she mentioned. "It adds an hour and forty-one minutes." I groan. "Can't she take a train?"

"You said you loved to drive," she says. "That's why you refused to take the jet, which would have gotten you back here light years faster."

"Send the jet for her," I say. "Wouldn't that be better?"

"She's distraught," Holly says. "She needs a friendly face as much as she needs a ride."

"Who is this person again?"

"It's my dear, dear friend Rob's little sister, and beyond that, she's my friend. She's here to play the piano on tour with Henrietta Gauvón—which means that she's an accomplished pianist. Thanks to circumstances beyond her control, the tour was delayed. She's had a run of bad, bad, *bad* luck. Certainly you can spare an hour of your precious, non-royal time. Plus you'll have her delightful company for half of your drive."

I sigh heavily. "Fine, but if I do this, you can't pull the pregnant card for the rest of your trip."

"But I haven't had this much fun since. . . Well. I've never had this much fun."

"Take it or leave it."

She sighs heavily. "Deal, I guess." Holly hangs up and sends me a flurry of text messages with the details.

Elizabeth Graham—that's the name of the pathetic kid sister Holly's sending me to save. Could the name be any more American? She's sitting, broke and lost, in the middle of some Frankfurt hotel lobby because she doesn't want to call her mom and dad and ask them for help. At least I can relate to that sentiment. I reluctantly plug the address into my GPS and hit go.

Maybe it won't be so bad. Maybe she'll even be cute, like Trudy who Holly had me help before. And maybe she's also already in love with some other guy. That's sort of my pattern. Not that I have had any dates to fashion into a pattern lately. It's been more than two years since I took out someone who I was excited to see. Which is pathetic.

It occurs to me for the first time that this might be a setup.

What exactly did Holly say about her friend? She's an

accomplished pianist. She used the word delightful at least once, I'm sure she did. By the time I turn off the 3 to head for her hotel, I'm more excited than I should be. When I was living at home, Mom and Dad incessantly set me up with titled lords and ladies. Princesses, the daughters of dukes, and the daughters of earls.

Snobs, all of them.

Most of them quickly decided that if I wasn't even a prince of Liechtenstein, they were wasting their time with me. After all, a marquis in Belgium with tenuous ties to a prince who's in poor health? Worthless. I couldn't even argue with them. My father left me shares in several business ventures that haven't done too badly, a townhome in Antwerp, the Château Solvay, a home in Vienna, and an apartment in Paris. I have a decent trust from him, and a trust from Mom's grandfather as well, but none of it compares to the Liechtenstein family wealth.

I'm small potatoes.

But Americans don't care about all that. Americans want someone who works hard, someone who will treat them well, someone who has a nice smile. I meet those criteria and then some. By the time I reach the Hampton on Grussonstrasse, I'm almost. . . excited. I slide my Range Rover into a space in the car park beneath the hotel and take the elevator upstairs, my eyes scanning the lobby eagerly for this distressed damsel. Will she have long blonde hair? Short dark hair? Dark, dramatic lips? A little pouty, maybe.

A man with grey hair glances up from reading a newspaper. He crinkles the pages and frowns. I look away quickly. The only other person in the lobby is slumped into the corner of a sofa, her face propped on her hand, asleep. And drooling. Her hair, the color of dark chocolate, surrounds her head in an enormous halo of frizz. Her shoes are off, and her feet are resting on one of her suitcases. It's a good

46

thing I drive a Range Rover, because she has a lot of luggage. Her bright yellow dress looks like it could be quite cute, if it wasn't rumpled, and if it didn't have streaks of something dark that begin at the collar and run downward in uneven and clearly unplanned swaths.

Clearly *not* a setup.

I walk toward her and tap her lightly on the shoulder. "Uh, Elizabeth?"

Her head jerks upright, and she wipes at her face dazedly.

"My sister asked me to pick you up."

She inhales sharply and squeaks. When she looks up at me, I realize what the streaks on her dress are from— mascara has run down beneath her eyes and covers her cheeks.

"You are Elizabeth Graham?"

She nods and stands up, looking around frantically.

"Is everything alright?"

"I'm so sorry," she says. "I didn't mean to go to sleep, but I flew in last night, and I didn't sleep very well, and I know it's past noon here, but it's barely six a.m. back in Atlanta."

"I've been jet lagged on numerous occasions," I say. "Please don't worry about it. Can I help you carry any of this? My car is just downstairs."

"Oh, no," she says. "I can get it all. When Paisley told me you were driving right past here." She makes a sound that closely resembles a hiccup. "I am really very grateful. Truly."

"It was no big deal." Shame over my irritation washes over me in a wave. It might not be a setup—indeed I may not find Holly's friend the least bit attractive, but that's no reason I can't extend a helping hand.

She stands up and her head reaches almost to my shoulder. She's much taller than I expected. She slings a purse over her body crosswise, a backpack over her shoulders, and then stacks a smallish rolling bag on top of a large one. "Ready." She beams at me.

"Oh, no, I'll grab those." I snatch the rolling bags from her before she can object, knocking the smaller one off in the process.

She bends down to try and grab it.

I hold out my hand and wave it at her. "No, no, please. I insist. Let's go to the elevators. I hear you've had a rough twenty-four hours. The least I can do is navigate these to my car for you."

"Thank you." She gulps, and even with the halo of fluffy hair and the mascara streaks, there's something endearing about her face. Like a chipmunk with a half eaten acorn, or a dog caught digging up a bone. Nervous, eager to please, grateful, and unaware of her own vulnerability.

She doesn't say a word in the elevator, or when we approach my car. But when I'm swinging her bags up into the back of my car, she stares.

"Is everything alright?" I ask.

"Oh, yes, for sure," she says. "But I just noticed how tall you are."

"You're fairly tall too," I say. "It's a good thing I don't drive a sports car."

Her laugh is like a trio of nightingales. I could listen to it all day. "If it was a convertible, the paparazzi would think you were on a road trip with Hagrid."

I know she's making fun of herself, her height, her frizzy mop of hair, but I can't help chuckling anyway.

She's smiling when she slides into the passenger seat, but she notices her face in the rear view mirror and stiffens. "Oh no." She flips the visor down and whimpers. "Oh my—"

I slide into the passenger seat. "Your mascara might have run a bit."

48

"I didn't even have that much in the tube," she wails. "I look like an ugly version of Marilyn Manson."

I have no idea who she is. "It's not that bad," I say. "Honestly."

When she turns to look at me, the only word for her expression is stricken. "I'm a licensed cosmetologist. Do you know what that means? I don't know the word for it in German. It's literally my job to do people's hair and makeup. I bought waterproof mascara, I'm sure I did." She begins rummaging around in her bag and then yanks out a little black tube. "See?" She squints and groans. "Oh, no. They must've changed the packaging. This is mortifying."

"If it helps, I doubt anyone in there suspected you were a beauty expert. Or whatever the word you used means." I certainly never would have guessed it.

She shuffles around in her purse again until she finds a package of something and pulls a tissue from it. She begins wiping on her face, but a moment later she squawks again. "It's all over my dress. This day couldn't have gotten much worse." But instead of crying, or complaining, she begins to laugh, the same beautiful, lilting, melodious laugh.

"Are you alright?" I ask.

She finally stops laughing and finishes wiping the makeup residue from her face. "You have no idea how much I love Paisley right now. She is just the best person in the world, and you too, by extension."

When she turns to face me this time, I'm shocked at the transformation. She's not a supermodel, but she no longer resembles a clown.

"I'm not an idiot, Cole. I'm pretty sure you weren't driving right by my hotel, and I know that picking up an idiotic twenty-something who is a complete and utter mess wasn't high on your list of things to do for the day. I really appreciate it."

I'm a completely selfish jerk who does not deserve her

gratitude. "If we're being totally honest, I should confess that Holly basically twisted my arm to get me here."

When I glance her way, Elizabeth is frowning. "Who's Holly?"

"Right, she's Paisley to you. My sister goes by her middle name in Atlanta. Her first name is Holly, which is what we all call her."

"I heard that at some point, I think," she says. "But I'm a little slow today. I'm sorry."

"Stop thanking me and stop apologizing," I say. "Or I'll have to gag you, and I doubt Holly would appreciate that."

"I wouldn't say a word about it," she says.

When I look her direction, her lips are compressed. So it was a pun about being unable to talk because of the gag. She has a strange sense of humor, but I like it. Now if I could get her to laugh again.

"What do you do, Cole? When you aren't driving to and from Frankfurt at a moment's notice?"

"Uh, well, that's a little awkward," I say. "I'm sort of between jobs right now."

"Well, what was your last job?"

"It was more of an unofficial position," I hedge.

"As what?" she asks. "Because I'm beginning to wonder if you're, like, smuggling drugs and I'm a conveniently frizzy cover for your whole operation. Maybe that's why you needed to put my luggage in the back yourself."

"Actually, I've been filling in for my dad, since he's been sick," I say.

Her eyes widen. "Right, because Paisley's a princess. So you're a prince, but you're working as the king, basically?"

"Actually, Liechtenstein is sort of a strange country," I say. "Or, compared to the bigger ones you probably studied at school it is."

"Well, we have plenty of time," she says. "Why not give me a primer?"

I smirk. "You need another nap?"

"Oh please. I'm American. We find all of this fascinating."

"The first time you yawn," I say, "I'm done."

"Deal," she says.

"So the Liechtenstein family started with just the Liechtenstein castle in Vienna. Various ancestors of my Dad, whose given name is Hans-Michael, advised the Habsburgs, whom you likely have heard of, one of the most famous royal houses of Austria. In America, I believe they say Hapsburg. Their family held the throne of the Holy Roman Empire for over three hundred years, from 1438 to 1740 when the House of Bourbon replaced them."

"Still awake over here," Elizabeth says.

I roll my eyes. "I should hope so, as I'm just getting started. So, my dad's ancestors gave good enough advice that the Habsburgs gave them quite a few valuable lands, but none of them gave them a position in what you'd call the Parliament, but we call it the Diet, spelled d-i-e-t, but pronounced dye-et."

"And they wanted that position?"

I nod. "Badly, actually. So back in 1699, an enterprising relative arranged to buy a nearly worthless lordship, Shellenberg, as well as the County of Vaduz, both of which reported directly to the Holy Roman Emperor himself. Good old Charles VI decided to combine them into a Principality for his dear friend Anton Florian, and he called that Principality 'Liechtenstein.'"

"So, it's not its own country?" she asks, rather astutely.

"It wasn't in the early 1700s, that's for sure, and as a funny bit of trivia, good old Anton and his family didn't even set foot in their shiny new Principality for decades."

"You're kidding."

I shake my head. "They didn't care about it at all, just the privileges and power it would afford them."

"Wow, that's wild."

"Well, Dad's family sort of wobbled along, not really caring much about their Principality, other than the title it bestowed of 'prince.' In 1788, Johann Joseph decided to become a military man. He turned out to be quite good at it, and the Napoleonic wars afforded him the opportunity to prove himself admirably. After his father passed away and he became the reigning Prince, he kept right on fighting. In fact, he attained the rank of General three years after he took over as active prince. He fought and fought, but eventually negotiated two different peace treaties with Napoleon that the Austrians felt were a little too good for Napoleon."

"Did he betray his own people?" she asks.

I shrug. "Depends on your perspective, I suppose. He was fairly forward thinking. He had to resign from the military when the Austrians got mad at what they felt were not very aggressive treaties, but as a result of his impressive service and Napoleon's favor, Napoleon made Liechtenstein a sovereign state in his Confederation of the Rhine." I smile. "And good old Johann Joseph went on to create quite a few rights for his people that were fairly liberal for the time. He also fostered a lot of agriculture and forestry, both of which still benefit the country today."

"It sounds like you admire him," Elizabeth says.

"I suppose I do," I say. "He did a lot of good. He didn't ever live in Liechtenstein, but he visited and was quite generous with his firewood and other resources. He wasn't perfect, but he tried his best, and he wasn't afraid to jump in and work—and fight—whenever necessary. No matter the risk to himself."

"A decent role model," she says. "I could use a little more risk tolerance in my life."

"I don't know," I say. "Holly tells me you flew out here to join a tour without ever having been to Europe. You might have had a few bumps, but I imagine you'd have worked something out, even if I hadn't been close enough to give you a ride."

"I was researching hostels," she says. "But my credit card had been frozen thanks to some jerk in Texas who stole the number. It was going to be a very bumpy few weeks before Paisley called. Or, I guess, Holly. Sorry."

"It's fine," I say. "I'm used to hearing Paisley. Her husband James calls her Paisley, too. Honestly, I mostly say Holly out of a combination of habit and the desire to annoy her."

"Ah yes," Elizabeth says. "That instinct runs deep with brothers."

"So you clearly have a brother or two."

"One brother was plenty for me," she says.

I wish I still had a brother, but there's no way for her to know about Noel. I shake it off—it's not a great road trip story.

"So what happened after good old Johann passed? At some point, someone has to move out to Liechtenstein, right? Once they realize what a beautiful little bucolic country it is?"

"Have you ever seen Liechtenstein?" I ask.

She blushes. "Uh, no. Did I use the wrong word? I realized after I said it that I'm not actually sure what that word means."

Adorable. Utterly adorable. "It means cute and country, I think, but you shouldn't quote me on that. English is my third language and I struggled, honestly."

"Third?" her eyebrows rise. "Are you serious?"

"I learned Dutch first, and then shortly after, German. I don't count Alemannic, as it's only a dialect of German. I'm dyslexic, so learning new languages is a misery, but Mom insisted I learn English after I mastered the other two. It took a decade to become fluent enough to manage on my trips to the United States. If I hadn't done a year of school on an exchange in New York, we probably wouldn't be talking freely right now. I find that learning to read and write something is worlds harder for me than simply speaking."

"That's impressive," Beth says. "Honestly."

I shrug. "Charles Schwab is dyslexic. Albert Einstein was too. Your president, John F. Kennedy, dyslexic. And Walt Disney. I could go on."

"I didn't mean to say you aren't capable," she says. "Sorry if it came across that way."

"Not at all, but I don't like telling people." I have no idea why I told her. "They look at me differently."

"Are you sure they're not staring at your nose hairs?" she asks.

My hand flies to my nose and she laughs. That captivating laugh keeps me from being annoyed. "My nose hairs are fine."

"Your nose hairs aren't at all visible," she agrees.

"Anything to distract me from droning on about the family's rise to prominence?"

"Oh, not at all. I was about to ask you what happened after Napoleon made you a sovereign state."

"It is quite exciting," I say. "And good old Johann Joseph was very dutiful. He and his wife had fourteen children."

Her jaw drops. "Wait, all with the same woman?"

"Viennese women are sturdy," I say. "Like, seriously impressively fertile."

She shakes her head. "I can't even."

"Can't even what?"

Her brow furrows. "Excuse me?" She pauses. "Oh, sorry. That's an odd American expression."

I smirk.

"You're messing with me now."

"Maybe, but I'm finding that it's quite entertaining."

And I want her to laugh again, even if it's at herself, which she does quite freely. It's refreshing, a woman who laughs at herself. "But his oldest son Aloys took over for him."

"Boring. Oldest son, oldest son, always the oldest son."

I don't disagree.

"But then," she says, "maybe I only think that since I'm the youngest daughter."

"Well, good old Aloys married another Viennese woman and they had eleven kids."

She shakes her head. "He couldn't even match his father. Sad, really."

"Well, it must have been a very vexing few years for him," I say, "because his first five children were female, as were the four after the oldest son. Can you imagine? *Nine* daughters?"

"I hope they had a lot of bathrooms."

"He must have been a very patient man."

"My father only had three girls," Elizabeth says, "and he says he barely survived raising us."

"I do believe fathers today are expected to do a great deal more in the way of interaction and nurturing than good old Aloys. He probably foisted them off on nannies."

"Now I have a burning desire for a nanny," Elizabeth says. "But do I need to have *eleven* children to justify it? Because I don't want one that badly."

"You just need to marry a prince," I say.

"Know of any eligible ones?"

When I glance her way, her eyebrow is cocked, the side of her mouth turned up, and I realize she's flirting.

"Actually," I say. "This is a little awkward, but I'm not a prince."

Her mouth drops. "But Paisley is a princess, right? Or is that just a media thing, and she's not really?"

I clear my throat and tighten my hands on the steering

wheel. Apparently even Americans care. "Oh, she's a princess alright, not that she can inherit from Dad either."

"Aren't you the oldest boy?"

I flinch, but I doubt she notices. I don't mention Noel. "I was born during my mother's first marriage, to Gerard, the Marquis of Béthune. He died when I was barely a year old."

"Oh, I'm so sorry."

"I don't remember him at all, but from what Mom says, he wasn't a wonderful person. And her second husband, the Prince of Liechtenstein, has always treated me as his own son."

Her eyebrows rise. "But that's not good enough for the sovereign Principality of Liechtenstein."

I shake my head. "It's not, and that's okay. I've been helping my dad out for way too long, but I recently told him it was time for me to press play on my life again. It's time for him to let go."

"Let go of what?" she asks.

"A few nights ago, Dad unveiled his plan to name me as his successor."

"Whoa, I thought you said you can't—"

"I can't. You're right about that." I squeeze the steering wheel so tightly that my knuckles turn white.

"You look upset, and I don't want to make it worse, but if your dad—"

"His plan would never work," I say. "He wanted to adopt me formally, and then petition the House to change the law so that an adopted child could inherit."

"It sounds like it's about time," Elizabeth says, "for the house law to be changed."

"You're so American."

"What does that mean?" I can hear the frown in her voice.

56

"It means that most things in life can't be fixed. They just are what they are."

"Is that an American thing?" she asks. "Or a young thing?"

Great, now she thinks I'm ancient. At thirty-three, I'm probably almost ten years older than her—which means I'm way too old to even be considering the age gap. Even if Holly is nearly ten years younger than James. I focus on the road ahead.

"So, good old Aloys had two sons and nine daughters."

I chuckle. Right back to the Liechtenstein primer. "His oldest son, Johann the Second, took over after him. He gave the people their first constitution. He took over really young and was the longest reigning monarch in Europe who never employed a regent of any kind."

"But the real question. . ." Elizabeth meets my eyes. Hers sparkle.

I don't want to look away, but I have to watch the road. "Yes?"

"How many kids did good old Johann the Second manage to father?"

"Ah, well, he was a bit of a disappointment there, truth be told."

"Do tell," she says.

"He didn't have any children."

"Was he. . ." Her voice drops to a whisper. "Gay?"

I laugh. "Doubtful, but I guess there's no way to know for sure. He had one younger brother, though, if you'll remember."

She nods, sitting forward in her chair, her head turned toward mine.

"Well, good old Franz was an ambassador, and at the tender age of forty-three, he fell in love with a. . . Jewish widow."

"Oh no, the horror." She rolls her eyes.

"And of course, Liechtenstein is Roman Catholic," I say. "So Johann the second did *not* approve."

"He ruined his brother's romance? Oh man, that's sad."

"Not quite," I say. "See, the widow converted, but that still wasn't good enough. But after twenty years of loving her against his brother's wishes, Franz married her in secret."

"Whoa, how old was he then?"

"Almost sixty-three," I say. "Which is a little depressing, honestly."

"How long were they secretly married?" she asks. "And did Johann the second, who I don't like much anymore, find out?"

"I don't know whether he discovered it, but he finally died in 1929, when his younger brother was seventy-three, and plucky little Franz finally married the love of his life publicly, the widow. He went on to rule by her side for nine more years after that."

"That's tragic. I feel like there's a movie there or something."

I chuckle. "Maybe if they weren't so old. Do you want to watch a geriatric love story?"

She sticks out her bottom lip. "What if I do? Love is love."

It makes me like her even more, but I don't say that.

"Wait." She swivels to face me, her eyes wide, her lip still stuck out. It sounds like she's holding her breath when she says, "Did they have children?"

I shake my head. "Nope. None at all, which means that in spite of his eleven children, poor old Aloys didn't manage to keep his line going."

"Geez," she says, a little bitterly. "All those worthless girls."

"You'll like Francis Joseph II," I say. "He took over when his dad, the next dynast in line, passed on the throne.

And he was brilliant—turned around the family fortunes himself. He also gave women the right to vote, and he moved the family to Liechtenstein. He thought if we were ruling the Principality, we ought to be living here, too."

"Smart guy," Elizabeth admits, almost reluctantly.

"You don't know the half of it. We stood to lose everything in the wake of the world wars. The family was balanced on the edge of a knife, but he managed to extricate the bulk of the family's art from war-torn Germany, and then using the sale proceeds from a few notable pieces, he refilled the coffers, transforming Liechtenstein into a financial powerhouse."

She smiles. "Did you ever know him?"

"I have a photo or two of my diapered little self sitting on his lap, but I don't remember them. But his son, Hans-Adam the Second, is my dad's father, and he was nearly as good a man as Great Grandfather Francis."

"Sounds like you were blessed," she says. "And also cheated."

By the time we reach the palace, I almost don't notice her frizzy hair, or the streaks down her yellow dress. When Lars shows up to take her bags, I almost stop him and make a joke about needing to retrieve my drugs from them first. I don't, and when I examine why, it makes me uneasy. I don't want to share her laugh with anyone else. That's when I realize that, although Holly probably wasn't trying to set me up with Elizabeth Graham, I almost wish she was.

❧ 5 ❧

BETH

If Paisley had told me that her brother looked like Liam Hemsworth, I would *not* have agreed to the ride. My hair, my running mascara, my ruined dress, my pathetic, forlorn, jet lagged nap in the middle of Frankfurt.

My one hope is that he didn't notice that I was drooling all over my hand. Please let him not have noticed that. Not that I can do anything about it now. I laugh out loud at myself. As if a semi-prince-legit-marquis who looks like a movie star and speaks three languages fluently would ever date little old dowdy Beth Graham from a suburb of Atlanta. It doesn't matter whether my hair was done, or my makeup, or whether I looked organized and impressive.

And in any case, I am *not* organized and impressive.

I'm a beautician who dabbles at playing the piano. I live with my parents. And my birth mom may be famous, but she can't even be bothered to pay for my hotel and food when the job I flew out for is postponed. I'm not bold enough to demand she cover my costs, seeing as she's the reason I'm in this mess. If Rob hadn't made friends with a secret princess, I'd be scouring the streets of Frankfurt looking for the most inviting park bench—until it got bad enough I had to call Mom and Dad and ask for money.

Humiliating.

I look around the room to which Paisley led me. A canopy bed with a rich, embroidered blue bedspread rests on the back wall with one hundred and seventy-four pillows piled on top of it. Okay, I didn't actually count them, but it's close to that. A chaise lounge at the foot of the bed with matching embroidery. Tapestries on the wall, honest to goodness *tapestries*. And the window opens on the town of Vaduz below. This entire room should be photographed for a magazine.

Although, the bathroom doesn't have a shower—just a clawfoot tub designed for the Jolly Green Giant. It's at least nine feet long. Who needs a tub that long? I can't even remember the last time I took a bath, so that will be interesting. But for now, I plonk my makeup bag on the counter in front of the vanity and start over from the ground up.

A moment later, a tap at the door warns me that Paisley is here with the flat iron she promised. I hop up and run over.

"Thank you." I take the flat iron with greedy hands.

"I swear, they really should have a 'travel to Europe' primer or something. It's like a whole new world over here."

"This room." I spin around. "I have no words."

"Words like, old?" Paisley asks. "Musty? Cluttered?" She smiles. "I can help. I have plenty of words."

"You're bonkers," I say. "I couldn't possibly love it more. It's breathtaking, charming, elegant, and it has gravitas. That's a word, right?"

Paisley laughs. "I'm glad you like it. This is the blue room, very cleverly named." She looks pointedly at the bedspread, then at the blue vase collection on top of the armoire.

"I need a blue room, now," I say. "I mean, really. And the canopy bed!"

"It eats up way too much space," Paisley says, "and it's so old that it squeaks, even though I made Mom replace the mattress."

"Who cares if it squeaks?" I ask. "It's a piece of history."

"I like history well enough," Paisley says, "but I prefer a good night's sleep."

"I'm sure I'll sleep fine. Thank you," I say. "Truly. I can't thank you enough."

"I'm glad you could come," she says. "None of my real friends have seen any of this. It's kind of fun to see it through your eyes."

"Does James like it?" I ask.

She laughs. "He grew up in the Boston version of this, so he's as jaded as me. He thinks the word 'antiques' is just good marketing for old junk."

My mouth drops.

"We have furniture that is just as high quality now— look at Rob's stuff—and it's not creaky and worn out. Give me new, thank you very much, and let great great uncle Heinrich keep his fifteen billion dollar rolltop desk." She snorts. "I'm not saying there isn't a place for it. I just don't appreciate it, clearly. Luckily, the world is a vast and beautiful place with room for all kinds."

"Speaking of beautiful." I raise one eyebrow.

Paisley frowns. "Huh?"

"Your brother?" I roll my eyes. "A heads up might have been in order. I was asleep on my arm and *drooling* when he arrived. No lie."

Paisley laughs. Then she laughs some more.

"I had mascara smeared all over my cheeks, and look." I point at my dress. "I looked like I was wearing a horrible Medusa costume." I pause. "I don't even know if you celebrate Halloween here."

She shakes her head. "Not really, no."

"And you know, it wouldn't be so bad, except—"

"He's so utterly and completely, devastatingly handsome?"

I sigh. "It's not fair, like, at all."

"It really isn't. Do you know how obnoxious it is that some people get all the looks?"

Paisley is nearly as cute as her brother. Meanwhile, I'm average in every way. Which I'm mostly fine with, but not when, at my very worst, I'm shoved up against the cover model for Ralph Lauren Polo, Europe. "And he's so stinking tall."

"Which you should like," Paisley says. "What are you? Five ten?"

I guffaw. "As if your brother would ever see me as anything but a charity case." I toss my hair.

"So flatten it. Or curl it. Or whatever, but do it quick. Mom sent me to tell you that we have dinner in twenty minutes, and that was at least five minutes ago."

I race across the room to plug the flat iron into the wonky European outlet.

"You can keep that one," Paisley says. "Mom had three. She said she doesn't like that one because the plates are too wide."

When I wait for it to heat up this time, I touch up my makeup, and wonder of wonders, nothing melts or smokes or anything. Thank goodness. I flatten my hair faster than I ever have, and then I change into my very favorite dress— black with a thick, simple, lace-ringed bodice that looks even more dramatic against my porcelain skin. With my eyes outlined in burnt ember, I look about as good as I can. Which isn't much, but it's light-years ahead of my Hagrid/Medusa/Marilyn Manson look.

I take the massive staircase slowly, not eager to add to my earlier humiliation with a tumble downward. I've

63

nearly reached the bottom when something catches my eye.

Something I can barely believe.

In a spacious, light drenched western facing room, lit by the lowering sun, is a reddish masterpiece. I know I'm expected at dinner. I know that Paisley's family is proper and fancy and formal, but I can't keep my feet from rushing toward it. A Grand Fazioli Brunei. The nicest concert piano in existence, barring random one-offs. I reach out and brush the burl case, inlaid with mother of pearl flowers, and run my hand over the diamond inlay on the lid.

My fingers curl and uncurl, itching to play just one song. Just one.

"Beth?" Paisley calls from the entry.

"I'm coming," I say. "I'm so sorry—I was sidetracked."

I tear my hand away and force my feet to move toward her voice. But there must be some way I can obtain permission to play on it. Maybe when the family is out, sometime. Surely they have outings planned, and fancy occasions. Things that will take them away from the palace.

"You okay?" Paisley asks.

"You have a Grand Fazioli Brunei," I say, my voice breathier than I'd like.

"A what?" Paisley scrunches up her nose.

"Only the most elegant, rich sounding, meticulously engineered, mellow piano—in the world, really. Paolo Fazioli engineered it for the Sultan of Brunei originally, you know."

Footsteps behind her alert me to more people on their way toward us.

Paisley raises her voice. "Uh, hey, Mom, Cole, did you guys know we have, like, a famous piano?"

I laugh. "It's probably not famous to normal people, but it is for music nerds. It's like having a Rolls Royce in your music room."

Cole steps out of the dining room, his long legs eating up the parquet floor. He halts abruptly, his eyes traveling to my face and then back down to my shoes. He frowns and his eyes widen and then his mouth opens, but no words emerge.

"I'm sorry. I didn't mean to make a fuss. Let's go," I say.

"Elizabeth?" Cole says.

"Beth, please," I say. "I'm not fancy enough to merit such a long name."

"I heard you played piano," he says. "And Rolls Royce or not, you're welcome to play that one anytime you'd like."

"I have a lot of new music to learn," I say. "But it might not be amazing to listen to—it's just the supporting melody for the songs I'll be accompanying on tour. It feels wrong, somehow, to practice them on this." I glance over my shoulder. "Like doing donuts in the parking lot with a Rolls."

Paisley's mom ducks her head around the corner. "What's going on?"

"Mom, my friend Beth wants to know whether she can practice some of her pieces—she's about to be on tour with Henrietta Gauvón—while she's with us. Cole and I told her it's fine, but she's worried because apparently Dad spent way too much money on our piano."

Mom laughs. "These two certainly never appreciated it."

I look at Paisley. "I had no idea you played at all."

She swallows. "I don't."

"None of us do," Cole says. "Not anymore."

A weight seems to settle in the room at that comment, like a blanket has been tossed over us, a dampening, depressing blanket. There are way too many people for me to pry, but I make a note of it to ask Paisley later. I'd like to avoid all the land mines I can.

"Are we eating?" Paisley's father shuffles around his wife and stops beside her. "Ah, this must be your friend, Holly."

"Right," Paisley says. "This is Elizabeth Graham, who is joining Henrietta's tour. It was delayed, which gave her some time to spend with me. I can't wait to show her around."

"What do you want to see?" her dad asks.

I shrug. "Literally anything. Other than a few family vacations to the beach and to Disney World, I've never left Atlanta."

"Well, our daughter seems to like Atlanta well enough," her mom says. "But we think our little spot in the world is also quite nice." She clasps her hands together. "Oh, Holly, will she be here for the party?"

Paisley's mouth compresses and her eyes tighten. "Mom, I told you it's too early for anything like that."

Her mom lifts one eyebrow. "But you won't be back for months! It won't be a big deal, I promise. Just a few very close friends."

"Warning," a deep voice from inside the dining room says. "I can't be left in here alone with the rolls for much longer if you expect there to be enough for the rest of you." It must be James threatening us.

"We haven't blessed the food yet," Paisley's mom says, aghast.

Paisley grins. "We better go inside."

I follow the others inside, and try my best not to blush when the open seat is at the end of the table, right next to Cole. I utterly fail when he pulls my chair out for me. "Uh, thanks."

"Uh, you're welcome," he says with a smirk.

I am such an uncultured American. I've never minded before, but it's glaringly obvious right now. I wish I could be sitting next to James instead. Even if he's basically American royalty, at least he doesn't have any official titles.

"So tell us," Paisley's mom says after she offers a beautiful prayer. "How did one of Holly's friends from Atlanta come to join Henrietta Gauvón's European tour?"

This does not make me look better. "Well, it's a strange story, but I'll just share the highlights. I haven't even talked to Paisley, er, Holly about it yet. I always knew I was adopted, but I didn't realize my birth mother was—"

"Henrietta herself?" Paisley is practically bouncing in her seat. "Are you serious? That's amazing. She must have been quite young when she had you. She barely looks thirty now."

I shake my head. "I don't know about that. I haven't spent more than an hour talking to her, in my entire life. It's kind of why I agreed when she offered me the job."

"She showed up out of nowhere," James asks, "and offered you a job as her pianist?"

"Well, she called me out of nowhere, and then she saw me play at my night job at a steakhouse, and she got the news then that she needed a new pianist as hers is pregnant and feeling quite sick."

"Must be going around." James nudges Paisley's elbow.

My eyes widen. "Wait, are you?"

"I'm barely eleven weeks pregnant." Paisley sighs so hard that her hair shifts off her forehead. "You're not supposed to be telling anyone. I haven't told Mary, or Geo, or Trudy, or Rob yet. You and my mom are the worst."

"We're not the worst," her mom says. "We're excited. No, delighted. No, ecstatic. There's a difference."

"Mom, I do not want it splashed across the nightly news before I've told my friends."

Her mom gulps at that, and folds her hands in her lap.

"I won't tell a soul," I say, "but I am really, really excited." I want to tell her that Brekka's expecting too, but I figure that's Rob's news, not mine. I keep my mouth shut.

Dinner is as delicious as I imagined it would be. I ought

to limit my consumption so I can more closely resemble my svelte, pencil-thin bio mother, but it's too good. I can't do it. When I reach for my third roll, James catches my eye and smiles. "Can you believe they rarely ate rolls before I joined the family?"

I shake my head. "I'm not sure my life will ever be the same, now that I've had these," I say. "Do you think your mom would share the recipe?"

Cole's laughter rings from the rafters.

"What?" I ask.

Paisley's mom looks horrified.

"Is it an old family recipe?" I ask. "I'm sorry, I didn't know."

Cole's still laughing, and now Paisley is too.

"They employ a chef and three cooks," James says. "I doubt Paisley's mother does a lot of baking."

I'm such an idiot. I wish I could sink into the intricately woven carpet under my feet. Of course she doesn't. "Well, maybe the chef wouldn't mind sharing, then. When I go home, I'd love to try and make them."

Paisley wipes her eyes and shakes her head. "I can tell you the number one ingredient." She meets my eyes. "Butter. Anything that tastes this good is at least forty percent butter."

"Mom can't make toast," Cole says. "She'd starve if the chef and the cooks all got sick."

"Of course that's not true," I say. "She could always order take out."

Cole and Paisley start laughing again, and this time her dad and James join them.

"I'm glad my general incompetence in the kitchen is so amusing," her mom says, although she doesn't look very annoyed.

"I'm sure you spend your time doing other things that are much more complex and important than baking bread."

This time, Paisley's mom laughs too. "Not really," she says. "And now I have an overwhelming urge to take a baking lesson."

All in all, by the time dinner is done, I'm more than ready to race up the stairs to my opulent blue room and go right to sleep. I'm about four stairs up when Cole stops me. "Do you have plans tomorrow?"

I shake my head. "Not unless you count testing out a few ideas for new and more horrible ways to insult my hosts."

Cole chuckles. "Oh, please. Mom has never been talented in the kitchen. She burns popcorn, oversalts and overcooks eggs, and undercooks everything else. Trust me when I say we're all better off if she steers clear. And don't worry—her self-esteem doesn't suffer. She thought it was nearly as funny as we did, but the joke loses its potency if she laughs. It's much funnier if she scowls and postures instead of laughing along with us."

I hate how quiet my voice is when I ask, "So you don't think she hates me?"

Cole takes steps up twice so we're standing eye to eye. "Not at all. I think she likes you, nearly as much as I do."

My shoes suddenly feel too tight, and there's an odd tingling between my shoulder blades. "Oh."

"I wanted to see whether you might be interested in accompanying me tomorrow."

"Normally I'd love to, but Paisley said—"

His voice drops an octave, as he shifts to a whisper. "She makes a lot of plans, but she's been here four days, and so far, she's always in and out of the bathroom until one or two in the afternoon."

"Morning sickness?" I ask.

Cole nods. "The baby does not like mornings. My sister rarely does what's expected, but in this instance, it appears she's quite traditional."

Oh no. Paisley probably asked him to babysit me. "It's okay," I say. "I don't need to be entertained. Unless it bothers someone, I can simply practice my songs in the morning."

"What if *I* need to be entertained?" He cocks his right eyebrow.

Uh. "What?"

"I haven't laughed as hard as I did today in a very long time. I find that I quite like an American perspective on things."

I frown.

"I'm not making fun of you, to be clear. I simply love seeing what you think about some of the things that have been as they are for ages—sometimes for no better reason than we haven't thought to change them. Americans rush toward change in every aspect."

"That's not fair," I say. "We like things to be done right, and if that's different than the way they're already done, well, then we change. But if something works, we aren't afraid to keep doing it."

"Really?"

I think about the new items on every fast food menu, the new cereals on the grocery store shelf weekly—frequently in horrifying combinations—and the ever-changing fashion trends. "We might like a little variety now and then, but I'm sure that's human nature, not Americans specifically."

"Alright," Cole says. "But back to tomorrow, I'm meeting with the National Assembly to review a treaty with France. I thought you might be fascinated, given that you had so many questions earlier today."

A treaty with France? How different his world is from mine. "I'd love to see that."

"I'm due there at ten in the morning, but if you're up earlier than that, you're certainly welcome to practice the piano. Any time after eight in the morning, everyone should be up and working."

"Thank you," I say. "For everything."

"It was truly my pleasure," he says.

I hope he's not just being polite—because somehow, with a flash of his bright, grassy green eyes, my day went from epically bad to Cinderella good.

❧ 6 ❧

COLE

"Why aren't you part of the EU?" Beth asks. "Because then you wouldn't need to use the Swiss franc, right? And when travelers came to visit, it would be easy for them to eat and shop and whatnot."

I shake my head. "We don't care much about tourism. It's barely a line item in our gross domestic product."

"Really? With as adorable as Liechtenstein is? With such a rich history and such friendly people?"

"We are quite friendly," the prime minister says, "but not to outsiders."

Beth's eyes widen, and I remember that she's an outsider. How could I have forgotten that?

"Of course, we're always happy to welcome Holly's friends," I say.

"Right, of course." Adrian Hundinger, Liechtenstein's Prime Minister for almost seven years now, swallows. It's a good thing he's so fluent in English, or bringing Beth along might have stressed him out. "I hope you didn't think I was referring to you."

Beth shrugs. "Well, I am an outsider, so it would be silly

to be offended by it. So far, everyone I've met has been cordial and welcoming."

"What Cole hasn't told you," Adrian says, "is that we are not well equipped for tourists, so the inconvenience of the Euro not being accepted works in our favor. We have more businesses here per capita than any country on earth. We like to work, we like to play, and we like to keep to ourselves."

"And the EU sets tax brackets, which would ruin our very attractive twelve and half percent corporate and eight percent value added tax," I say.

Beth shakes her head. "Well, it's good that you know what you're doing." She switches to German. "I need to practice my German, so please don't need to speak English."

I correct her as kindly as possible, and she repeats the phrase, properly. "German is a confusing language," I say slowly. "But you will pick it up if you stick with it."

She nods. "Thanks. Talking slowly helps a lot."

"Many of the citizens here in Liechtenstein do speak English," Adrian says. "And we love the United States, so don't feel bad if you need to clarify anything."

Beth asks fantastic questions, and she waits naturally for a pause to ask so that she never slows down our progress. Since the Landtag is out of session, the members of the National Assembly fill in, which expedites everything.

"I think this is done," I say, finally. "Unless you have any questions. Hopefully they'll approve our changes, and if they do, I'll get my dad's signature."

"Perfect," Adrian says. "It'll be nice to finish with this."

"I probably ought to tell you," I say, "that I've accepted a job working for Argenta. I'll be moving to Antwerp in the next two weeks. That's one of the reasons I wanted to finish this up. Well, this and the details of the small business initiative."

I've worked with Adrian directly for three of the last seven years he's held his position, and even before that, I came with Dad to every meeting. In all that time, he has never been flustered, or distraught, or upset. No matter how frustrating the opposition, no matter how childish the Landtag or the citizens or the trade delegates, he smiles and navigates through the worst until things are smoothed over. It's what makes him such a wonderful Prime Minister.

He splutters now, his eyes bulging. "You're leaving? Just like that?"

"You know that there's nothing for me here," I say softly.

But it's too late. Beth is watching us, her head tilted, her sharp brain trying to interpret what we're saying.

"How can you say there's nothing for you here?" Adrian gestures out the window at the Alps behind us. "Liechtenstein is your home, and it may not strictly be in your blood, but it's—" He stands up and begins pacing. "You belong here." He whips his head around and pins me with his famous stare. "Your people need you."

"Franz will—"

Adrian throws his hands in the air. "Pah, Franz. He hasn't lived here in. . . How long? Since he was eighteen years old. And he married that *American*, and lived in New York and now in Munich. He doesn't know us, and he doesn't care about us. He cares about dollars and cents and buying and selling the world."

I stand up. "Now see here. It's largely due to Franz's expertise that Liechtenstein remains in such a strong position internationally. The banking group would never have acquired—"

"Being Prince of Liechtenstein is about more than

balancing the budget. It's about more than making smart business moves."

"Well, that's good," I say, lowering my voice. "Because under my stewardship, Berg Telecomm nearly *died off*."

"But it didn't," Adrian says, "and it was in a nose dive long before you were tasked to resuscitate it."

"Holly saved it," I say. "I can't take a lick of credit for that. You'd be better off appealing to her. The dynasts might actually vote to change that archaic law and allow a female to inherit. Holly would be an excellent ruler."

"You're the one who stayed when things were hard, and you're the one who brought her back when we were struggling," Adrian says. "We had all given up on her years ago, but you inspired her to step up. And beyond that, if Berg had died, you'd have gladly donated whatever was required of your own personal wealth to create a new entity to fund the Distribution. Because you love the people, and you know them. You play football with them. You go for jogs and wave and chat with them." Adrian grabs his briefcase. "You do what you want. Your father always has, as the good Lord surely can attest. But you think about this before you simply bow out and pass the governing of our people off to your uncle Franz. No one else, not even your father anymore, knows more about the forty thousand people who live here. And we love *you*. Not your dad, not your mom, or even your sister. We have watched as you have been there for every single thing as soon as we needed it. You are as royal as your father, your grandfather and your great grandfather, and we have noticed."

"So what?" I ask. "Even if that's all true, there's still no place for me here."

"There's always a place for a son of Liechtenstein here," he says. "I'm not a prince. Does my contribution not matter?"

I sigh. "Of course it does."

"So run for a position on the Landtag—any party would support you. You'd be a lock to win, you know you would."

I laugh. "It's a part-time position, and at the end of the day, my place isn't here. It's in Belgium, where my father was a lord. That's the future for me."

"Your future is always wherever you take it." He marches out the door with stiff shoulders and a severe frown frozen on his face.

Beth's eyes follow him out before circling back to me. I wonder how much she understood of our interchange.

"He doesn't want you to move to Antwerp?" she asks.

Too much, clearly.

"He'll get to know and respect my uncle Franz soon enough. Dad said he'd be reaching out to him, to let him know he's preparing to transition the rule into his hands. Uncle Franz went to Harvard Business School. He worked for the top banks in the world, and he's commanding, impressive, regal even. He's eminently more capable than me at all the governing, and the economics, and probably everything, really." I shrug. "Honestly."

Beth doesn't offer any opinions, but she doesn't have to —with her eyebrows raised and her quirked mouth—she's as skeptical as the day is long.

"I've been doing my best to fill in for my dad, but believe me. Franz will be able to do what I've done with one eye closed."

"Sounds like he'll have to, what with all his other responsibilities. I hope a tenth of his time will be as effective as all of yours has been, for the people of Liechtenstein's sake."

"It will be."

Her brow furrows. "I thought you couldn't stay, since you weren't his biological son—"

"I can't," I snap.

She flinches, and I wish I could take it back. She didn't

deserve that, not when she's merely responding to Adrian's frustration. And probably my own, because if I'm being honest with myself, I've wished for nearly thirty years that Mom had just married Dad from the start. I wish I were really his son, his oldest child, an actual Prince of Liechtenstein, and not this pathetic placeholder, not quite at home anywhere. Never really belonging with anyone.

However, the daydreams of a child don't alter the real world, and it's time I give up on impossible dreams. Past time. "I'm sorry if I was short with you."

"You wish you were your dad's child, biologically. I get it."

Of all the people I've met, Beth might actually understand. So I just nod.

"But even if you can't take over as prince, I'm sure your dad could adopt you." Her words are so soft I can barely hear them. She has no way of knowing that after thirty years of wishing and hoping, that my dad finally offered me papers naming me as his son.

Or that I already turned him down.

"If I were to be adopted, I would forfeit all claim to my biological father's titles and estate."

"That can't be right," Beth says. "In America, you can inherit from your birth parents, but you're also entitled to a fair share from your adoptive parents."

I shake my head. "Trust me, the title would pass, as would Château Solvay."

"And you love it, this Château?"

I snort. "I've been there three times, I think."

She tilts her head and purses her lips.

"Look, you can't understand because you're not from here. It's different in Europe. Titles, lands, they still matter a great deal."

"Well, my mom used to tell me something. She would say, 'money can't buy happiness.' And I think you could apply that to titles and vast and impressive estates. You look happy with your mom and dad. You look happy here, working with Adrian. Maybe you're just a happy person and you'll find joy anywhere. I don't know. I know better than most that adoption papers are just a formality." She drops to a whisper. "But sometimes those formalities make a difference."

I grab my briefcase and walk toward the door. "You don't know me," I say. "And I care a great deal about the formalities that provide me with my title, my lands, and consequently, my value. In America, you worry a great deal about being happy. Here in Europe, we worry a great deal more about things that are less transient. We care about things that last."

I hate the hurt in her eyes, and I hate that I caused it. "I'm sorry if that was harsh, but things are very different here. I appreciate your concern, but I have things very well in hand."

"I'm sure you do," she says.

When we reach my car and she climbs into the passenger side, she still hasn't said anything else. No questions about the snow in the mountains. No badgering about the origin of the family castle, or our healthcare system. I may not have known her long, but I already know that a happy Beth is a prattling Beth.

"We're in the center of the bustling metropolis of Vaduz right now," I say. "Would you like me to show you a few of the shops?"

She shrugs listlessly.

Oh no. Holly's going to kill me if I broke Beth. "Maybe a restaurant."

She shakes her head. "I'd better get back and check on Paisley."

"Right." My phone buzzes. "Speak of the devil. She's

feeling better and wants to know if we can bring her a Subway sandwich."

Beth scrunches her nose. "Seriously?"

I chuckle. "She loves them—turkey, mustard, which she didn't like until she went to America, double pickles, toasted with salt and pepper. She's obsessed."

"Do you have a Subway?" she asks.

I make a right turn and pull into a spot. I bob my head to the right.

Beth follows my direction and inhales. "You sure do."

"Can I get you anything?"

Beth shakes her head. "I'm not a huge Subway fan, but thanks."

I run inside to grab Holly's sandwich, and when I get back to the car, Beth isn't inside. There's virtually no crime in Liechtenstein, but my heart races anyway. I broke her, and then I lost her? I cast about frantically. She should be easy to identify, since very few women here are taller than a metre seventy. I've nearly given up when I notice people gathering in front of the Hotel Adler. I cross the circle and push through.

Beth's playing the piano absently as she chats with Jostli, the owner. He's practically fawning over her.

"Beth," I say more sharply than I intended. "There you are."

"Oh, Cole, I'm so sorry. I heard the piano, you see. Some kids were banging on it, and I just came to check—"

"You can play here anytime you'd like," Jostli says in English, but with a heavy German accent.

I roll my eyes. "Paisley's waiting." I figure using her middle name is better than a code, since no one here ever uses it. I'd hate for them to realize my sister was having cravings and out her secret before she's ready.

Beth stands up. "Thank you so much, Jostli," she says in German. "It was wonderful practicing casual conversation with you, and this is a very nice piano. Your aunt was very kind to leave it to you, and I'm very sorry for her loss."

"Your loss," I correct her absently in German. "You're sorry for his loss, not his aunt's."

Jostli doesn't look the least bit broken up about his apparently dearly departed aunt, but he certainly seems taken with Beth. I almost feel sorry for him when she doesn't even spare him a backward glance. Almost, but not quite.

We reach the car. "We have a piano at the castle. You don't need to find another one."

She nods. "But last night." She swallows abruptly and climbs into the passenger seat.

"Last night?" I raise both eyebrows.

"Well, it seemed like there was a reason that no one ever plays your gorgeous grand piano, and I don't want to pick at an old wound. Especially after you've all been so gracious and welcoming to me."

"It's really fine." And listening to her play the piano would hurt far less than talking about Noel.

"Okay," she says.

My guilt about snapping at her earlier kicks into high gear. "It's my brother," I finally say. "He used to play a lot."

"You have a brother?" I wonder whether Beth realizes she's leaning toward me, looking at me like she'd look at a stray dog.

"I had a brother." I can barely force the words out.

"Oh, I'm so sorry."

"Holly moved to Atlanta and forgot about all of us after he died." I'm surprised at how much bitterness invades my words.

"I wondered why she left in the first place, when I heard she was a princess."

"Noel and Holly were inseparable," I say stiffly. "They sort of filled our home with light, and then in the same month, they were both gone." My voice breaks on the last word, and I grip the steering wheel at ten and two and stare straight ahead. With the short distance between downtown Vaduz and our castle, I'm nearly home, winding up the curving road toward the front gate.

"That must have been terrible for you. Was he sick?"

I nod.

"I thought Rob was dead." When I glance her way, she's staring out the window. "You said Noel filled your house with light, well, Rob was the anchor in our family. When he decided to sign up for the military, no one understood *why*. Mom and Dad tried their best to talk him out of it, but when his best friend begged for him to do it too, there was no stopping him. And when we got word that his unit had been hit with an IED and two men died." She closes her eyes. "They didn't know which ones." A tiny choking sound escapes her lips. "But that was only for three days, and then we found out that he was alive. He had broken his back, but he survived."

"He broke his back?"

"Well, severed, maybe," she says. "I was in high school, and I didn't pay enough attention to all that. But he had a lot of scary surgeries and thanks to an inexplicable miracle, he recovered. And then he came home."

"Was it the same?"

She's still riveted on the window, even though all she can see is the gate surrounding the castle. "It was different, but maybe it was better. Rob wasn't the same, but he was just as solid, just as. . . I don't know. As reliable, maybe, but he was sort of. . .thoughtful. He cared more about everyone around him, as if he was mindful that at any moment, we could be gone forever. Does that sound crazy?"

"Not at all. My dad was almost the opposite of that, though."

"Was?" She turns toward me, her eyes impossibly wide.

"After Holly left, we muddled on, but Dad kind of checked out little by little. He went from being larger than life to. . . I don't know. He kind of shrank. Like, without them, he didn't care about life as much as he did before." And nothing I did helped. He just kept shrinking and shrinking.

"Did Paisley used to play piano?"

I pull the Range Rover into the garage. "Only to humor Noel. He played brilliantly. Wickedly fast and jaunty one moment, then slow and dramatic the next." I shake my head. "You stick the music in front of him and a few minutes later, he'd bang it out. I tell you, the world was so easy for him. He would have made a brilliant ruler. To know him was to love him, truly."

"To know you is to love you, too," Beth says. "So you must have that in common."

I twist sideways to face her. "Not even close. If you knew Noel, you'd get it. We're nothing alike."

"You might be more similar than you realize," she says. "I'm beginning to think you don't see yourself very clearly."

I open my mouth to argue when I notice a Bugatti parked at the end of the garage. Only one person I know drives a Bugatti. My shoulders tense.

"Hey, are you okay?" Beth asks.

She's far, far too insightful, and as much as I like her, I really wish she wasn't here right now. This is going to be hard enough without a loose, American, conversational cannon.

I'm ready to move, truly I am. I'm not rethinking my decision, but uncle Franz is a bit much. I had hoped he'd come after I was already gone. "I think we have company for dinner." I point at the car.

"Is that a Bugatti?" Her eyes widen.

"You know European cars?"

She shrugs. "We own car dealerships back home. Occupational hazard, maybe."

"Well, the driver of that particular car is my Uncle Franz."

Her mouth drops open. "Next in line for the throne, Franz?"

We don't have a throne, but I don't bother correcting her. "The oldest of my dad's younger brothers, yes. He's also the CEO of the Banking Group, and a lawyer, and a financial genius. He's a little. . . imposing. I'm going to apologize in advance if he's rude to you. He won't even notice."

"Okay," I say.

"In case you're one of those super whizzes at reading people, we all think he's probably on the spectrum. Mild, but he's blunt to the point of being painfully rude sometimes, and he doesn't ever seem to care, as if he doesn't even notice."

"I won't say a word about anything, I swear," she says.

I'm not sure that's a promise she can keep, but at least she'll try. I'd hate for her to get attacked again today.

When we pass through the door, Mom immediately seizes me. "Ah, Cole, you're back. How'd it all go?" She beams a little too intensely, which is how I know she's barely hanging on. The more stressed Mom gets, the nicer she becomes. Forced cheer is her defense mechanism, like a squid inking, or a porcupine throwing needles. Mom lobs smiles and compliments, but she can't mask the crazy in her eyes, not from me.

"Aunt Andrea." I bob my head at Uncle Franz's wife, who's ten years his senior. "Where's Alejandro?"

"He had school commitments," she says.

Beth's head snaps toward my aunt, immediately recognizing another American. Even if Andrea was born in Puerto Rico, she emigrated so young that the United States is all she knows.

"Three Americans in one house," Holly says, walking down the stairs. "If we aren't careful, they'll stage a coup."

Uncle Franz chuckles. "I barely got to say two words to your husband at the wedding. I can't wait to talk shop with him today."

"He's got one call after another for the next little while," Holly says. "I'm afraid his smaller bank and invest-ment bank don't run quite as smoothly as your megaliths yet."

Uncle Franz shakes his head. "Nonsense. We've acquired a few new banks that have allowed us to expand into far-flung markets, but what James has built from the ground up in a decade is excessively impressive. Truly. And the way he wields it like a rapier, shredding his enemies and friends alike." Uncle Franz inhales and exhales slowly. "He's an inspiration, and I need to pick his brain on several things. The exchange market in—"

I stop listening and start reviewing a list of things I need to accomplish in the next two weeks before I leave for Antwerp.

Thank goodness for Holly. She carries most of the interactions with Uncle Franz and Aunt Andrea. After-noon tea stretches out far longer than I like, but eventually it ends, and we're released to change for dinner. I catch Beth on the way upstairs, jogging up two steps at a time to pull even with her. "Sorry about that," I say. "I had no idea they were coming, or I'd have left you at the Adler to prac-tice piano or something. Jostli is obnoxious, but he's harmless."

"I didn't understand most of what your uncle and Paisley talked about, and your Aunt Andrea was nearly as intimidating with her fashion lines, but they were perfectly polite. And now I can boast that I've met three princes."

"Still only two," I say. "I'm not a prince, remember?"

She shakes her head. "You're a prince to me."

I laugh. "That's exactly the kind of thing you shouldn't say at dinner, though."

"Are you sure you want to give up and hand everything off?"

"Of course I am."

She shrugs and purses her lips.

We passed my room, rounded the corner and are standing outside her door. "What does that mean?"

"What?" She lifts one eyebrow.

"That shrug and frown thing you just did."

"Oh, good grief. Nothing."

I cross my arms. "That meant something. I have a sister —I know when a girl's dying to say something."

"I've already been fussed at once today." She pulls her thumb and index finger from one corner of her mouth to the other, like she's zipping her mouth closed.

"You don't really have a zipper on your mouth. . ." I lean against the doorway.

"You Europeans are obnoxious, did you know that?"

I smile. "We're persistent, and we're elegant. Is that what you meant to say?"

"Right, that was it." Beth ducks inside her room.

"See you in a bit," I say.

"Just be sure," she says. "Before you do anything final. There are some things you can't take back, no matter how badly you wish you could." She closes the door before I can ask about the story behind that cryptic remark. Which is probably for the best, because I barely change in time as it is. Beth and I reach the staircase simultaneously, and I offer her my arm.

Her incredulous smirk is priceless. "I can walk on my own."

"That's not the point."

"These heels are stupidly high." She takes my arm until the bottom of the stairs and tries to let go.

I tighten my hand on hers. "You must allow me to lead you into the dining room. After all, we can't have you loitering around the piano again."

Her mouth rounds into a perfect o. "Hey, I could *play* the piano during dinner," she says. "Then you don't have to worry about what I'll say, and maybe some music will improve the atmosphere."

"You don't work for us, you know."

"But I'm just taking and taking and taking," she says. "It would be nice to be useful in some way."

"I'll let Marta know to add you to the rotation to mop the floors tomorrow," I say.

"Of course."

I laugh. "I'm kidding."

Every eye in the room turns toward us when we walk inside. The smile falls from both our faces and we take the seats at the end of the table, just like last night. But this time, Uncle Franz and Aunt Andrea are seated across from us.

"How long has it been since this room was redecorated?" Aunt Andrea asks. "Because it's awfully dark, isn't it?"

She'll be measuring the curtains next. Have Mom and Dad already told them why they invited them here, or are they simply assuming? I thought we agreed that I'd tell them about my plans to work for Argenta first.

"Would you like living in a castle?" Mom asks.

Aunt Andrea arches one eyebrow. "Castles are dreary, but I can make it work. My bigger concern is that I don't know how you've survived in Vaduz."

"You don't like small towns?" Beth asks.

Aunt Andrea and Uncle Franz both stare straight at her. She bears up under the scrutiny better than I expected.

"Stuttgart was too small," Aunt Andrea says. "And Munich is—" She scrunches her nose. "Tolerable. Neither of them are New York."

"James misses New York too," Holly says, kindly drawing fire from her friend. "I think once you've lived there for a while, it imprints on your DNA or something."

In spite of Holly's deft steering of the conversation, Aunt Andrea circles back around three more times to mention the terrible burden it must be to live in Vaduz. I've about had it.

"You may be wondering why we asked you out." Dad folds his napkin and looks at his hands. "I know it was short notice, and I appreciate you accommodating my request."

"Of course," Uncle Franz says. "When the Prince commands, the rest of us obey."

I hope he's kidding.

"Obviously that's not at all what I meant," Dad says.

"What did you ask us here for?" Aunt Andrea asks.

"Well, you know that I'm dealing with some health issues," Dad says.

Beth's words ring in my ears. *There are some things you can't take back, no matter how badly you wish you could.* That's a lesson I've already learned. I was so sure, absolutely positive in fact, that I shouldn't gamble my future on this crazy, last-ditch effort. I knew that it would hurt too much to hope and then fail. I'm better off bowing out and letting Uncle Franz take over.

But sometimes we don't do what's the best for us. Sometimes we do what we must.

"And for the past four years, I've been managing nearly every part of the day-to-day affairs of the Prince," I say.

Uncle Franz and Aunt Andrea's heads swivel toward me in a satisfying manner, their eyes wide, their lips barely parted.

"Dad didn't formally adopt me in the past, as I was unwilling to forgo my biological father's extensive lands and title. But last week, he decided he couldn't live with that oversight. He has drawn up papers to have me adopted, and we plan to petition the dynasts to vote on an amendment to the House Law. We wanted to ask you whether we'd have your support, since you're next in line to inherit."

Uncle Franz's eyes narrow. Aunt Andrea's hands ball in fists next to her plate.

"I know this feels sudden, but with as involved as you are, integral really, to the management of the LGT Group." I pause. "I can only imagine that you barely see your family as it is, what with being CEO of the group and chairman of the board for the bank, not to mention the trust."

"You want to change the *House Law?*" Uncle Franz asks. "To allow adopted children to usurp the laws of primogeniture?"

Dad squares his shoulders. "Cole is every bit as much my son as Alejandro is yours."

Uncle Franz's nostrils flare. "Except he's not. My blood runs in Alejandro's veins. My DNA comprises every one of his cells."

"Do you know that for sure?" Beth asks in perfect German. "You had his DNA tested?"

My jaw drops.

Holly snorts.

"Of course not." Uncle Franz's face is red.

"Perhaps you didn't get it tested because the certainty of the blood matching doesn't matter, as much as the fact that you raised him."

"Who is this again?" Andrea asks in English. "Because I don't appreciate her insinuations or her tone."

"Oh, I'm a nobody, don't mind me." Beth's eyes flash.

Uncle Franz wipes his mouth and stands up. "Thank you for dinner, Hans-Michael. It's always wonderful to see you, but I'm afraid I should warn you. I won't support this kind of change and neither will the other heirs, I'm sure of it."

After Dad sees his brother out, he shuffles back to the

foyer where I'm waiting for him. His shoulders are slumped and his eyes downcast. "That was exhausting."

"I'm sorry," I say.

He looks up at me then, his eyes finding mine. "Never apologize to me for being my son. I'm very proud of you Cole. We may not win this fight, but I'm honored to prepare for battle alongside you. And if Franz insists on toppling me, well, perhaps he'll find it difficult to succeed as both a prince and a CEO."

"Are you saying—"

Dad shrugs. "If he beats us here, maybe we take his precious CEO position away. After all, I own a controlling interest."

Beth may not have made the night go more smoothly, but she's the one who pushed me to change my mind. For the first time in a very long time, maybe since Noel's death, I feel like I might actually belong right where I am.

❧ 7 ❧

BETH

I'm plugging my phone in for the night when a text comes in from Rob. YOU AWAKE?

BARELY.

BREKKA WANTS TO DO THE GENDER REVEAL. TWENTY WEEKS ULTRASOUND WAS EXCELLENT. WOULD NOW WORK?

My excitement quickly burns through my exhaustion. ABSOLUTELY.

Rob sends a zoom link to my phone, and I boot up my laptop. This isn't really a tiny-phone-screen kind of event.

"Hey, Beth!" Brekka waves at me.

Rob's sitting right next to her. "We figured if we waited this late, your show might be over." He leans closer to the camera. "Whoa, where are you? That's a pretty amazing hotel."

I probably should have told my family that everything was delayed, but it's too late for that right now. "Thanks for making sure I didn't miss this," I say. "It's going to make my whole day."

Rob angles the camera on the laptop a little bit so that I

can see Christine, Jennifer, Mom, and Dad who are all sitting behind him.

"I'm the only one who's not there?" I try to avoid sounding as whiny as I feel. I don't really succeed.

"My parents will be on shortly," Brekka says. "Or, my mom will, anyway. Dad's in Hawaii, and I'm not sure what his schedule's like. My mom's at Geo and Trig's house right now. They'd have come, but she just had her baby last week."

"Whoa, Geo had her baby?" I ask.

"Yeah, the day before Paisley left for Europe. He was three days late and we were all worried she'd miss meeting him," Brekka says.

"And, how is he? Everything okay? Delivery go alright?"

"Little Mark is absolutely perfect. Dark, dark hair, like you'd expect from Trig and Geo. He was only six and a half pounds at birth, but in nine days he's already gained weight like a champ. He's just shy of seven pounds, which the docs say is amazing."

"Does he sleep yet?" I ask.

Brekka shrugs. "Not much, but Trig's mom hired a full-time night nurse—for some point in the future when Geo will actually take a break. To hear Trig talk, little Mark is never out of her arms."

Geo sounds happy. I'm such a lightweight that tears well up in my eyes at the thought of Rob and Brekka's baby playing with little Mark.

Brekka wipes at her eyes and shakes her head. "Do not cry, Beth. I will lose it."

"Speaking of, we are keeping things pretty low key," Rob says. "We bought one of these candles." He holds it up. "It's either pink or blue underneath, and we'll light it once everyone is here. Then you guys can make your guesses and tell us which you think it will be, one by one. By the time you're done, it should be showing the color."

"What, no paintball guns or balloons as big as my head?" I shake my head. "I'm a little disappointed. I was expecting a little more from my rich family—maybe a skywriter, or like, acrobats."

Christine raises her hand. "I offered to bring a balloon, but only because the party store didn't have a confetti cannon. They turned me down."

Jennifer swats at Christine's hand. "They could have at least done cupcakes, right? I'm starving over here. Who has a party and won't let you eat food until *after* it's over."

Jennifer's always hungry, so when I roll my eyes, I'm in good company. Mom, Dad, Rob, and Christine all roll theirs too.

Brekka's mom pops on then, her face less than two inches from the camera. I suppress my laughter. Trig's face appears next, his irritation plain on his face. "Hey, guys. Let me get this set up. Just a second."

He disappears, and the screen bounces all over, but eventually it's set up right, and Geo comes into view. She's holding the tiniest little blue-wrapped baby I've ever seen. The hair poking out from under his deep blue cap is nearly black.

I can't help myself. "Awwww."

I'm not the only one gushing.

And even without me starting her off, Brekka starts crying. "He's so beautiful, Geo."

"He looks exactly like his father," Geo says.

"But with your eyes, thankfully," Trig says.

"Okay, let's get this started," Brekka's mom says.

"Conference call?" Brekka straightens and shakes her head. "Really?"

"Nothing like that," her mom says. "But this little guy needs tummy time."

"Would you believe she's made us a schedule?" Trig's eyes widen and the corner of his mouth turns up. "For everything. Feeding, tummy time, burping, diaper changes. All. Of. It."

"We're sticking with it perfectly so far," Geo says. "And actually, it's been sort of helpful."

"Don't take this the wrong way, Mom," Brekka says. "But no schedule for me, thanks."

"We'll see," her mom says. "But let's get moving."

Brekka turns toward Rob. "A year ago, she'd have been basking in our news, but now that she already has a grandchild, we're chopped liver."

"Can't we be chopped brisket at least?" Rob asks.

"That's the point," Brekka says. "No one wants liver."

"Ah, right."

"Light the candle," Mom says. "I want to go first. I'm sure that I know what it is."

Rob leans toward the end table and lights the candle.

"It's a boy for sure," Mom says. "You're carrying high, and you're not sick at all, and Mark needs a best friend."

"Dad?" Rob asks.

"Boy," Dad says. "Your mother's never wrong."

"I hate to be boring," Trig's mom says, "but I think it's a boy too. I have a sense about these things, you know. I knew Geo was having a boy, and she did."

"Alright," Rob says. "What about you, Beth? You seemed the most excited of all the family. Any intuition?"

"It's a girl," I say.

"Why do you think that?" Brekka asks.

I shrug. "Because Jennifer has Liam and Owen, and now Geo has Mark. Mary and Luke had a boy, too. I think it's time someone has a little girl to pamper and spoil and dress up."

"I'll second that," Christine says.

"Liam and Owen have been praying for the last week that the baby can be a boy," Jennifer says. "So I vote boy."

"You know it's not actually a vote, right?" I ask. "I

mean, the gender has already been chosen. We're just guessing."

Jennifer arches one eyebrow. "You knew what I meant."

I shrug. Siblings. Gotta pick at them, or they don't know you love them.

"Is that everyone?" Rob asks.

"Aloha." Brekka's dad pops up on the Zoom meeting. "Am I too late? I'm afraid I didn't hear my phone alarm and just realized what time it was."

"No, Dad," Brekka says.

"Is something on fire?" He squints at the screen. "Oh, never mind. That's just a pink candle."

"Whoa," I say. "Pink? It's a girl!"

Suddenly, I can barely pick out individual voices for all the whooping. Rob blows out the candle and picks up his tiny wife, dancing around the room with her. I watch the hoopla for a few moments before begging off and calling it a night. I fall asleep the second my head hits the pillow, dreaming of pink booties and purple and pink blankets.

A strange sound wakes me up as the sun's rays are barely illuminating my window. A chugging? Heaving, maybe? I pad across the carpet and open my door.

Paisley's on her knees on the ground in the hall, puking.

"Oh, no," I say.

She wipes her mouth and turns toward me. "Oh, I'm so sorry. I hope I didn't wake you up."

There's a small pile of puke on the carpet. I duck back into my room and grab a wad of toilet paper, wet a bathroom washcloth, and snag a hand towel. I race back out to where Paisley's staring, dully, at the ground.

"Please don't apologize. I'm sorry you feel so lousy."

She wipes the back of her hand and wrist across her mouth. "This baby is trying to kill me."

I kneel down in front of her and wipe up the puke with the toilet paper and set it aside. I scrub the carpet with the washcloth, and then I pat it as dry as I can with the hand towel.

"You're efficient at that," Paisley says.

"We have a Persian cat," I say with a smile. "It hocks up hairballs pretty often."

"Oh good," she says. "I'm now on the same level as a fluffy feline."

"What can I do?" I ask.

"I wish there was something to do."

I flop backward and lean against the wall. "Where's James?"

"He's still asleep. Poor guy has been staying up half the night handling work calls—the time change is hard on him."

"Can I get you something?" I ask. "Subway sandwich?"

Her eyes light up. "I can't eat the whole thing, but little nibbles help keep me from being so sick."

"Are there keys I can borrow to someone's car?"

"Take mine," she says. "They're hanging next to the door. Do you know how to get there?"

I smirk. "It's not far. I think I can manage."

Paisley sighs. "Can you grab an extra baguette? I love their bread."

I don't laugh, but it strikes me as hilarious that the *princess* of Liechtenstein is obsessed with a place as pedestrian as Subway. "Will anyone be upset that I'm coming and going?"

She smiles. "Nope, you're on the list of people who are allowed."

"This may be the first time I've ever been on an exclusive list in my life."

"You were at Rob's gallery opening."

"That's true, I am a little fancy." I clamber to my feet. "Do you need a hand?"

"I'm going to lie down in the room next to yours. That way my vomiting won't wake up James."

"True love's test: pregnancy."

"That's truer than I expected it to be," Paisley said. "Count your blessings that you're so young. No pressure for you to have babies, even if you got married sometime soon."

I think about Mary, Brekka, Geo, and Paisley. My sister Jennifer and her two boys. The joy on Brekka's face as Rob spun her around. Even a puddle of puke at my feet or the prospect of countless sleepless nights doesn't deter me. "I want babies. Lots and lots of them." And I would never give mine away, not to anyone, not under any circumstance.

"You really must want them," Paisley groans. "To be saying that now."

"I'll go so fast you'll barely notice I'm gone."

The trip to Subway is quick, and it's open, thankfully, and within moments I have exactly what she asked for in my hands. I'm jogging back to the car when I notice Jostli at the Hotel Adler. He waves and smiles.

It would be rude to ignore him, so I pause. "Good morning. What are you doing out so early?"

"The hotel is closed right now. There was a plumbing leak, so we're doing some spring cleaning." He gestures behind him where there are several people setting up scaffolding.

"Painting?" I ask.

He nods. "But first we clean windows. You want to practice your songs today?"

I have a work of art waiting for me back at the palace, but there's a sleeping husband, a sick friend, and Cole to think about. "I need to deliver something, but if you're okay with it, I'll be back."

Jostli beams and nods.

"Great, see you soon."

I drop off Paisley's sandwich and bread and make sure she's alright, and then get her permission to use her car again. "You can play here," she insists, "but that's also fine. Whatever you want."

"I'd rather not risk bothering anyone."

The scaffolds are up and a man and three women are scrubbing windows and squeegeeing them off when I arrive.

"Are you sure this is fine?" I ask.

Jostli ushers me into the main dining room. "We're excited, actually. Is nicer than the radio, to have live piano."

"Your neighbors won't care?"

"They will love it."

"Unless they're still sleeping," I say.

He chuckles. "We work hard here—not sleep long in day. Is fine, I promise."

No one seems to notice I'm even playing for the first few songs of the playlist, but when I play a few of Henrietta's more well known songs, the cleaners wave at me and toss thumbs ups my direction through the now sparkling glass. I play those songs a few more times than strictly necessary, but it won't hurt for me to be over prepared. With this delay on the tour, I need to make sure my part is utterly perfect. I don't want to disappoint my bio mother after knowing her for just two weeks.

I play until my fingers begin to tire—more than three hours. I gather up all the sheet music Paisley helped me print yesterday and stand. That's when I notice the people.

Dozens and dozens of them, gathered outside the cafe.

Jostli crosses the room to where I'm standing, my mouth hanging open.

"You gather many fans."

"I'm just playing the supporting music."

"We have many musicians here in Liechtenstein," he says. "More than where I am from in Switzerland, and many, many more than in Germany. We have good taste, and we all think your playing is very special."

"Thank you," I say. "I'm just glad no one minded."

"If you can stay for lunch, I can pay you. Two hundred francs?"

My eyes bulge. "For lunch?"

"It's almost eleven now. Can you play until one?"

"I need to check with the friend I'm staying with to make sure it's alright."

Jostli shrugs and walks toward the kitchen, presumably to talk to his kitchen staff while he waits to hear my answer.

I whip out my phone and text Paisley. No reply after five minutes. Which I take to mean that she doesn't need me. This random two-hour lunch gig would double my cash on hand, and it's fifty bucks more than I make for three hours at Parker's. I'd be a moron not to do it. I wave Jostli down. "I'd love to stick around, but what do you want me to play?"

Jostli shrugs. "Whatever you want."

I start by playing the songs from Henrietta's new album, and then I play a few fan favorites, like "Piano Man." But the stakes are so low here. Everyone in the room keeps smiling at me and bobbing their heads in time with the music. It appears Jostli wasn't kidding. They love music. I'm in a foreign country, surrounded by people whose language I barely know, and they're as kind an audience as I've ever seen. It's now or never, really.

I've been secretly writing my own songs for years. One or two a month, melodies and lyrics, but I've never played them for anyone. Until today. I start with the lightest one, "She Skates," a song I wrote about Paisley, actually. She's the first adult I've ever met who didn't care what anyone else thought. From mixing four kinds of ice cream, to wearing roller skate sneakers as an adult, she always breezed through her life, happy, carefree, unfettered. I've always admired that about her.

When I finish, the patrons break out in a round of applause, which startles me.

But it encourages me, too. So I play another. "Why Cry," about finding the sunlight after a storm, the sugar at the bottom of your tea. It's light too, and they clap again. It's not the "Piano Man," but I'm playing *my* music, and they're, seemingly, enjoying it.

I play a dozen more songs, growing progressively more angsty as I go, but the diners don't seem to mind. When I glance at the clock, I realize it's half past one. I played too long. I stand up, but before I can take a step, Jostli's by my side. "That was even better than I expected, and you played for extra time. Thank you."

"I wasn't paying attention," I confess. "Sorry about that."

"What songs were at the end? None of us have heard them."

I swallow. "That's because they're my songs."

His eyes light up. "Several people asked if you might have an album for sale? Or can we download your music online?"

I shake my head. "Sorry, no. You were the first people to have heard it. Ever."

"Will you be here again tomorrow?" a ruddy-faced man behind Jostli asks in heavily accented English.

I shake my head. "I haven't even been asked."

Jostli presses money into my hands. "I would love to have you here any day, for lunch or dinner. And I've packaged up some food for you to take. That was very, very good."

"And we've had double the patrons we usually have," Hannah, the hostess says in German. "Good for business."

"Even on the patio," Jostli says.

"You should ask for more money," Hannah stage whispers. Then she winks.

"Oh hush, you," Jostli says. "I was already going to offer her more. How is a hundred and fifty an hour?"

"Um, well, I'll only be here for a few days," I say. "I'm going to be touring soon, remember?"

"With whom?" the ruddy-faced man asks.

"Henrietta Gauvón."

Startled gasps and murmurs.

"Can I get your number and let you know?" I ask.

Jostli beams again. "Absolutely you can." He writes it down on a napkin. "And any morning you need to practice, feel free to come here."

"Maybe we should start selling pastries and coffee," Hannah says.

"Perhaps we should." Jostli winks at me. "And if we do, you'd definitely get a cut."

I count the money once I reach my car, and I'm startled to see that it's three hundred francs, not the two hundred we agreed upon. It's nice to have more than doubled my cash—for a few hours work. Plus, the sandwich and cucumber salad he packed for me is amazing.

Paisley's awake and sitting at the kitchen table when I reach the palace.

"How are you feeling?" I ask.

"Much better, thanks." A half dozen plates with varying types of cake cover the dining table in front of Paisley and her mom.

"Finally sick of Subway?" I ask.

Paisley's mom smiles at me. "I also think the daily Subway sandwiches are humorous." She points at a chair. "Do you have time to help us?"

I sit down quickly. "What kind of help involves cake?"

"We decided to throw a *very small* baby shower," Paisley says. "For family exclusively. Only because it will be a good chance to mention Dad's adoption of Cole, which is being finalized today."

"Today?" I raise my eyebrows. "Didn't he decide he wanted it done like twenty minutes ago?"

Paisley smiles. "One of the benefits to being the supreme member of government is that you can expedite things. Also, Dad had the paperwork drawn up weeks ago."

"Ah. And the cake?"

"We need the food to be quite excellent," Paisley's mom says. "Because I want everyone in a good mood when we start asking how they feel about revising the House Law."

"Could I recommend alcohol, instead?" I laugh. "Although. Maybe not for a baby shower."

"Oh, there will be an open bar with cutesy themed drinks." She winks and shoves two plates toward me. "Try this one, it's hazelnut and chocolate. The other is mint and chocolate."

I pick up a fork. "How could the family members really oppose allowing legally adopted children to be included?"

Paisley's eyes widen. "Do you have any idea how many things in Europe are done a particular way, for no reason other than it has always been done that way?"

"No." I take a bite of the hazelnut. It's amazing. "But I'm assuming you expect some resistance to the idea."

"There's very little chance this will succeed," Paisley's mom whispers. "But we have to do our very best. Cole deserves it."

I taste the mint next. "This is good, but not as good as the hazelnut."

Paisley swaps those plates out for two more. "Now try the vanilla and honey, and the white chocolate raspberry."

I feign a frown. "Are you trying to fatten me up?"

Paisley laughs. "You can't fault me for trying. Even with all the puking, I've gained six pounds already."

"Well, as it happens, I'm always willing to eat cake of

pretty much any flavor." I try both. "Vanilla and honey is much better than I expected. Light and airy, but still fresh. Almond flavoring?"

"I think so," Paisley says. "Which kills it for me—too bad, because I'm not a huge chocolate fan either."

I shake my head. "It's my favorite by a wide margin."

"Which is fine," her mom says. "Because we will have three different options."

"Three?" I grab two more plates and dive in. "So what can I do to help? Anything that I need to say or not say, you know, as the bumbling American?"

Paisley and her mom exchange a look.

"We'll work up some talking points," Paisley says. "It's not a bad idea. Liechtenstein and America are on excellent terms and do quite a bit of trade. They would likely value the American view on this. A reminder of the importance of maintaining the family image in the midst of modern views wouldn't hurt."

"Liechtenstein is a very modern country," I say. "From what I've seen."

"I agree," her mom says.

"Well." Paisley pokes her fork into the remains of the hazelnut cake over and over.

"What?" I ask.

"Women could vote in the United States by 1920, but here, they couldn't vote until nineteen-*eighty-four*. And—"

"Holly, that's quite enough."

"I'm just saying, Mom, we're not exactly progressive."

"The concern with the adoption and the women as dynasts is the same," her mom says. "If they begin to expand who can inherit, where does it end? My husband could conceivably adopt anyone."

"So add a requirement that the child be raised for at least ten years in the home of the adopting parent—but allow the adoption to be formalized at any time, or it'll be too late for Cole."

Paisley's mother tilts her head at me. "You're smarter than you look."

"Uh." I decide to take it as a compliment. "Thanks." I stand up. "Well, I left the house pretty early and then spent most of the day practicing. I ought to shower and actually make myself presentable, unless you need me for something else."

"Not at all," Paisley's mom says.

I feel like I ought to curtsy or something, but in the end I just walk out. I'm halfway up the stairs when Paisley catches up to me. "Hey, thanks for this morning. Did you actually work at Adler's?"

"It was so fun."

She continues up the stairs, so I follow. "Look at you, more work than you can handle."

"Actually, he wants me to go again tomorrow. It would be great for me to earn a little more cash, if it doesn't bother you."

"Please," she says. "Go ahead. I'm glad you've found something to do here. Mom's scoffing aside, Liechtenstein is really small. It's not a good fit for most people."

"Most people being you?" I lift my eyebrows.

She shrugs. "Yes, definitely including me. Now that I've been elsewhere, I could never live here. I love the hustle and bustle and variety and energy in America."

I get her point, but there's also something wonderful about a small place, where everyone knows you, and where you have a real community. "Do you think Cole has any chance?" I hate the idea that he'll give up his plans and job and probably be left with nothing. "Or if he doesn't succeed, can he get his job again?"

Paisley laughs. "You're so American." She waltzes

through my doorway and sits on one of the embroidered armchairs in my room. "But no, I doubt that he has any hope at all, no matter what we do. That's why I didn't argue with him about his decision to go to Antwerp in the first place."

"I think this is about more than winning," I say. "I think maybe he needs the adoption to feel like he fits in."

Paisley freezes. "Cole has always known he's as much Dad's child as I am."

"Really?" I shouldn't say anything else, but I've never been one to keep quiet. "He mentioned a brother who played piano. I got the distinct impression that he felt like he was a poor replacement now that he's gone."

Paisley flinches, and I wish I'd kept quiet.

"I'm sorry. I have a big mouth."

"I shouldn't have kept his existence a secret," she says. "I think ignoring his death kept me from really recovering from it. Talking about him hurts, but it also feels good, like lancing a boil, maybe."

"Nice image," I say. "I bet your brother appreciates being compared to a boil."

She cocks one eyebrow. "I'm not comparing Noel to. . . Well, maybe I am." She laughs. "That would have killed him, actually. He had the best sense of humor." And between one second and the next, she's bawling.

I crouch down next to her, but she waves me away.

"It's the hormones," she says. "I'm a complete mess all the time."

I'm not sure that's it, but I don't argue. "I don't mind."

"You're a really good person," she says. "Which isn't a surprise. Rob is solid gold."

"He really is."

Paisley inhales and exhales several times until she's not crying anymore. "You know, Noel was just as good a person as Rob, and I don't say that lightly."

"What happened?" I ask. "You don't have to answer, but I'd like to know. Cole just said he passed."

"He got sick, cancer. He went into remission, but then. . . it came back. He was so young, too. Twenty-one. He just couldn't go through it all again."

"Not enough energy to fight?"

Paisley closes her eyes. "Actually, he committed suicide, I guess."

She guesses?

"I mean, he didn't, like, blow his brains out or leap off a building. But he needed this medicine, and it was miserable, and he just stopped taking it. Everyone blames me for not realizing that he was hiding it."

"You couldn't possibly—"

She opens her eyes and glares at me. "I should have. I blame me, too. He would have told me, if I'd paid enough attention to ask."

"Paisley. It's not your fault he died, and that is *not* suicide, either."

She sighs.

"And you have no idea what would have happened if he took the medicine. The result might have been the same."

Tears roll silently down her cheeks. "I would give every dime I have for an extra month with him, but you're right." She places a hand over her belly. "Now that I'm pregnant, I've been thinking about this a lot. If my baby were sick, I would do *everything* that could be done. I would try anything, endure anything. But I think time is a little bit like a pile of coins, the currency of life. We all get a pile when we're born, but some of us have larger piles than others. But that time can be good time, like if you're healthy and happy and learning and growing, or it can be bad time. For instance, if you're stuck in prison, or if you're being abused, I bet you don't value the time quite the same. And Noel." She sniffles. "We all wanted to ration out his last weeks, days, and hours. We wanted to stretch them as far as we could."

Paisley dances and sings and spins. She occupies all the energy in every room. Every eye is usually on her, like she's a movie star. . . or a princess, I guess. But seeing her like this, listening to her, I realize that I undervalued her depth and her insight. "I like that. Time as a currency that we all share."

"I missed Noel so much that it caused me almost unbearable pain. And as much as I loved him, I guess I hated him a little bit too. For not fighting, for not telling me when he gave up, and for dying and leaving me behind to suffer with a world I didn't recognize, a world where all the joy had disappeared." She wipes her eyes. "But maybe he spent that money the way he should have. Since he wasn't taking his medicine, we had a picnic the week before he died. He played piano most mornings. He sat in the garden and read. I don't know whether he could have done any of that while struggling with the medicine's side effects. So maybe he was right, and we should have forgiven him and accepted his decision long ago."

"The world would be a much happier place if we could all forgive a little more."

Paisley stands up, and I hug her tightly.

"I know it has been hard for you," she says. "But I'm glad your birth mom's tour got delayed. Maybe I needed you here a little bit."

And maybe I needed it too.

COLE

"We need to leave right now to go over the details with the caterer," Mom says.

"Do you really need me for this?" I check my watch. "I'm supposed to meet Adrian later to give him the signed treaty and review a few details of the process we need to follow to execute it properly."

"Cole Gerard Béthune, your sister only agreed to this baby shower to help you."

I hold up my hand. "I think you need to rethink what you call me when you're upset."

Mom's hand flies to her throat, and a smile spreads slowly across her face. "Cole Michael Alois of Liechtenstein, you will come with us, and you will smile, and you will not complain about it."

I roll my eyes. "Oh, fine." I follow Mom and Holly to the garage. "I notice that Dad's not being badgered into coming."

"Your father doesn't feel well today," Mom says.

My phone rings and I hold it up to ward off any protests. "This is my boss. You know, the one I have called twice, asking him to call me back so I can tell him that I'm not actually going to be working for him like I said I would."

Holly waves at me. "Take it. Stay here. We'll be fine." She slides into the car and closes the door.

Mom exhales and does the same.

And I hit talk. "Russell, thanks for calling me back."

"Cole, I hope everything's alright."

I clear my throat. "Actually—"

"Don't tell me you aren't coming."

"I wish I could do that."

"What's going on?" Russell asks.

Russ and I went to school together years ago, before I went back home to help Dad and he set out to conquer the world. "Dad's adopting me, and we're going to push to change the House Law so I can take over for him."

Russell whistles. "What are the odds it'll work?"

"Not great, probably," I say. "But Dad asked, and I couldn't tell him no."

He swears. "I doubt I'd pass up the chance to be a prince either, if it came to that."

"It's not about that." I mean, it kind of is, but not in the way he means.

"Well, here's what I can do." He groans. "I really need someone soon, but I can lean on my boss to let me keep using his assistant for another month. Maybe that'll buy you some time."

He's willing to hold the spot for me? "I don't want to make your life harder."

"If you had seen the imbeciles who came in for the interviews." He huffs. "When I heard from you, it was a Godsend, believe me. I'm just trying to figure out how to keep you."

"Thanks," I say.

"Good luck," he says. "I mean, if I prayed, I'd be praying for it to fail, but as your friend I hope it works out."

Typical Russell.

Of course, the second I hang up, my doubts set in. What are my chances? Fifty-three dynasts. Dad will vote to change the law, but he may be the only one. Clearly Franz won't, and I'm guessing that his son Alejandro won't either. Dad called Josef this morning, and that's when he started to feel lousy. If his two sons vote against it too, that's already five against. One hundred percent of the people we've approached have refused to support the change.

Most people spend their entire life doing whatever they can to avoid being outright rejected, but not me. I look failure in the face and say, hit me, please.

I'm such an idiot.

I wish Noel were here. He'd know just what to say. Of course, if he were here, I wouldn't need any words of advice. He'd already be Dad's Regent.

As if I've entered the Twilight Zone, as if thinking about him summoned him here, piano music floats across the family room. It's light, it's mellow, it's magnificent. It's Noel, it has to be. No one else I've ever heard play sounded so balanced and simultaneously rich, like he had four hands with which to play instead of only two.

Even the beats, the pauses, the rests between one note and the next are impeccable. Not too long, not too short.

In a word: perfect.

I should walk into the conservatory and see who's playing. It has to be. . . My feet are moving, my heart in my throat. Beth is a hairdresser. She plays part-time at a restaurant. But it is Beth. She's so engrossed in the song she's playing that she doesn't notice when I enter the room. I quietly take a seat. She plays three more songs before she sees me, jolts, and stops playing.

We both spin around when we hear the clapping sounds coming from the foyer. The cooks, the chef, the housekeeper and her maids, and the butler are all gathered outside the door to the conservatory, but Dad's standing in front of all of them, tears leaking down his cheeks. "I thought. . ."

I close my eyes. I know exactly what he thought.

"You sound so much like Noel," Margaret says. "Thank you for playing such beautiful songs."

Beth stands up, her face white as snow. "I'm so sorry—Paisley told me it was fine if I worked on a few songs in here."

"Don't apologize," I say. "No one has played since Noel died, and I think we all missed it. More than we realized."

Beth gathers up the papers in front of her, sets them on the bench and practically bolts. But instead of heading upstairs toward her room, she beelines for the side door, toward the garden.

"Someone should talk to her," Dad says. "Don't you think?"

I'm already headed for the garden, weaving my way in between the various members of the staff who closed around her exit as if guarding her from paparazzi. "I've got it, Dad."

"Wonderful," he says. "Because I have no idea what to say to the girl."

Neither do I, but at least she knows me a little. It takes me ten minutes to find her—because our lawn is far too large. I pass dozens of benches, but no Beth. I finally spot her, leaning against the base of a huge Elm tree, sitting cross-legged on the ground.

"Hey there, Mozart."

She snorts. "Hardly."

"Mind if I sit?"

"It's your house."

"Well, technically it's entailed, which means I'll probably be tossed out—"

"You know what I mean."

I circle the tree and slide down next to her, my back leaning against the same trunk. "You told me you played 'back up' piano."

"I do," she says. "I cut hair."

I snort. "Sure, but what we heard in there." I shake my head. "You are extremely talented. You should be, I don't know, at Juilliard."

"I almost went," she whispers.

My head swivels around to face her. "I knew it. Why didn't you?"

She shrugs. "My GPA, uh, grade point average—"

"I know what that is," I say.

"Well, it was kind of borderline and Juilliard made my acceptance contingent on receiving Bs in every class my last semester."

"And?"

"I almost failed Algebra. I barely got a C—I wasn't even close to a B."

I whistle. "Well, I won't be hiring you to handle my accounting any time soon, but that was a big mistake on their part."

"Yeah." She leans her head back against the stump, her eyes looking into the branches above. "Juilliard is probably still reeling from the loss of Beth Graham."

It's a little dark, but her humor is solid.

"It's fine, though. I mean, if I'd gone, I wouldn't have been around when my brother came back from the war. Or when my dad nearly lost the car dealerships. Or when my sister Jennifer had a baby—she had a really tough six months after her first son was born, and I stayed with her to help with the nighttime feedings. I would have missed all of that if I'd been a little better at math."

"But you would have been brilliant at Juilliard. I've never seen the entire staff quit working and stand around listening to music, not in my entire life."

"It reminded them all of Noel, that's all. Which is exactly why I haven't been practicing there," she says. "But I had a few ideas and wanted to try them a few times before playing in front of people." Her laugh sounds almost strangled. "Backfire. I ended up playing my songs for the first time for the Prince of Liechtenstein."

"I'm not a prince," I say. "Not unless an awful lot of people are swayed enough by delicious cake that they decide to change a law that's centuries old."

She smirks. "I was talking about your dad. Not everything is about you, Cole of Liechtenstein. I should congratulate you, though. I don't remember my adoption day, but I imagine it felt pretty good."

"You're right about that." I can't even describe how it feels, not in a way that will make sense. "But it almost makes it harder."

"What?"

"Knowing that I could basically be booted from this house, the house my dad owns, at any time, it felt fine. I mean, I wasn't even his son, not really. But now I am, and it feels more unfair to me. I resent it more than I did last week."

"Booted? But only if he dies, right?"

I grin. "Maybe you should pack your bags. Our eviction notice could arrive any time."

She rolls her eyes.

"But in all seriousness, Dad's been sick. He could die at any time, really."

Beth gasps. "He's sick?" She licks her lips. "I noticed he doesn't seem to see very well."

"His eyesight has been breaking down for a while now, but it's his heart that's life threatening."

"I'm so sorry. I didn't know." She glances at her knees. "But maybe that's one of the reasons he decided to do this. So you would know, even after he was gone, that you were his. That he loved you."

"I've always known that," I say.

"But now you *know* it." Beth looks up at me, her impossibly long lashes framing the biggest, darkest brown eyes I've ever seen.

She may be the first person I've ever met who really understands how I feel. As if I'm being drawn by a bungee cord, my head ducks. Lower. Lower.

Her face doesn't waver, but she inhales and her lips part, infinitesimally. Which, of course, draws my eyes. I know that I shouldn't kiss her, my sister's American friend. She's too young, she would never move to Liechtenstein, and she's so *American*. Especially if I want to rule here, I should *not* be involved with an American.

Dad spent twenty minutes last night telling me that Franz's marriage to an American was our best weapon in this fight.

But I don't care about any of that, not right now, not while Beth's looking up at me with those eyes and that mouth. I wrap one arm around her and lift her toward me as my head lowers the few inches that still separate us.

And our lips touch.

Hers warm, soft, full. Mine hungry, desperate, urgent. She tastes like strawberry shortcake and sunlight. Her body curls toward mine naturally, her head tipping up, her lashes fluttering down, and I forget everything else. The House Law, the dynasts, my job in Antwerp, my brother Noel, none of it hurts, none of it worries me, not right now. There are only Beth's smooth arms, Beth's inviting mouth, and Beth's smooth cheek beneath my fingertips.

"Looks like he cheered her up," Holly says.

Beth springs away from me like a birdshot blast in hunting season, sprawling backward onto the manicured lawn. Holly and James are laughing so hard I'm worried they'll suffocate.

If they don't, I might take care of it myself.

❧ 9 ❧

BETH

I scramble to my feet as quickly as possible. I'm sure that the back of my khaki slacks is now covered with grass stains, so I make sure to face Paisley and her husband directly. "That was. . . I mean, we were. . ." I swallow. "I wasn't upset to begin with. I'm fine." I glance down at my watch. What excuse can I give to escape? Then I can either sink into the ground forever, or I can pretend this never happened. I'll place even odds on both. "Oh wow, I didn't realize how late it was. I need to call my sister Christine. She had some questions for me." About what? I'm such an idiot. "Hair emergency."

I should spin on my heel and run away, but then they'll see the grass stains I'm positive are spread across my bum.

"You can call her out here," Paisley says, her eyes still sparkling. "We'll give you some privacy." Her eyes sparkle with suppressed mirth.

Cole stands up and brushes off his pants. "We certainly will." He glares at Paisley.

Some kind of bizarre nonverbal communication takes place between the two of them, and then Paisley takes James' hand in her own. "We better head inside. If I don't eat some crackers soon, all those hors d'oeuvres might come right back up."

James and Paisley walk away, their shoulders still shaking, Paisley still glancing over her shoulder intermittently. Still, they give a reasonable approximation of leaving us alone.

"Sorry," I say. "I know that was. . ." Actually I have no idea what it was.

Cole steps closer.

My heart hammers in my chest. I like him way, way too much.

"I'm sorry. I shouldn't have done that." His voice is low, gruff.

"It's fine," I say. "I mean, obviously I enjoyed it."

He clears his throat. "Me too. I've been thinking about that for longer than I—you aren't sticking around here, and I am, at least for now, and—"

"Paisley already told me that the family sort of freaked out when your Uncle Franz married his wife."

His eyes widen. "It's not because she's black," he says, "or because she was born in Puerto Rico or didn't have a title."

I sigh. "I know. It's because she was American."

He laughs. "I mean, yes and no. We love America, we really do. We love Germany and Switzerland too. But for so long, the monarchs in our family sort of eschewed Liechtenstein, so the people here are a little wary of anyone who doesn't have roots here. It wasn't long ago that we used Swiss judges to adjudicate our own disputes."

"I didn't realize that." I can see how dating an American would be. . . complicated. Even if you weren't sort of campaigning to get chosen to be a prince.

"Which, you know, wouldn't have mattered to me two weeks ago. Or even three days ago."

"Before you were trying to convince fifty-five snooty dynasts that you're fit to take over for your dad."

"Fifty-three." His Adam's apple bobs when he swallows. "But yes, basically that's right."

"I totally understand," I say. "You don't need to worry about it. I'm leaving in like three more days."

He nods.

"So, still friends?"

He smiles. "I certainly hope so, and I'll talk to Holly to make sure she's not going to be idiotic about it." His eyes light up as though he's recalled something he forgot. "The whole reason I came out here was to make sure you know that we appreciated the piano music. You are welcome, very welcome, to play at any time. It has been. . . missed. Please don't worry about everyone's response. It's just that you played so well that it filled some kind of empty hole none of us knew we had."

"Thanks," I say, "but I doubt I'll need to play again."

He frowns. "Aren't you supposed to be practicing for the tour?"

"I've actually been doing plenty of that." It's a good thing my fingers are used to playing for long stretches, or I'd nearly have played my fingers raw in the last few days.

"How do you mean?" Cole asks.

"Do you remember Jostli, the owner of the Hotel Adler?"

Cole's eyebrows draw together. "I do."

"He's sort of paying me to play for meals over at his hotel's restaurant. With the hotel closed right now for some kind of remodeling issue, it's been really helpful for them to have the extra patrons that live music brings."

"You've been playing there?"

I can't quite help the smile that curls the side of my mouth. "And singing. It has been really fun. The people here are so kind."

"When do you play next?"

"I've been doing lunch, but Paisley's mom wanted some help with the shower plans earlier, so today I'm supposed to leave in a few minutes to play for dinner."

"I'd love to come listen," Cole says.

"Uh, I'd prefer you not. . ."

I hate seeing the hurt look in his remarkable green eyes.

"It's not personal, but I don't really know any of the people who come, and that keeps me from stressing about playing and singing."

"Playing for me would make you nervous?" Now he's smiling.

"Not usually," I say, "but I've been playing my own songs and my own lyrics. It's different somehow."

"Well, I'm not giving up," Cole says. "I'd still like to hear you, but if you want your first dinner to be lower stress, that's fine."

"Thanks." I head back for the palace.

Cole falls into step beside me. "I hope he's paying you well."

"Better than I deserve, I assure you," I say. "He's paying me close to double what I make for the same thing back home and playing my own stuff is much more fun than doing covers all the time."

"As long as it's fair."

"Although, I probably shouldn't admit that it's in cash. Does that mean I need to report my earnings here? Will you hand me in to the authorities now that you know?"

Cole rolls his eyes. "I might let it slide, just this once."

Once we reach the palace, I head upstairs to change, and Cole leaves for some kind of meeting with the Prime Minister. I'm on my way upstairs when I see his Range Rover circling around the palace and down the hill. I understand why he can't pursue anything with me, but it still sucks. My fingers brush against my mouth, remembering our kiss.

The best kiss I've ever had. Times ten.

I'm glad I have a job to do today so I can't moon around the rest of the night. And tomorrow I play at lunch again, and then I have the baby shower. Then just one more day and I'll be heading back to Frankfurt. I'm pretty sure. I text Henrietta and Uwe to make sure nothing has changed.

Uwe replies a few moments later with the details of when and where I should report.

I change clothes, putting on the black dress I wore the first night here. Since I'm performing for a dinner crowd, I figure I should look my best.

When I walk downstairs, Paisley tosses me her keys with a half smile. "You sure you don't want Cole to give you a ride?"

"Why would she need that?" her mom asks. "It's barely more than a mile away and he's not even here."

"No reason," Paisley says. "Good luck!"

"Thanks." I glare at Paisley over my shoulder on the way out, and she winks. When I slide across the buttery black leather of her Mercedes, I worry it might ruin me for my eight-year-old Honda Civic when I go back home. A girl can get used to living in a palace and driving like a princess. I've also grown accustomed to simply driving down the mountain and around the corner and easily pulling into any spot, but when I arrive today, the little circle is already packed. I end up parking on the street two blocks away, which stinks since my heels aren't low. I wonder what's going on—or maybe Sundays are just busy days around here.

When I arrive, every table is already packed—inside and out. My eyes widen. "What's going on?"

Hannah waves me back, her smile sly.

"Is there some kind of special event?" I ask.

"You're the special event," she says in German. "Word of your playing has spread and many people have been making reservations. Jostli has hired four new servers, and two new cooks to keep up. He wants you to stick around."

I blink. "My German isn't very good. Can you repeat that? I think I misunderstood."

But when she repeats herself, I realize that I didn't misunderstand.

"They're all here. . . because of me?"

Jostli strides toward us. "All because of you!" His voice booms, his grin almost painfully wide. "And I need to know how to keep you here. I think I can expand. Move the parking lot a few streets away and make my courtyard bigger. During the winter, we'll put heaters on the patio. It'll be lovely." His English is definitely better than my German, so I'm grateful he always switches to English with me.

I shake my head. "I can't stay. I live in America, and I'm only here because I'm going on tour—"

"With Henrietta Gauvón, I know, I know." Henry spits on the ground. "I hate Henrietta Gauvón."

I laugh. "You don't, but I appreciate the compliment. I already told you that I can be here for lunch tomorrow, and then maybe one more performance the day after, and then I have to leave."

He sighs. "If you don't like that tour, you can come back here. Yes?"

"No, I have two jobs and a family back home! In Atlanta, Georgia." I look around at the gathered crowd. "I do love it here, and I'm delighted that everyone enjoys my music. In fact, I wrote a song today about Liechtenstein. The people, the mountains, the genuine warmth, all of it. I am so grateful that you've all come to listen to me."

Jostli's eyes light up. He repeats my words, but in German, and applause breaks out.

"My German is really bad, but I tried to write a German version, too."

"We want to hear it both ways," Jostli says, "Yes?"

A few dozen people cheer.

He repeats it in German and everyone claps. "There you have it," he says. "Let's start and end with the new song."

"It could be really bad," I say. "What if they hate it?"

He rolls his eyes. "They don't hate any of your music, and this is about them. They will adore it."

He's right. When I sit down to play, the talking quiets to a low murmur. And when I begin to play the bright, cheery song I wrote about this stunningly beautiful country, nestled in the Alps, people stand up outside and crowd around the doorways. Their faces press against the windows.

When I finish, they cheer and clap and hoot and howl, which makes me cry.

I almost can't sing it in German. I butcher at least three words, and my voice wobbles, and my heart races, but they don't seem to care. "Noch einmal, bitte," they shout. "Play it again, please!"

And I do, but only one more time before moving on to other songs. It's an unbelievable high that they prefer *my* songs to "Hey Jude," and "Sweet Home Alabama," and "Piano Man."

But they do.

It's hard to drive back to the palace that night, to tell their eager faces that I need to stop playing, but I don't dare stay out past ten. I have no idea whom I might inconvenience.

"I am charging them a cover," Jostli says once I finally duck into the kitchen. "And so I decided to pay you more."

"A cover?" I ask. "For watching me through windows and doorways?"

He shrugs. "We don't get concerts here, and we love music."

"It's okay, you don't need to pay me more than we agreed." Having people who love to listen is enough.

"They paid an extra fifty francs per person to be inside for two hours, and you stayed an hour and a half later than we agreed—which means I got to charge that for everyone inside twice."

"Fifty francs?" I realize my mouth is dangling open and snap it shut.

"So I think a thousand francs is fair."

"Uh, yes, I think it's generous, even. Thank you."

"Are you sure you can't stay longer?" he wheedles.

I shake my head. "They won't be this excited for very long, not if I'm a permanent fixture."

"I was thinking of making this very fine dining. Nights out. Then citizens from high country, the Oberland, and the low country, the Unterland, will all come."

"It's a very kind offer." I hug Jostli. "But I'm afraid my answer hasn't changed. I came to Germany to be near my birth mom. I only came to Liechtenstein to visit a friend when the tour was delayed. I'm really sorry."

He hangs his head. "Alright, alright."

The next morning, Paisley's family barely notices when I escape to do my lunch performance, and it's at least as packed as it was last night. I'm pretty sure Jostli is helping things along with fliers or emails or calls, but I don't mind. He pays me a thousand francs again, and it takes forever to escape. Dozens of people want my autograph on napkins, which is beyond baffling. The only thing I've ever signed before was a credit card receipt and my report card—and then I was forging my mom's signature.

When I finally arrive back at the palace, everyone's loading into cars for the baby shower.

"I'm sorry to have taken so long," I say.

"Don't worry," Paisley says. "And if you're tired, you don't have to come. I'm sure I'll have a real shower back home, and I'll make you come to that."

"After everything you've done for me, I should *host* that one," I say.

"It's a deal." Paisley starts for the door to the garage. "You're welcome today, but it's going to be pretty boring, I'm afraid. All in German, and a lot of snooty people even *I* hardly know. If I told James he could skip it, you'd see a blur headed upstairs."

I glance down at my simple brown skirt and cream blouse. "Is what I'm wearing okay? I would love to come, but I don't want to embarrass you."

She shakes her head. "You look just fine, and believe me, James will be giddy to have another American there."

"Other than Aunt Andrea, you mean?"

"Someone who doesn't have her claws out," Paisley says. "Yes, other than her."

I follow her toward the door. "Great, then let's go. I'll stand in the corner and be James' security blanket."

We all pile into Cole's Range Rover, which puts me knee to knee with his mother, who's wearing a very elegant, very expensive suit. Cole is wearing a black suit, and his father's wearing a dark grey suit. I'm terribly worried I might be underdressed—although Paisley said I'm fine. Maybe they're all dressed so nice because they're the hosts.

"It's a good thing you got the sport version," James says. "Or we'd have to take two cars."

"Maybe we should take two cars," Paisley's dad says. "Then we have an escape vehicle."

"It can't be that bad," I say. "And I know for sure the cake will be amazing." No one refutes me, so I assume they agree. But when we pull up to the Government House of Liechtenstein, there are far more cars parked in the exclusive lot out front than I expect.

"How many guests will there be?" I should have paid more attention during the planning. I've been to dozens of baby showers, at least five in the last two months. Even the ones thrown for Geo and Mary, whose husbands are practically billionaires, featured silly things, like memory games with trays of baby items, baby food tasting, and the diapering of dolls. *It's just a baby shower,* I remind myself. *It will be fine.*

I quash my fears and follow them inside.

But I should have gone with my gut. Because this baby shower is nicer than my high school prom, and we held that in the capital building. Everyone milling around has a fancy drink of some kind in their hand and is wearing some kind of designer dress or suit.

I've never seen this many diamonds gathered in one place. At least, not since Rob's gallery opening. Instead of freaking out, or badgering Paisley on her big day, I slowly work my way toward the back of the room. I find a small table with two tall seats and claim one. A few minutes later, as she said he would, James sits down next to me.

"You found the American bubble of shame," I say.

He chuckles. "That I did, and may we both stay safe in here as long as possible."

"Aren't you supposed to be up there, chatting with the fancy people and supporting your wife?"

"I have no idea what any of them are saying. Your German may not be perfect, but at least you can follow the conversation. All I hear is block snock ach bon blickenheim."

"You just told me that my nose is ugly."

His eyes widen.

I laugh. "I'm kidding. You said nothing—which you know, because Paisley already told me you speak pretty decent German."

He sighs. "I can speak pretty well, but I struggle to

understand, especially when they start talking a kilometer a minute."

"I should be listening in," I say. "Practicing."

"I could too, I guess, but this whole thing is really about Cole, not about our baby. I refuse to feel guilty."

"How's that going?" I ask. "Any new allies?"

"I have no idea." James leans toward me, his elbows on the table. "You know, maybe you should wander around and listen in on what people are saying. No one knows you, and they have no idea you speak German."

"An American spy?" I ask. "Pass."

"Spoilsport."

"So are they going to have any games?" I ask. "Or, like, have baby-themed anything?"

James shrugs. "I've never been to a baby shower in my life. I managed to avoid Luke's and Trig's by setting up big meetings in New York." He spreads his arms. "The difficulties of commuting."

"I've been to loads of them," I say, "but this is the first I've ever attended with an open bar."

James laughs. "They went back and forth on that one. Apparently the family really gets along better with a little social lubrication—plus." He lowers his voice. "They want everyone to be in a good mood when they start talking about Cole and the house rules or whatever."

"How are they going to broach that subject?" I ask. "I mean, it's not really an easy transition."

"We've spent hours and hours discussing that one," James says, "and—"

But the clinking of a glass distracts me.

Paisley's standing at the front of the room, gently tapping on a wine glass. "Don't worry," she says in German. "It's only orange juice."

Soft laughter.

"I know this is a little early in my pregnancy to do a

baby shower. Mom and I went back and forth, back and forth. But since I don't come to visit as often as I'd like, and I don't come even half as often as Mom would like, and there's no way to know how long I'll be able to fly as this little parasite grows inside me, we figured we'd better take this chance to celebrate the expansion of our little family with all of my big family."

Several people clap, and others tap their glasses. It feels more like a wedding toast than a baby shower.

"I know it's not typical for a mother-to-be to give a speech at a baby shower, but I've been thinking a lot as I prepare for motherhood. You all know that in the corner over there—" She points. "Mom set up a table where you can leave me advice and tips. Today I wanted to share some thoughts with all of you as well. You've probably heard by now that Dad has adopted my older brother, Cole. Mom and Dad married when Cole was three years old, and he doesn't have a single memory of his birth father. In reality, Hans-Michael, my dad, is also Cole's dad. For years we avoided putting that in writing out of *fear*."

Murmurs. Lots of murmurs.

"What fear, you ask? Well, let me tell you. As the son of Gerard, the last Marquis of Béthune, Cole had a significant inheritance, a title, a beautiful property in Belgium. But thanks to the way the Liechtenstein House Law works, as my father's legal son, he has. . . nothing."

Paisley pauses.

I had no idea she was such an impressive speaker. She's leading us all right down the path.

"I've been living in America, and you all know I basically ran away to hide there ten years ago. When Noel died, it broke my heart and shattered the path I saw for myself. I should have stayed here and helped Mom and Dad, but I didn't."

She pauses again. No one says a word.

"Do you know who did stay? Do you know who bore up under all his sorrow and also carried others? Can you guess who sacrificed his plans and ten years of his life for no pay, and no real thanks?" She clears her throat. "Well I can tell you. Cole did. My brother. And last week, when my dad said he wanted to adopt him, Cole declined. He felt that it was time for him to move on, to try and find a new place to belong." She sets her glass down and folds her hands across her mostly flat belly. "My brother already belongs. My brother already has a home. My brother should be my father's heir. And what I learned from spending years in America is that when things like this rear their ugly heads, when injustices become glaringly apparent, we can't simply kick the responsibility on down the line. We need to *do something* to fix them. So I'm asking all of you, on behalf of my dad who has served tirelessly, on behalf of my brother who is the most worthy ruler I've ever met, to vote to change the House Law so that an adopted child can inherit and take over in title what he has already been doing in reality."

Almost the entire room bursts into applause.

"Okay, fine, I'll do it," I whisper.

James blinks. "Do what?"

"I'll walk around and spy on them."

"I couldn't follow all of that, but it sounded pretty moving." He beams at me. "I helped her write some of it in English last night."

"Have you seen *Braveheart*?" I ask. "Next to that freedom speech that Mel Gibson gave, her little message was just about the most motivational thing I've ever heard. And my pastor at church is phenomenal—since we live in the South, that's saying something."

"People mistake Paisley's joy and energy for a lack of intelligence sometimes," James says.

"Those people are stupid," I say.

James leans a little closer to me. "I love when that happens. Her brilliance always rolls back around to bop them on the nose."

"Well, if any of them were listening, I bet they support Cole."

I hop off my chair and begin to walk around, but the more I listen, the angrier I get. Some of the women agreed with Paisley—most of them in fact. But every single man I pass smiles and shakes his head. They say it's a slippery slope. They say an adopted child is not the same as a blood relative. They say it's not about them, but about the future. They say they're going to vote the way they need to—for their sons.

I expect to be angry.

Instead, I'm profoundly sad. Not just for Cole, but also for myself. Because maybe they're right, and if they are, it confirms every single time I've felt uneasy, felt left out, felt like I don't quite belong among my own family. I know they love me, but maybe, just maybe. . . Like Cole, like all adopted kids. . .

I don't really belong anywhere.

❧ 10 ❧

COLE

fter last night's party, I'm thinking this was an epic mistake, but it's too late to take it back. I dial the number.

"Hello?" Karl answers.

"It's Cole," I say. "Can you talk right now?"

"Sure," my cousin says. "Let me step out of this cafe so I can hear you. Is everything okay?"

"Yes, we're all fine, although I hate to interrupt your lunch. We can talk later."

"I was just grabbing something to take back to the office. It's fine."

"Right," I say. "Well, I have some news to share."

"News? Your dad's fine, right?"

"It's good news, Karl. Relax." Karl is kind, considerate, hard-working, and bright, but he panics over paper cuts. "My dad decided that even if the odds of my ruling after him are slim to none, he wanted to formally adopt me."

"Adopt you?"

"We took care of all the paperwork earlier this week, and it's final. I've been preparing the paperwork to transfer the title to you."

"The title?"

If I didn't know Karl fairly well, I'd think he'd had a stroke. But he's always like this with anything even remotely shocking or strange. "This is where you say, 'wow, what great news.'"

"Well, is it good for you? I mean, if you can't rule, you're giving up your family home and estate and everything. For nothing."

A good summation of my epic mistake, yes. "Right, and that's probably what I've done. Nevertheless, it is done, and you will benefit. Your joy won't hurt my feelings, I assure you."

"But you're such a good person. It can't be good karma for me to take your inheritance from you."

I grit my teeth. It's like he's won the lottery and he won't take the money. "Karl, I don't even have a say, not now. It's all yours."

"Why don't you hold off on the paperwork? I would be fine with not filing it, if say, things go badly. Then you can just reverse the adoption. I'm sure your dad could do that. Isn't that the benefit to being a prince?"

First my old friend holds my job, and now Karl doesn't want a ten million dollar home and title. Is this a message? Providence? God telling me not to keep aiming for something that won't happen?

Beth.

If I wasn't doing this stupid thing. . . that kiss.

But I think about how it felt, signing the papers to be adopted by Dad. Signing my name Cole Michael Alois of Liechtenstein. Knowing that, legally at least, I'm Dad's child. If fate thinks I'm an idiot, well, maybe I am. I don't care. For the first time in my life, I'm an idiot with a family —even on paper. That's worth more than a sprawling house with too many gardens and a ridiculous title I never wanted.

"I appreciate your consideration for my future," I say. "I genuinely do, but holding off isn't necessary, I assure you."

"Well, if you're sure, alright then. Mum is going to be over the moon. I bet she'll start packing her bags this very second."

His mother has never forgiven me for being born. Perhaps now she'll finally smile at me at family functions. A thought strikes me: I don't have to *go* to my dad's family functions anymore. I'm not obligated to host them, or appear, or anything. I genuinely liked Karl, but he was very nearly the only one. "I wish you and your mother every happiness at Château Solvay. Truly."

"I will be praying for your success, Cole, and so will Mum."

I'm not sure I'd stretch her goodwill that far, but perhaps she won't be lighting candles against me either. "Thanks. Keep an eye out for a certified letter, alright? Don't want to throw that one away."

"Will do. And next you're in Belgium, please let's do lunch. We may not have the same last name anymore, but you're still my favorite cousin."

"Mine too." Surprisingly, I mean it.

I force myself downstairs to confront Mom and Dad. Holly will be puking, more than likely, but the rest of them will want to do a post mortem. No one said anything last night after the shower, but I could tell by the forced smiles from all the cousins and uncles and great uncles that in spite of Holly's amazing speech—the outlook is bleak.

Mom's waiting in the kitchen to offer me fresh squeezed orange juice.

"That bad, huh?" I take the glass.

"We have some work to do," Mom says.

"No one knew who I was," Beth says from the corner. "And I know my German isn't perfect, but it's improving. I did a lot of listening in, and a lot of the women actually support you."

"Several of the men approached me near the end, one by one," Dad says. "They each acted like this was a major epiphany, something they had never considered before."

"What?" Mom's eyebrows are raised.

"Alfred, Leopold, and Eugene, and right before I left, Heinrich as well, suggested that instead of changing the law to allow adopted children to succeed, that I should focus on allowing women a place."

Mom collapses into the chair. "But Holly wants nothing to do with ruling."

"Which is what I told them," Dad says. "It's a pointless change, for our family at least."

Beth's eyes are on her tea, but I can tell they're flashing. "But think about Holly's daughter, if she has one, or even if she has a son, what message does it send, that women are excluded?"

"If they're willing to budge on that, maybe we did make some progress," Mom says. "We just need more opportunities to talk to them, and we need to do it smaller. I think the shower was a great way to send out a cohesive message, and Holly was brilliant."

"She really was," Beth says. "I only understood about 85% of it, and I was ready to go to war."

"War?" Mom asks.

"I think she meant that it moved her," I say. "That Holly appealed successfully to her sense of justice."

"But you're American. And you're adopted too," Mom says. "So of course you support the sentiment. It's all these people who don't understand because they're too selfish to imagine caring for, sacrificing for, or welcoming in someone who isn't their obligation who worry me."

"I think it's fear," Beth says. "Or possibly narcissism, but I didn't get the feeling it was that overt."

We all turn to face her.

She blushes, but she soldiers on. "You said there are only fifty dynasts, right?"

Mom nods. "Go on."

"I heard several people saying that Holly would be a fine ruler. Part of that might have been that they were impressed with how well she spoke. But even so, it doesn't account for so many people supporting her instead of you."

"Why not?" I ask.

Beth bites her lip. "Well, if you allow women, the number of dynasts doubles, right? Sort of devaluing the importance of being one."

"Sure, probably," Mom says. "Although we do tend to have more boys than girls for some reason, but something close to double."

"But if you say that you can adopt children as well, that doesn't change much. You'd think the men would be more likely to support something that barely impacts them at all, other than perhaps Uncle Franz, who stands to take over if this proposal fails. But for the others, it adds exactly one person to the list, right?"

Dad scratches his head. "We aren't big on adoptions in our family—I hadn't even thought of that, but I believe Cole is the only one. Except didn't Alfred adopt?"

"Okay, so maybe it adds two new people, instead of fifty." Beth taps her lip. "Either way, it should be the more attractive option—allowing the existing dynasts to retain their power and importance. So I thought about why they would oppose it. It could be that they love their wives and daughters and wish they had fair representation, maybe. But I think nobility at its heart has always operated on the assumption that something about the ruling class made them better than everyone else. Special. Unique. Smarter."

Beth is a genius.

"America was sort of hated for a long time for tossing

that basic belief out the window. Maybe that's why I'm so quick to assume this, but if you open the royal line up to adoptive children, it's almost like you're saying their right is based on. . . well, nothing. Luck, essentially."

Dad and Mom are speechless.

"Is there anything we could do about that?" I ask.

She shrugs. "Maybe you could figure out how to circumvent their pride? Aren't all your noble houses intermarried like 500 times? Could you say that the person must have common ancestry with, I don't know, someone that you would meet the criterion for?"

"Where did you attend school, young lady?" Mom asks.

"Aveda Academy in Atlanta."

"It must be a very fine institution," Dad says.

Beth's eyes sparkle. "I think it's one of the best, for teaching how to cut hair and do highlights."

"Excuse me?" Mom asks.

"I never went to college," Beth says. "I take care of hair —trimming, color and so forth."

"You also play piano," Dad says.

"That too," she says, "but as a hobby. Speaking of, I had better get ready. Apparently Jostli wants to start early today —more of a brunch performance."

My phone buzzes. It's a text from Rogan, the captain of my football team. SCORED US SEATS INSIDE AT THE ADLER. YOU IN?

"Beth?" I ask.

She turns back toward me from the doorway.

"How many people are actually eating over there while you play?"

This time, she blushes much darker than she did earlier. And she swallows. "I don't know. A few."

"My buddy just texted me an invite to eat there."

"I'm sure a prince wouldn't want to go and eat at a

134

random hotel restaurant with a bunch of normal people." Her lip twists just enough that I know she's kidding.

"Good thing I'm not a prince," I say.

"Now, see here," Dad says. "I went jogging every morning past most of the businesses in that area, for forty years or more. All of the citizens know me, and most say 'Hoi' as I pass. We're not snobby here, whatever may be true over in England."

"Well then, if it's not beneath you, you should take him up on it," she says. "I hear the hamburgers are pretty good."

"The hamburgers?" I ask.

Beth smiles. "They've been the best seller, what with the American theme they have going on over there."

"American theme?" Mom asks. "Isn't it a Swiss restaurant?"

"I think it's because of their live entertainment," I say. "The American singer/song writer, Beth Graham."

"Well, maybe I'll see you there," she says over her shoulder as she escapes.

"You can count on it," I say.

Mom and Dad, thanks to Beth's analysis, dive right into a discussion of whom we could contact and in what circumstance they might be most receptive. Beth comes downstairs in a light blue top and black skirt, looking like an ad for a summer women's clothing catalog, but she sneaks past and waves on her way out. Mom and Dad go on and on and on, compiling a list of our attack plan. When Mom goes to the library and brings back two enormous tomes and begins poring over the family tree from both her family and Gerard's, I stand up.

"I'm willing to do whatever you want, tomorrow. Beth leaves in a day, and my entire football team wants to grab lunch there and see what the fuss is about. I told them I'd be there, and I don't want to be late."

Mom frowns. "Can't Beth bring something back for you?"

"Dad's the one who determines when to call for a vote, which means this planning is important, but it's not urgent."

Mom's lips compress into a thin line, but she doesn't argue.

Dad says, "If the hamburgers are good, bring one back for me. Adeline makes amazing soups and salads and her fish is beyond compare, but her burgers and fries taste like under-salted rubber."

"Rubber should be heavily salted, should it?" Mom asks.

I roll my eyes and walk out the door before they can ask me to look up any more minutiae about Gerard's great great grandmother's children. I'm actually excited as I drive downtown and look for a parking space. In thirty-some years of living here, I don't recall ever needing to park three streets away from anywhere downtown.

Beth is the reason all these people are here? My Beth?

I scrub that thought from my brain. She's not my anything. She's just Holly's friend. Actually, Holly's friend's sister. And she's American, and she's leaving in a day. So.

My phone rings, and it's Rogan. "Cole! Where are you? If you're not here in five minutes, they'll give your spot to someone else."

"I'm around the corner. Two minutes, tops."

"Oh good." He hangs up.

Rogan's an amazing forward, but he's not much for the small talk. I expect our seats to be right near the piano, since Rogan said I owe him fifty francs for mine, but when he waves at me, his blond hair flopping in his eyes from the movement, he's in the furthest back corner. There's nowhere inside the restaurant walls that is further from the piano. At least we're not outside. I walk past table after table after table, all full. There are, at least, a few speakers sprinkled around, the wires taped to the concrete of the patio. Ostensibly that ensures that even out here, they can hear Beth clearly. If I hadn't already heard her play, I'd think my people had all gone mad.

"Beth will start playing for the lunch block in less than five minutes," Jostli announces. "So if you haven't placed your orders yet, you probably ought to do it quickly."

Our waiter takes our order, burgers all around, and I make sure that my chair affords me a view of Beth's hair at least, if not her face.

I'm remembering the first time we met, her hair three times as large as it is now, her face streaked with makeup, her movements perpetually startled and unsure. And I watch with awe as she welcomes everyone, easily, calmly, with such confidence. Her eyes sparkle, her arms are grace personified, and her mouth.

I want to kiss her again. Badly.

But when she starts to play, I don't care about kissing her any more; I just want to be near her. When she plays a song she wrote, about Liechtenstein, when she sings about the snow on the Alps, the wind sluicing down the mountainside, the smell of fresh laurels, the playful laughter of children and the waves from the passersby, my heart soars.

She has captured it, the essence of what makes this place home to me.

The song is everything that made me want to be adopted, that led me to gamble my future on an impossible dream. Her insight, after being here for such a short time, is remarkable. Glancing around the room, it's patently obvious that everyone gets it. They know that she *sees* them. She may not have a lofty degree, she may not have the airbrushed face of a supermodel, but she cares about people.

She belongs here.

And yet, she's leaving. Soon. And I can't even do

anything about it, not when I'm already teetering on a knife's edge. Not when my family already thinks I'm less than, not good enough, not really royal. Her words from earlier repeat in my mind.

It's almost like you're saying their right is based on. . . well, nothing. Luck, essentially.

If my mom had met Dad first. If she had waited to have children, would I have been Hans-Michael's son? There's no way to know, but it's a terrifying thought, that the entire world and our position in it has nothing to do with our real, intrinsic value, and everything to do with luck. Some call it fate, but either way, it's something entirely outside of our control.

But life is also a sequence of decisions. Calculated gambles. Guesses. I doubt that my dad's family, that Holly's family, will welcome me. But I still hope they do, I yearn for it. Something about Beth's music speaks to me, and is it any wonder? We're both adopted, me by one parent, her by two. We both feel we don't quite belong. But it's not only me. Something about this hairdresser from Atlanta speaks to all of these people, to my friends, my family, and the entire staff at the castle. Like Noel, she gets people.

And they adore her for it.

When she finally stops playing, the applause is crazy. The people outside stand up, and then, like a wave crashing, we all do. So she plays one more song, something I've never heard. Something about searching and searching and finally, in the end, finding a place where she belongs. "Finding Home," she says. "That's what I'm calling that one. I just wrote it this morning, so it's rough, and I haven't even tried to translate it into German yet."

And all the citizens, most of whom don't speak English, still get it, no, they *love* it.

I try to approach her after that, now that she's done, but she's mobbed. I can't even see her head in the middle of all the people. About half an hour later, Jostli's gruff voice rises above the murmurs and the shouts and the chatter. "It's time for Beth to go, but as you all know, we have one last chance to see her. Tomorrow she'll be here for a final show. Talk to me and Hannah in the far corner booth outside, but do it quick. We only have a handful of seats left."

I head outside, figuring that they'll smuggle her around back. Which is how I'm waiting at the end of the street where the alley empties when she skips around the corner.

"A few people?" I ask. "You said a few people come."

She blushes again, and I love it. "Well, I never really have any idea if anyone will show up. I still can't believe they do."

I shake my head. "Of course they do. That was an amazing show, and no one does anything that. . . simple anymore. It's all drums and lights and smoke and mirrors and glitter and bangles and poles."

"Yeah," she says, "we had a budget of zero. In fact, the people first started showing up when I was just practicing in the mornings."

"And Jostli was too pleased to capitalize on that," I say. "That guy."

She glares at me. "He gave me two thousand francs today. Don't slam him. It's ten times what I make back home for the same amount of time."

"Don't give him too much credit," I say. "He's raking in the dough."

"So what? He should. It's his place, and his people and his initiative that made it possible." She looks at her feet. "I don't think I've ever had this much fun before. I hope the tour is like this."

"Oh, it'll be way more exciting," I say.

But secretly, I hope it's not, because even more than Jostli, I wish Beth would stay.

BETH

I'm shocked when Cole is already up, dressed, and waiting in the kitchen at six a.m.

"Uh, hi," I say. "I was going to grab a muffin and be on my way. Margaret said she'd leave some—"

Cole extends a basket in my direction. It's full of muffins.

"Thanks. I hope I didn't wake you." I don't know how I could have. I showered last night to avoid waking Paisley this morning. She gets so little rest, I didn't want to cut it short in any way.

"Oh please. Holly's puking is way more likely to wake me up than you, tiptoeing around like a little mouse."

"Thank goodness it wasn't me." I snag a large blueberry muffin with a crumble topping of some kind. "It's a good thing I'm leaving. I think I've gained ten pounds while I was here."

"You look exactly the same."

"Exactly the same?" I cock one eyebrow. "I certainly hope not."

He laughs. "Well, maybe not *exactly* the same. You weren't really at your best when I drove through Frankfurt.

140

In case I haven't apologized, I'm sorry I was grumpy about picking you up."

"You had a right. I checked it out on a map, and you had to completely reroute to go by Frankfurt. I didn't realize how much of a nuisance I was being. It added at least an hour and a half to your trip, maybe more." I stack my bags so I can head for the front drive.

"Not that way," Cole says. "You need to go through the garage."

"Paisley has your driver, Roger, taking me," I say. "She said it wasn't a big deal, that you guys didn't need him today. She said to meet him out front." I glance at my watch. "In about four minutes."

Cole smiles. "I'm afraid Roger won't be able to take you."

My heart races. "Oh no, then I need to call an Uber or something. Gosh, how long do you think that'll take?" I try not to panic. I wonder what Henrietta will say if I'm late.

"Calm down. I told him his services weren't necessary, because I'm going to take you myself."

I shake my head. "Oh no, I can't let you do that. The tour is moving right along to our second stop and that's Milan. It's more than three and a half hours away, and then you'd still have to drive back."

"Why do you think I took my car to Antwerp when we have a private jet?" he asks.

I shrug.

"I love to drive. It's calming, and it lets me think. I have a lot to think about right now."

I can't be sure, but he seems to stare right at me when he says that, almost like he's thinking about—but that's ridiculous. We already talked about this, and we aren't a fit, in any way at all. He's eight years older than me—Paisley's sly smile when I asked was nearly insufferable—and he's far more educated. Plus, he's an actual titled noble, whether he's accepted as a prince or not. Or he was, anyway. And he lives in *Europe*, and he can't date an American or it will ruin all his plans.

Silly or not, I wish he was thinking about me.

I've been thinking about him altogether too often. When I sleep, when I eat, even when I play. He's creeping into my songs, into my dreams, and if I'm being honest, into my heart. I wish his path and my path weren't headed in opposite directions. Which reminds me that today, finally, after twenty-five years, I'm going to be spending time with my birth mother. That's the whole reason I came in the first place.

My purpose is clear, my course set, but I certainly don't mind his company for the drive. "Alright, well, thanks then. I'm paying for gas."

Cole's eyes sparkle. "Here, we call it petrol, but fine. You can pay when we stop for petrol."

"Petrol? Seriously?"

"When I first began studying English, I learned the word 'gas' for a bodily emission. The first time a human used it to mean fuel for the car, I was mightily confused."

"I can't believe you're fluent in three languages," I say.

"Neither can I." Cole practically snatches my bags and carries them to the garage.

"What do you mean?" I ask.

Cole loads my bags into the back of his Range Rover. "I'm dyslexic, as I mentioned, and Mom hired tutor after tutor, but learning Dutch was hard enough."

"Dutch was your second language?"

He pulls the car out of the garage, but once we're on the driveway, he looks at me sideways. "Dutch was my first language, and even that was hard. Do you know what dyslexia is?"

"Of course I do," I say. "It's a learning disability where letters get jumbled in your head."

"It's a little more complicated than that," he says.

"Tell me."

"Do you really care?" Cole raises both eyebrows and glances at me.

"Absolutely, I do."

"A lot of people think that we can't see words or letters right. They think our words are 'jumbled', like you said. But actually, our eyes are just fine. I see the exact same thing as you. A group of researchers not long ago took a bunch of Hebrew letters none of the students had ever seen and asked them to reproduce them after seeing them and the children with dyslexia did just as well as those without."

"So if it's not jumbling words or letters, what is it?" How could I never have known this?

"Teachers used to say that if you reversed your letters, that was a sign for young children, but letters written backward is actually really common. Tons of early readers and writers transcribe things backward."

"Okay."

"Do you know the words phonic and phonemic?" he asks in English.

"I've heard of phonics, but I don't know what it means." I scrunch up my nose. "Sorry."

"I'm not sure anyone other than my mom has really ever cared what I dealt with. When I was a kid, I could speak Dutch alright, for the most part, but when I tried to learn to write it, we realized that—well I got ahead of myself." He laughs. "Phonic is the relationship between a sound and a letter or a letter combination. So an 'a,' by itself, makes a hard 'a' sound. 'Eh,' or something like that. But phonemic awareness is when you can identify the different parts of a word and the sounds that comprise them."

"Um."

"I lost you."

I nod.

"That's fine. It's not really something that most people have to worry about."

"I want to know. Is there a way you can explain it, like you're talking to someone who's not very bright?" I ask. "Like someone who didn't go to college and learned to do hair instead?"

"First of all—"

I wave my hand through the air. "I was totally kidding."

"Okay, how about this. One of the first things I had to learn was my vowel sounds. When you think about apple, not writing the word, just saying it aloud, the 'a' makes an ahhhh sound, like apple, or snap. But if you put 'a' in another word, like pray, or say, then it's a different sound. The apple or snap 'a' is what they call a short vowel sound. That whole concept confused me. I struggled to process the relationship between sounds and the words they formed. That meant that when I started to try and learn phonics, I was already doomed."

"So people figure this out when kids start learning to write?"

"There are signs to watch for earlier, but yes, usually. See, phonics is learning the sound a letter or combination of letters makes when they're joined. Early readers don't *know* words yet, they are sounding them out. A child reading new words will sound out each letter of short combinations. They may know that 'p' makes a puh sound and 'i' makes an ih sound. 'G' makes a guh sound, and so on. They string them together and get pig, but it's slow and laborious. That is phonics, but you have to possess the underlying phonemic awareness or the phonic training won't work."

I shake my head. "That's making my head spin. I can't even imagine how hard it was for you as a child."

Cole laughs. "It took four years before we started

making any progress. See, the first few tutors were trying to make me memorize every word in the language by spending hours reading every day."

My mouth drops open. "Seriously?"

"A lot of people with dyslexia are still shoved into the same position. They never become strong readers, or even capable readers, because it's all straight up memorization for them. When Mom hired Fräulein Hagner, my world brightened considerably."

"The Mary Poppins of learning disabilities?"

"The who?"

"Never mind," I say. "What did she do?"

"At first I was angry. She took me back to the very beginning, not reading, not writing, just speaking. We sat at a table and she taught me hand signs that corresponded with short vowel sounds, and then with long. I hated it. I felt like she was treating me like a baby, like I was stupid, but she pushed me along anyway. She made me work on saying things in the right way, for the right reasons, and consistently identifying the sounds. It took me about four years with her to master Dutch; Mom threw me a huge party."

"I bet that was exciting."

He frowns. "I was happy that Mom was relieved, but it was a little embarrassing. I was a thirteen-year-old who could finally read with something close to ease. Not extremely well, mind you, but without everyone around me cringing. And then, the next week, instead of sending Fräulein Hagner packing, Mom announced that we'd be moving along to German."

"Oh."

"We had been in Liechtenstein for almost ten years, and I had barely reached the point that I could read and speak my native tongue. But everything here was in German."

"How long did that take?" I ask.

"Probably because I could already speak it fairly well, and I had the sounds in place, only a year and a half or so."

I groan. "Don't tell me. A big party and then a new language?"

Cole shakes his head. "Nope. Mom told me she knew what a hard time I had, and even if Holly could speak English as well as she and my father, and even though we valued our relationship with the United States, I didn't have to learn."

"Oh."

"But I felt like she said that because I wasn't really important." Cole's fingers tighten on the steering wheel, his shoulders tense. "So I learned it myself."

"And?"

"It took me a long time. A lot of connections in English are counterintuitive."

"But you're so fluent I can barely tell you even have an accent."

He shrugs. "I did a one-year study abroad."

"When?" I ask. "Where?"

He smiles. "Hawaii."

"Are you kidding?"

"I didn't say that I didn't enjoy it."

"And I almost felt sorry for you," I say.

"Don't ever do that," he says. "More than five percent of the population deals with this, and most of them never had a Fräulein Hagner. In fact, I've been working with Mom and Dad to set up the very first program specifically for kids identified with dyslexia here. If they work on the underlying problems early, the rest of their lives will be much smoother, and they won't be limited by anything."

"So you have no trouble, say, reading aloud?"

He chuckles. "I still avoid it, in any language."

"Probably fine," I say.

"Except that means I have to memorize any speeches I give, or just use an outline."

He asks me about hair school next, and before I know it, we've nearly reached the concert hall Uwe sent to me. "They're supposed to be setting up for tomorrow night's show."

"What's the venue called?" Cole taps on some buttons on his GPS.

"The Alcatraz, which is the name of a huge prison in the United States."

Cole frowns. "A prison?"

"It was a high security prison that was on an island. Actually, I bet Mom will get a kick out of the name, when I tell her I'm being escorted to Alcatraz."

"I think in Spanish, that word means a big brown bird."

"A big brown bird?" I ask. "Like, just any brown bird?"

Cole bites his lip. "It's a specific one, that's brown and scoops up water in its beak, but I don't remember the name."

"Pelican?"

"Yes." He nods his head. "I think it means pelican."

"Well, that's good. I'm glad the venue is named for birds, not the rock island prison off the coast of California."

"And today you will practice?" he asks.

"I certainly hope so. I've never played with Henrietta's people and I'm worried—"

"Don't," he says. "I have one hundred percent faith that you will be perfect."

"I would settle for seventy-five percent," I say, "but thanks."

"Are you excited?"

Mostly, I'm nervous. "Sure, a little."

When we reach the front, Cole tries to park and walk me in, but the guard keeps yelling at him in Italian.

"It's fine," I say. "I can get my bags from here."

"Are you sure?" Cole asks. "Because I think I can take him."

I shake my head and roll my eyes. "Stop." I open the trunk and grab my bags. I wish he could at least hug me bye, but the guard is glaring at him even now. I wave. "Thanks for the ride, both times, and good luck."

"It was truly my pleasure," Cole says.

And then his car is driving away, and my heart is sinking far more than it should. The rest of the day is chaotic, but Uwe takes things in hand steadily. He handles sending my bags to the local hotel, and he shows me to the room where lunch is waiting for the band members and staff.

I've been here for two hours, but I still haven't seen Henrietta. I swallow the last bite of my sandwich just as Uwe pokes his head around the doorway.

"Henrietta is coming. Be ready in fifteen."

A man with a shocking amount of white hair pivots to stand directly in front of me. "Elizabeth, yes?"

I nod.

"I'm Peter Hamm, the production manager. It's nice to have another American around."

"Oh." My eyes widen and I worry that I look like a deer about to be splattered by a semi.

"It's a lot to take in—but if you know the music, you'll be fine. Everyone here is very professional. In fact, other than you, Henrietta's had the same band playing with her for more than four years."

"That's impressive," I say. "She must not be hard to work with."

Peter stifles a laugh. "She pays well. Very well."

Not quite as promising. I hadn't even thought to ask what I'd be paid. "I'm excited to be here," I say.

He shakes his head. "We still can't believe she hired

someone to fill in for Ginger just because she liked your playing in some dive joint."

Parker's is hardly a dive joint, but I don't argue. Clearly she didn't mention that I'm her daughter. "I feel very lucky to be here."

"Had you heard of her before?" he asks. "Because my family in Cleveland has no idea who I'm working for."

I glance around, worried that someone else overheard and will take offense.

"No stress there, angel. We're the only fluent English speakers, other than Her Royal Highness. I mean, they know a few words, but they won't be able to key in on random conversation without really focusing. And even then, it's hard. Do you speak German, I hope?"

I gulp. "Some, yeah."

"It's about to get a lot of use."

"No one seems super friendly," I say.

"They're being stupid. They don't want you to take over Ginger's spot."

I realize that if they find out I'm Henrietta's daughter, they'll really hate me. Maybe that's why she didn't tell anyone. "They don't need to worry," I say. "I know this spot is temporary, and I have no intention of stealing it from anyone."

"Says the naive, fresh-faced ingénue." He chortles. "But keep that up. I almost believed you, so they might buy it too."

Peter takes it upon himself to introduce me to the crew. I try to memorize all the names. There's another Uwe—this one handles lights. And two women named Anna. But the rest of the names begin to blur together in spite of repeating them in my head several times the moment I heard them. I had no idea that a concert required this many people. And that's before the dancers show up. Apparently they get ready on the other side of the stage.

All told, between the musicians: guitar, bass, drums, and bizarrely, a harmonica, the managers, the light techs, the sound crew, and the dancers, there are at least forty people milling around, chatting, making jokes, and scowling at one another. I sit down at the Steinway and play the first few measures of the first song in the new album. The grand piano has a decent sound, but the hammers are on their last legs. I bet they're at least four years old. "Hey Peter," I say. "This is running pretty bright, for me at least. Is there someone who handles the venue who I might be able to talk to about adjusting the voicing?"

Peter snorts. "Trust me, Bach, no one else will notice."

"Uh, okay."

Uwe said fifteen minutes, but after twenty, I start running through entire songs. No reason to waste time. The guitarist and the bass player are looking at me and snickering, but I try not to care. After the fourth or fifth song, the noise around me has become almost familiar. Until it completely dies. I finish the song and look around to see what happened.

Henrietta's standing on stage, tapping her shoe. "I hope everyone here will welcome Beth," she says in German. "Cleary she has no problem with musical ability, but this is her first tour. I'm sure she'll quickly figure things out, but if she has questions, please be helpful."

I'm such an idiot.

Henrietta continues, "I know we had a bit of a rough non-start, but since we spent over a month preparing before our brief interlude, I hope a simple run-through will get us back on track."

Peter hands me a set list and whispers, "We changed the order some."

I glance down, scanning the songs. "Uh, there are two songs on here I don't know."

He shrugs. "Good luck."

When Henrietta approaches the microphone, I realize that no one introduced me to a director.

"Psst," I say to the guitarist whose name I cannot for the life of me recall. "Who am I supposed to follow? Where's the director?"

He flips me off.

Tears threaten, but I will not start sobbing before we've even played a song. I square my shoulders and channel my inner Brekka. She wouldn't give up. She would double down. I fumble the first four measures looking around for someone to follow, but I quickly realize there's no director. The drums start, and then the guitarist plays the opening chord and we play—taking our ultimate cues from Henrietta. By the third song, I'm feeling the rhythm much better, and Henrietta even smiles in my direction.

But the fourth song is one I don't know.

And apparently the piano is kind of important, because when I don't start playing in the first fifteen seconds, Henrietta lowers her mic and shakes her head. "What's going on?"

"Uh, well, I don't know this song," I say. "It wasn't on the list Uwe sent me."

She closes her eyes and pinches the bridge of her nose.

"I sent her everything," Uwe says.

I will burn him to the ground. "I must have missed it." I barely grind the words out.

Henrietta says a few words I don't know, and I file them for later investigation. They didn't exactly teach me swear words in school, so the unknown words aren't promising. "You better know this song cold by tomorrow."

I nod. "Absolutely, I will." She lifts the mic again, and I can't bring myself to tell her that I don't have the four-teenth song, either.

She doesn't smile at me again, but I survive the next nine songs with sweat on my brow and trembly fingers.

Even so, I could handle that. But when the drums start for the fourteenth song, I can barely hold my fingers steady.

Henrietta is going to lose it on me, and it's not even my fault. I learned every single song Uwe sent. When I hear the solid bass drum and the opening notes of the guitar, I decide that if I'm going down, I may as well really do it. I lock in with the drummer's slow and easy rhythm, steering clear of the bass clef so the bassist doesn't hate me, and move up one register to highlight the rude guitarist. I focus on chunky chords, punctuated by staccato notes to emphasize Henrietta's melody.

She doesn't stop the song in the middle, but when it ends, she glares at me. "What was that?"

I open my mouth to say that I didn't get the music, but I can't bring myself to say it again. It didn't help the first time, anyway. "I thought I'd try something different."

"I liked it better," the bass player says. "The old piano part was boring."

Henrietta shrugs, and we move right into the next song.

By the time we finish, my hands are shaking, and it feels like I've run a hundred miles at a sprint.

"Not horrible," Henrietta says on her way past me. "But I expect better tomorrow night."

And then she's gone. No dinner invite, no questions about what I did for the last twelve days. Nothing.

Even Peter steers clear of me after my blistering set down earlier, but the shuttle takes us all to the hotel. I struggle, but I manage to lug my bags to the lobby and then to my room. By then, I'm too exhausted to go back downstairs and try and act like I don't want to bawl during dinner. Luckily, Paisley sent me with a whole bag full of snacks.

Trail mix and potato crisps for dinner? Why not. I eat three bags of chips to console myself while listening to the two songs I didn't know on repeat over and over to try and get the piano part down. The bassist was right—my line was better on *Eternity*, the second song.

I shower and collapse into bed, ready for this day to end. I'm nearly asleep when my phone chimes.

Of course, now that I know someone sent me a message, I need to know who it is. I texted Mom and Dad and Rob and the twins to tell them I was going to bed, so it's not one of them.

BOO.

Boo? Who would text 'boo' to me?

WHO IS THIS?

THE QUEEN OF ENGLAND.

I TOLD YOU I WOULDN'T PLAY AT YOUR TEA PARTY ALREADY. TWICE. Eyebrow raised emoji.

WHAT IF I LET YOU WEAR MY CROWN?

My heart races. I'm pretty sure I know who this is, but I didn't give him my number. He never even asked for it. CAN I KEEP IT AT THE END?

DEPENDS.

ON WHAT? I ask.

WHETHER IT WILL STAY ON YOUR HEAD.

I THINK I CAN MANAGE. I'VE ALWAYS WANTED A CROWN.

Dots. And then finally, IF YOU WERE TO HAVE REALLY FLUFFY HAIR, LIKE A LION'S MANE, IT MIGHT STAY ON BETTER.

Now I know. HOW DID YOU GET MY NUMBER, COLE?

A LITTLE BIRD GAVE IT TO ME.

I have no idea what to say now, but I'm beaming like an idiot. A few goofy words from him, and my horrible day has transformed into a decent one.

HOW DID IT GO? NOCK THEIR SOCKS RIGHT OFF?

He didn't put the k in front of knock. For some reason,

I find that so precious that I want to hug him. Or maybe I've wanted to hug him since the first day we met. TODAY SUCKED.

IT WILL GET BETTER.

I HOPE SO, BECAUSE IF IT GETS WORSE, I'M FIRED.

WHAT HAPPENED? he asks.

EVERYONE HATES ME, AND I SCREWED UP TWO SONGS.

I REALLY DOUBT THAT.

IT'S TRUE.

YOU'RE NOT USED TO PLAYING WITH A BIG BAND.

He's making excuses for me, which I appreciate, but that wasn't actually too bad. It was fun, honestly. THEY WERE SONGS NO ONE EVER GAVE ME.

SO TELL THEM THAT.

BELIEVE ME, I TRIED. BUT REALLY, I SHOULD HAVE GONE AHEAD AND LEARNED ALL HER SONGS, JUST TO BE ON THE SAFE SIDE.

YOU'RE TOO NICE. IT'S OKAY TO GET ANGRY.

Something about his words clicks, and a ridiculous fury I had been denying grows inside me until I hit my pillow. Then I hit it again. Then I start to cry.

YOU STILL THERE?

I'M OKAY, BUT I CAN'T SPEAK FOR MY FEATHER PILLOW. NEXT TIME, BEFORE YOU TELL ME ANGER IS THE ANSWER, THINK OF THE POOR BED COVERINGS.

Laughing face emoji.

THANKS FOR CHECKING IN. GLAD YOU MADE IT HOME SAFELY.

YOU KNOW I LIKE TO DRIVE, he texts.

WHAT DOES THAT MEAN?

IF THOSE JERKS DON'T TREAT YOU BETTER,
I'LL DRIVE BACK AND SMASH SOME HEADS.

When I can't go right to sleep, for some reason I find myself pulling up the Liechtenstein government website. I can't find anything about the Family or House Law, but the Constitution is posted, in English no less.

I manage to read almost the entire thing before I fall asleep, and it gives me an idea. But of course, if I've had the idea, so has everyone else in Cole's family. I'm just a hairdresser—what do I know about thrones and titles?

But when I do fall asleep, there's a smile on my face.

❧ 12 ❧

COLE

I drink more tea and have more awkward family dinners in the next two weeks than I had in my entire life prior to now. Dozens and dozens of meetings, sometimes several with the same family member. I laugh at flat jokes. I smile at horrifyingly rude comments. I read and compliment a novel that is utter drivel, written by Dad's cousin. But the worst thing of all is that I doubt it will make a single bit of difference.

Because, of course, the same people I'm flattering could just as easily be lying to me.

"How do you feel?" Mom asks for the fourth time.

I drink the orange juice she poured me in one go and slam the glass on the table. "Mom, I know that it's very unlikely that the dynasts will vote in my favor. You're worried I'm going to have some kind of nervous break or something, but the only thing pushing me toward the edge right now is you."

She sinks onto a kitchen chair like I shoved her.

"I'm sorry. Maybe I'm not as zen about the whole thing as I want to be."

Dad puts a hand on my shoulder. "No matter what happens, I'm glad that you agreed to sign those papers."

"We could delay it," Mom says. "Spend a little more time—"

"It's time," I say. "I can't ask Russ to hold my job any more and if this doesn't work, I need to move on."

"I understand," Dad says. "Then let's go."

The Landtag meets in the Government Building, conducting hearings at an enormous round table with an open space in the middle. When someone has the floor, they can speak from the center.

When I arrive, thirty-one dynasts are already present. "We don't even vote for an hour," I say. "Looks like we'll have a good turn out."

Dad nods. "At least they're vested in this issue."

I do my best to keep calm and steady while I visit with the people already present. I've known many of them well for years, but others I've only met once or twice. At five minutes until noon, forty-six of the fifty-three have shown up, and six proxies have been registered.

"Gregor is sitting it out?" I whisper.

Dad shrugs. "I didn't think so."

As the clock rolls over, I stand and move into the center of the table. We placed extra chairs around the table, between the existing places. It's tight, but I can see every-one's faces as I spin around. At least as many women stand up along the walls as men.

Just before I begin to speak, Gregor slides in the door and stands in the back. Every dynast is now represented.

"Welcome, and thank you for coming," I say. "Dad asked me to say a few words before we vote today, mostly to explain why we've asked you here. You all know that Dad wants to change the House Law, which has existed for this principality for more than three hundred years, and was in existence for many centuries before in nearly the same form for Austrian houses." I pause and circle, meeting their eyes. "I do not make this request lightly."

Dad probably can't make out the features of my face, but when I look his way, his smile nearly cracks his face in two.

"Many hundred years ago, there were no DNA tests. There were no advanced scientific methods to determine if the child a midwife handed you was, in fact, yours. As the years have passed, many things have changed. Most of those things have been for the better. Women can vote. Refrigeration and antibiotics have saved and continue to save countless lives. Technology and banking have become international titans, and Liechtenstein has benefitted from that growth and progress."

"When my biological father died, I was too young to understand what I had lost. By the time I was old enough to miss a father, Mom had met Dad." This time, I'm the one smiling. "He never, not for one second, cared that I was not his biological son. Even when he and Mom were blessed with Noel, and then again with Holly, he never treated me differently. I was taught, cared for, nurtured, loved, and when the worst happened and Noel passed away."

I pause and breathe in and out a few times.

"When Noel died, Holly wasn't ready to step in and take care of our proud nation, so even though I had no right to inherit, I did it. And again, when Dad's eyesight began to suffer, I was here. You all know this already, but what you may not have considered is that our blood may not have been the same either way. Without blood tests from centuries ago, for all we know, we might be the children of the baker, or a local farmer. What matters isn't the DNA we carry. It's the loyalty we all share to this family. It's time that the house laws reflect that truth. It's time for parents who can't have children to be allowed to adopt one without a penalty. I hope you'll vote for this so that our family can continue to progress alongside with the world around us."

Dad waves and one of the clerks passes out ballots.

Gregor stands up. His brows are strong and dark, his jaw pronounced. He's wearing a sharp suit, which fits his job as CEO of a competitor bank. When he grew past the management level within the hierarchy of our family and there wasn't room for him to run things, he left. I imagine it was a difficult decision. "May I say a few words?" he asks.

Dad nods.

"I am not senseless to the justice in what you ask of us, Cole. You have exemplified the station of prince and son, and will one day make a great father, I'm sure. But I oppose this amendment, and I'll explain why. You act as though it's injustice for a couple to adopt a child and not have that child jump the line of succession, right to the top."

My heart hammers in my chest.

"The harsh reality is that not all men are created equal, no matter what Americans may tout. We are all different. Some smart, some unwise. Some healthy, some not. But our family line has proven to produce intelligent, capable, and devoted heirs. For generation after generation, we have kept our family at the top. Politically, in commerce and finance, across the board. Now, I'm not saying that Cole's genetic material isn't acceptable. I'm sure that it is. In spite of early struggles, he's been an adequate fill-in for his father. But contemplate what happens when he dies. Our job is to consider the possible future consequences. What if Franz and his wife, who married late in life and only had one child, had been unable to conceive? What if they had no children and adopted? What if that child wasn't bright? What if he wasn't hard-working? What if he resented us for bringing him here, from, say, China? Or India. Korea, Russia. It doesn't matter. Children who are adopted frequently have health problems and bumpy upbringings that lead to more issues down the road. Do we really want to build that risk into the house law in the pursuit of being 'progressive' or 'enlightened'? I know that I don't."

No one speaks after he sits down, but every head bows over the ballot. Most of them don't meet my eye when they bring the ballot to the box Dad's holding, which is why I'm not surprised when we count the ballots that I lose, thirty-eight to fifteen. I should be devastated. I gave away my father's property, my title, a reasonable living. I delayed a job, and if I ever worried that I wasn't good enough, well, this vote confirms those fears.

But I'm not.

My dad loves me. My parents believed in me. And now there's nothing keeping me from dating Beth. I've been texting her every day, and more often in the past week as I update her on my efforts to win over the dynasts. She has been unfailingly supportive, but my unease has grown with every day that passes. If I won today, I could never look for a job in finance in Atlanta. If I won this vote, when her tour ended, she'd leave and I'd be busy accepting and learning to manage a regency.

But I didn't win.

Many, many more than fifteen dynasts tell me how sorry they are that I didn't win. They thought I'd make an excellent ruler. They're so upset that the others couldn't see it. I know that most of them are lying to me, but all I care about is getting away as fast as I can so I can look up the tour schedule for Henrietta Gauvón. Almost two hours later, I'm finally free, walking toward the Range Rover, my eyes scanning the tour calendar—Paris tonight—when Mom calls my name.

"Oh Cole. I'm so sorry." She hugs me.

"I need to get out of town for a day or two," I say. "I'm sure you understand."

"Of course I do. Where will you go?"

"I was thinking Paris. Do you mind if I take the jet?"

Mom grabs my hand and squeezes. "Of course not. Take some friends. Do something fun for a change."

I text Rogan. HEADED TO PARIS TO SEE HENRI-ETTA GAUVÓN. LEAVE IN 90 MIN. YOU IN?

ERIK AND BEN ARE WITH ME. CAN THEY COME TOO?

I smile. SURE.

Which is how, less than three hours later, I've booked tickets on the fourth row and I'm in the air, halfway to Beth. I worry that maybe I should have warned her I'm coming, but it's too late now. Besides, it's not like this is some grand gesture. I've got three of my football friends with me. After we land, we have dinner at Mom's favorite restaurant to kill some time, but even so, we're almost an hour early when we pick up our tickets from the concert hall ticket office.

I wonder whether she'll be there, already out near the stage. "Let's go ahead and find our seats," I suggest.

"Seriously?" Ben asks. "We could walk around some and grab a crepe."

"We just ate," I say.

Erik shrugs. "I could eat."

I roll my eyes. "Here are your tickets, then. Meet me in there before it starts."

"You know there's an opening act." Rogan points at the top of the ticket. "Ever heard of 'Beneficio'? Because I haven't."

I am not going to miss a second of the concert. For all I know, Beth is playing for them too. "Show up late then, I don't care."

"Hey, that's a crepe cart opening up over there," Erik says.

"That's a hot dog stand," Rogan says.

"I like hot dogs," Ben says.

For the love. I walk inside, and I'm not even one of the first people finding my seat. Nearly twenty percent of the auditorium is already filled. I think about watching Beth in the tiny Hotel Adler restaurant, brand new fans peering through windows and doorways. I know it's her mom who's the draw here, but it's wild to think about the difference between that small restaurant and this.

I look around and try to count the seats. It's a testament to the amount of time that I have to kill that I reach five hundred and forty-three before giving up. Since I barely counted the first tier, I'm guessing thousands. Four different tiers, and seats that circle around on three sides. I wonder if Beth likes playing for Henrietta. She only tells me that she's 'improving,' whatever that means.

The minutes slowly tick by and people crawl across the stage, shifting equipment and setting up microphones. When eight o'clock rolls around, the time marked on the ticket, no one appears. No Beneficio, no one at all. The stands are more than two-thirds full, and I know it's a sold-out show, because I paid a hefty price to a third party for our tickets.

At fifteen minutes past eight, a small man in a banana-yellow suit walks out on stage. He says something in French I don't understand, then he repeats it, or at least, I assume he repeats it, in English. "I'm very sorry to inform you that Beneficio has fallen ill and will be unable to perform."

Murmurs, shouts, and even a few boos follow.

I have no idea what comes over me, but I don't think at all before adding my own shout to the mix. "Bring Beth Graham instead!"

Ben, Erik and Rogan are walking down the aisle behind me, but they're close enough to hear. "Yes," Ben says. "Beth Graham!"

They begin to chant her name, and the people behind them do the same. People are just stupid enough to start demanding something they don't understand. Within minutes, hundreds and hundreds of people are calling for Beth Graham. The banana man frowns and ducks back-stage. Eventually the chanting dies off, and people begin booing again. I can't understand everything that's being said, but much of it is in accented English. The young people don't eschew it quite as much as the older generation.

Someone a few rows behind me shouts, "We paid for two bands."

And in the tier above, someone else yells, "Beneficio sucks!"

At that exact moment, a tiny figure walks on stage. She walks slowly toward the microphone.

"You're not Henrietta Gauvón," someone yells.

"Beth Graham," I scream at the top of my lungs the second I recognize her.

Ben, Rogan and Erik pick it up immediately and soon others join us.

She glances around as if she's looking for something.

I sit down immediately.

She reaches for the microphone uncertainly. "I'm a piano player," she says. "My name is Beth Graham. I didn't believe it when Henrietta's agent told us that you wanted me to come out here."

The crowd has no idea how to react. I poke Ben. "Cheer, loudly. I don't want her to notice me."

He looks at me like I've gone crazy, but he's had enough to drink that he doesn't care how dumb he looks. When he starts shouting, so do Erik and Rogan, and then others pick it up too.

"Sing for us," I say, once there's enough other noise to disguise me.

Beth smiles. "I didn't plan anything, but I'm willing to give it a try if you are."

This time, I do nothing to prompt the applause.

"I'm sorry I don't speak French." She switches languages to German. "But I do speak German. I can sing a few songs in either. I hope that's alright."

More cheering. A few boos, but mostly cheers.

She walks toward the back of the stage, dragging the microphone stand behind her. Then she lowers it and arranges it close enough that she can sing and play.

"I call this one 'Sunrise.'"

I've listened to Henrietta's music. The piano exists to support the vocals, never rising up, never pulling attention from center stage. But in Beth's songs, it's a perfect balance, a delicate interweaving. In this one, the piano begins choppy, unsure. Dark, frightening. When she begins to sing, in German, her voice is angry, almost. She sings about being alone. Lost, afraid.

The piano is alone, the song one that no one knows. The audience came for a rock concert.

They're bored.

They're talking, some cheering, some jeering, none of them very vested.

But then Beth changes keys, and something shifts. Until. Until she met someone. Until the light began to shine over the horizon and she realized the world is a beautiful place. When she changes keys again, no one is yelling or cheering—they aren't even talking. I have no idea how many of them can speak German, but they grasp the tone, at least. Beth sings that when the sun sets again, she's not afraid. Thanks to this person, she knows what the world holds and she's unafraid. She'll be safe, strong, and ready. For her, the sunrise has already come and the sun will never fail her again.

It's perfect.

And I'm not the only one who notices.

Beth doesn't pause long, just long enough to say, "I call this song 'Chasm.'"

The piano in this piece is phenomenal. She plays so many notes, so many chords, that I wonder whether she has two sets of arms. The notes crash over me, pulsing, sobbing. I wonder whether the entire thing is instrumental when she finally begins to sing, this time in English. The world was safe, the world was strong, and light was in her life.

Then a chasm opened up under her feet and drowned her whole.

It so perfectly describes how I felt when Noel died that I'm embarrassed to have to wipe away tears. When I glance around to see if anyone noticed, I realize I'm not the only one crying. Hundreds and hundreds of people pull out their phones and turn on the lights, swaying with the slower tone of the song. This one doesn't end on a happy note, though, and I feel almost wrung out when the last notes fade.

Thankfully, she plays her song about Liechtenstein next, and the bone-deep sorrow from before eases.

When a little man in a yellow suit pops his head out on the side of the stage, I want to shoot him. He makes some kind of motion at Beth.

"This will be my last song," she says.

Boos, so many boos.

"I really want to thank you for being such an amazing audience. I wish I had known I'd be playing so I could have planned something better for you, but it has been an experience I'll never forget."

I hope she'll play the "Finding Home" song that I heard last time, but she doesn't. Instead, she plays a piece that would easily play on any radio in a large city. 'Her life was fine, her life was great, she had plenty of things to celebrate.' The melody is catchy, the cadence quick. It makes me want to bounce in my seat. 'She had real goals—all under control, but then.' The piano takes over, leaving me wondering what happened.

'You walked right in, all wrong and so right. You saved me that day and you loved me that night.' Oh no, it's a love song. Who is she talking about? Who loved her that night? I want to punch him, no, strangle him. It must be someone she met on tour. Could it be the guitarist? She mentioned in a text that he was young.

By the time it ends, people are clapping along with her. She stands up, holding the mic. "Thanks again. I couldn't have asked for a kinder audience."

The massive applause surprises even me, but I do my part to add to it, and Beth ducks backstage.

Ten minutes later, she and the other musicians sneak back on when the lights are dim, but I know to look for her, so I spot her immediately and shout, "BETH!"

Others take up the chant.

When Henrietta Gauvón walks on a moment later, everyone in the theater shouts and hoots and claps, but she glances behind her once, annoyed, and I realize I might not have done Beth any favors.

Twenty seconds later, with the lights and the smoke and the dancers, I stop worrying. The show Beth put on was *nothing* like this. There's no way Henrietta could be frustrated with a little piano performance, especially when her opening act cancelled. Henrietta hits every single note, and every song is flawless. The piano, especially, couldn't be better. It supports the vocals, enhances them, without ever overwhelming or distracting.

After she plays her last song, when the crowd keeps clapping, she beams. "Okay, I will do one last song. What do you want to hear again?"

"Beth," someone shouts.

"Beth Graham!" Others pick up the cheer.

Henrietta's eyes flash. "I knew you'd love my daughter once you figured out who she was. She really does take after me, doesn't she?"

The crowd goes *insane*.

"Beth, why don't you come up here and sing a song with your mother?"

Henrietta picks one of her biggest hits about a night out on the town, leaving Beth the part of back-up singer. But without the piano to support her, Beth experiments. She changes the words up, on the fly, and completely shifts the meaning of the song. Instead of singing about how fabulous Henrietta and her posse are out on the town, Beth makes it about the insecurity that's covered with a show, with sparkle, with bling. The tears behind the mask, she says at the end, and the crowd explodes.

I'm legitimately worried that the woman next to me is going to take her shirt off and throw it up on stage. Several people try to rush the security personnel and have to be shoved away.

Beth and Henrietta disappear shortly after, but I'm not ready to leave.

"Drinks, boys?" Rogan asks.

"I'll meet you in a few," I say. "I'm going to try and get backstage."

Ben rolls his eyes. "You're never gonna make it. She's famous now, bro."

I'm afraid he might be right.

I consider dropping my name or who my dad is, but I can't quite force myself to claim to be a prince when I'm so clearly not. Even calling myself the Marquis is a stretch these days. I settle instead for paying the bouncer a thousand dollars. Well worth it, if it works. Beth's deep brown eyes, her graceful fingers, her high-swept cheekbones, I'm hungry for all of it. My long legs eat up the ground, and I'm rounding the corner when I finally see her, leaning against a wall. I expect her to be deliriously happy, chatting, or maybe even being put upon by eager new fans.

Instead, she's frowning.

What's wrong? I keep walking, focusing on the words around her. It's loud back here, but I can hear someone shouting.

Henrietta.

"You planned it. You had to—else why would the audience call for you specifically?"

Beth shakes her head. "I have no idea why they asked for me."

"It ruined my show," she says. "And it made me look like a fool. I had to reveal you were my daughter so that the entire thing didn't fall apart."

So that the attention wouldn't be pulled from her, she means.

"I am very, very sorry," Beth says.

"You're always sorry. When you flub songs—"

"I only did that one time, during the first practice—"

Henrietta throws her arms into the air. "You are sorry when you change songs, but you keep doing it."

"You agreed they were better," Beth says.

Henrietta's eyes flash. Her voice is so soft I barely hear the words. "Will you be sorry tomorrow, do you think? Now that you have no place?"

"I don't understand," Beth says in German. Her German has improved a lot, but I imagine nuance is frequently lost even now.

"I don't understand," Henrietta mimics. "Let me be clearer. You're fired. Kicked off the tour. You have no job. You can go back home to Georgia and cut housewives' hair again."

Beth frowns. "I like housewives. I was raised by one." She steps closer. "And if you ever claim you're my mother again, I'll go on public record denying it. You may look down on housewives, but my mom is twice the woman you are. The best thing you did in your life was to give me up." She spins on her heel and marches away.

Glorious. Magnificent. Stupendous.

I've never seen someone I admire more than Elizabeth Graham. In fact, I'm pretty sure I love her.

13

BETH

My family puts together puzzles every single year at Christmas. Huge puzzles—the more pieces the better. We clear the kitchen table and the dining room table, and fit one on each. The puzzle takes shape on one side of the table, and the other side is the graveyard—the place for the unmatched pieces. As soon as school let out, we'd bust out the puzzles. During the break, we ate at the bar or on the sofas in the living room for a week or two while we worked puzzle after puzzle. Mom made Christmas cookies on every available counter space while we hovered over the tables working, our eyes scanning the options. I learned quickly, as the youngest, to start with pieces that had corners and then move to the edges. Once the outline was done, we'd move on to unique patterns or images. Only once the easy pieces were in place did I resort to looking for oddball shapes, like a piece with a flat end, or a wonky shaped tab, or triangular blanks.

Sometimes, not often but sometimes, we would complete an entire puzzle only to discover it was missing one piece.

I always felt vaguely betrayed. Had we lost it during the

time we had it out? Maybe I knocked it off with my elbow and Mom vacuumed it up. Maybe it fell and I kicked it under the bookcase. Or had someone put the puzzle away, knowing it was missing a piece and not caring?

No matter the cause, it robbed us of some of the joy in our accomplishment. We'd step back to admire a herd of horses running through a stream, but one eye would be missing. Or we'd want to show visitors that we'd recently finished a beautiful landscape, but they'd immediately say, "Um, there's a hole here." They'd point at the middle of the field of wildflowers where a single patch of kitchen table mocked us.

When we discovered a puzzle was missing a piece, we always threw it away. Shame on us for losing it, if indeed we had, but we would never inflict that on someone else by dropping off an incomplete puzzle to Goodwill, for instance.

Like those puzzles, I walked through my life feeling as if something was missing. I had a beautiful life, sure, with parents and siblings who loved me. I liked my job, I loved the piano, and I had great friends. I'm healthy and strong and smart enough, but I've never known who I *really* am. So when Henrietta showed up, sparkly and impressive and *famous,* well. I snatched that puzzle box out and tossed it down on the table in a blink.

I am such a moron.

A month ago, my stupidity might have been excusable as naiveté. A month ago, I didn't know Henrietta. I was bright-eyed and optimistic, and I came here hoping that knowing her would complete my perfect picture. That once I knew who I really was, everyone around me would finally admire me. I may not have gone to college like my siblings. I may not have perfect, shiny hair. I may not share their blue eyes. I may not have skin that bronzes in the sun, but it's okay, because I have something else.

I take after my bio mom, a breathtakingly beautiful, world-class singer and performer.

Except in the past month, she has made no effort to get to know me. She tossed me this job like a bone to a stray dog and never looked back. She didn't criticize the job I did, but only because I never made any mistakes. The guitarist, Alec, and the bassist, Frances, and the drummer, Roberto, were all regularly raked across the coals for missing notes or botching beats. I lived in fear of doing the same.

The dancers—I can't even imagine how they must feel. Too fat and they're fired. Too thin and they're ordered to eat. They must be attractive, but not *more* attractive than her. "I pay top dollar, and I expect top dollar performance."

But tonight, when I heard that people wanted to hear me play, I actually thought that she might be happy for me. She agreed that I could go out and perform in Beneficio's place. I worried that I wouldn't be able to play, but I did it, and they liked me alright. When they asked me to sing with her, I was elated. She seemed happy enough to welcome me up.

I scrambled for a way to take her somewhat silly song and make it something meaningful. When it occurred to me to sing about the things that she must be feeling inside while out partying, I thought it would make the song *real,* authentic for the first time. The crowd loved it, and they loved us, and then Henrietta finally admitted to the world that she was my mother.

I imagined we might have dinner, or hug, or maybe sit down and talk. Now that the staff knows that we're related, she can finally interact with me in a real way. How could I have been that stupidly optimistic? I know her now—I should have expected that even a beam from a flashlight next to the rays of her sunlight would cause a complete meltdown. But what really kills me is how disappointed I am to be let go. I have zero desire for smoke and mirrors and flashing lights. I don't want amps and electric guitars. I hate the dancers.

But I felt some of the audience connecting with my songs, with the pain behind them, with the hope, and it was one of the most thrilling moments of my life. I've spent the last five years defending my decision to cut and highlight hair. I will defend it until the day I die. There's beauty in serving others, and there's beauty in helping them see the gorgeous people they really are inside when they look in the mirror. I love that job.

Even so, the thought of flying home to cut hair and paint on foils instead of standing up on a stage to sing and play. . . it's deflating. Telling Henrietta off and defending Mom in the process was almost worth it, though.

"Beth?"

The hair on my arms rises at the sound of that voice. I've heard it nearly every night in my dreams. If I'm hearing it out loud now, well, I hope I'm not imagining things. I glance around the room, my eyes finally noticing that someone is standing in the side doorway. When my eyes meet his impossibly green ones, a thrill runs up my spine. "What are you doing here?"

He smiles. "I just saw the most amazing performance of my life. I'll never forget it."

"Shouldn't you be back at home?" He's got the vote on the House Law coming up fast. He didn't say when, but I know it's soon.

"I needed to see you." He walks toward me, his shoulders broader than I remembered, his hair darker. He stops less than a foot away from me, his hand reaching up to brush against the side of my face. "Not upset enough to cry?"

"Oh, I definitely shed a tear or two tonight," I say. "But I have waterproof mascara this time."

"Too bad," he says.

I snort. "Sure."

He steps closer. "I liked that Beth, you know. Small Beth. Unsure Beth."

"You did." I can't keep the skepticism out of my voice.

"I'll admit that initially, I was a little flummoxed."

"That's an impressive word for a third language," I say.

"I've been studying," he says. "See, there's this English-speaking girl I can't stop thinking about."

My heart quits beating. My eyelashes flutter. "We've been over this."

"What if I don't care?"

"I'm headed home. Did you hear?"

"I heard that your birth mom is an idiot. I'm sorry that happened, but it's all her issues, not yours."

"Either way."

"You were magnificent tonight. Everyone knew it." His head is leaning down, closer, closer.

My heart kicks back in, beating way too fast. "You did that," I whisper.

The side of his mouth curls up into a smile, and I know I'm right. He demanded that Beth Graham play tonight. It's because of him that I had that chance. When his face reaches mine, I turn upward and lean in. I'm still flying high from playing and singing my own songs for twenty thousand fans, but even that feeling doesn't compare, not to this. My hands grab his collar and yank.

I can't tell whether he groans or growls, but either way, I like it. His arms reach around me and slam into the wall on either side of me, pressing me more tightly against the hard lines of his chest. His mouth moves on mine carefully, slowly, but also with purpose. Like he came here to do just this.

"Why did you come?" I ask against his mouth.

"Surprised?"

174

I kiss him briefly. "In a good way."

"I couldn't stop thinking about you after you left."

"But isn't the vote—"

"It was today," he says. "And I lost."

My heart sinks. How could those family members not see that there's no one as prepared to serve the people of Liechtenstein as this man in front of me? "I am so sorry."

He shrugs. "I wasn't even that upset."

But now that he's not trying for a crown, he came straight here. . . to what? Am I some kind of consolation prize? Does he think we're hooking up? Am I his vat of ice cream after a breakup? That would be the only thing worse than my birth mother firing me and sending me back home —falling like an anvil to the bottom of the ocean for this guy who is a million and one miles out of my league, and then being cast aside once he's gotten over his loss.

I slide out from under his arms. "It was really nice of you to come this far." I try to keep the frost out of my voice, but it's there all the same.

"Beth?" someone asks from the main doorway.

My head feels stuffed with gummy bears when I turn to see who's calling me.

Mr. Ferrars, Henrietta's agent.

I close my eyes. "What now?" I'm angrier than I expect to be. "Does she want these clothes back, since they're a part of the costumes?"

Mr. Ferrars frowns.

"No, don't tell me—she's suing me for ruining her famous pop song."

"I heard the unfortunate news that my client, Miss Gauvón, has asked you to leave the tour."

"And?" I put my hands on my hips.

"I wanted to talk to you about an opportunity."

"I don't understand."

"Some fans put your songs online—on YouTube. They

have already generated quite a bit of interest, probably spurred on by Miss Gauvón's admission of your connection."

"What are you saying?"

"It's my understanding that the songs you sang are original." He raises his eyebrows.

"They are. I wrote them, both the melody and lyrics."

"I'd be very interested in signing you as a client. I can promise you a record deal at a bare minimum, but if these videos continue to generate hits, we could likely set up a tour very soon as well. We'd want to move fast to capitalize on the good press. Never lose momentum, that's my motto."

"The queen is dead, long live the queen?" I shake my head. "You're cold as death, aren't you?"

He folds his yellow-suit-coat-clad arms across his chest, and I struggle not to laugh. He looks like an angry, gay sunbeam.

"I am, at all times, extremely professional, and I'm offering you the opportunity to become very, very rich."

"Pass." I need to gather my things and get out of here. I cross the room, not looking back at Cole either, and push past Mr. Ferrars.

He catches my arm. "At least take my card. Think on it. If you change your mind, call or email me."

I stuff the card into my pocket. "Sure, yeah, okay." I smile. "Do me a favor and hold your breath until I call."

One less agent in the world would probably be a good thing.

I'm grabbing my bag when I notice that I'm not alone.

Cole followed me. "What happened before that guy interrupted?" His eyebrows are drawn together, his eyes sad.

I sigh. "I'm just exhausted."

"Come home with me tonight," he says.

"I'm not some kind of—"

He throws his hands up. "I came by jet, with Ben, Erik and Rogan. Friends on my football team."

"Football?" I ask. "I didn't think you guys liked football."

He smirks. "You call it soccer."

Right. "So you're saying instead of staying in the hotel Henrietta Gauvón is paying for with the rest of the band who *hasn't* been fired, go with you and sleep in the blue room. Alone."

He smiles. "That's exactly what I'm saying."

Oh. "I'll need to grab my stuff from the tour bus."

"I've got some drugs to smuggle," he says. "How about you let me grab it."

The joke I made when he picked me up in Frankfurt. He really is the good guy, the white knight. "I'm sorry." I step closer to him. "I'm so exhausted from today, from the last month, really. I don't know why I assumed—"

He wraps an arm around my shoulders, and I lean against him and breathe in the smell of Cole: sharp, clean, fresh. Like the mountain air of Liechtenstein. A place where the people loved me. A place where I felt safe.

"Let's go."

"Let me call a cab and text my friends to meet me at the airstrip."

Cole somehow gracefully manages all my luggage effortlessly. Everything is easier with him. "I'm glad you came tonight."

He hails a cab. "I am too. Your performance was—I have no words for it. It was everything."

Any concerns I had that Cole came here to try and hook up evaporate when his friends arrive at the airstrip. He wouldn't have brought Dumb, Dumber, and Dumbest to an attempted seduction. Although they're likely not as bad when they aren't quite so drunk. I spend half the flight trying to explain why I speak English. Raised in America seems to be a hard concept for them to grasp while utterly smashed, at least, after finding out Henrietta Gauvón was my birth mother.

By the time they all sit still long enough to understand, they fall asleep. One by one, like dominoes in a row.

"I never understood the American phrase 'sawing logs' until right now," I say.

"Erik has always snored like that," Cole says. "He blames a deviated septum, but I think he's never done anything about it because he likes the attention."

"Thanks for getting me out of there," I say.

"Happy to help," Cole says.

I stare out the window, but it's so dark that there's not much to see.

"Why did you turn that agent down?" Cole's voice is so quiet I barely hear it.

I turn toward him slowly. Sometimes, like right now, his beauty hits me like a club in a back alley. He's at least three levels hotter than I am. Why does he like me at all? He kissed me after I played the piano and all his employees were impressed. Then after he saw me play at Jostli's he gave me a ride to join the tour. . . And now tonight, he called my name aloud. The crowd would never have asked for me without someone prompting them first. He grew up in a castle and was raised to be a prince, proper title or not. Does he need me to be a rock star, to be worthy of him? Does he even like sweet, boring little Beth Graham? Or is he only interested in Elizabeth, daughter of Henrietta Gauvón?

"I don't want that kind of life," I say.

"You loved it up there, and the audience, they adored you."

"It's not who I am," I say.

"You don't need the dancers and the smoke and the

distractions. You don't need loud, busy music videos. Your songs have meaning and depth. You connected with people tonight. You can't tell me that you didn't feel that."

"I'm nothing like my birth mother," I say.

"You could have gone to Juilliard," Cole says. "I agree that you're much better served taking after your Mom and Dad than after her, but no one can deny that you inherited her musical talent."

"She craves the attention, the praise, and the crowds," I say. "I could have gone to Juilliard, but I chose not to."

"I thought you said that you didn't pass Algebra." Cole frowns.

My fingers knead the padded armrest of the plane's seat. "My dad was sick—he had arthritis and was having to step down from his business. We were interviewing managers when my brother Rob was hit with an IED in Libya. We thought he had died for two full days. I had my Algebra test during those two days, and I knew my family needed me. Juilliard was a dream—my family was real."

"You could have asked to retake the test."

"I failed that test on purpose. I could have asked to retake it," I agree. "But I didn't want to—I had made my decision. Rob needed months and months of rehab, and my mom and dad were struggling. I couldn't leave them, not then. And I don't regret it. I'd do the same thing again today."

"This isn't the same as that," Cole says. "And recording an album doesn't mean you're just like Henrietta. You're still you." He's right, about all of it, but it's also true that the person I really am and the person Cole wants me to be aren't the same. I'm sick to death of pretending.

It's time for me to go home.

14

COLE

No matter how many times I relive that moment, my kiss with Beth, it plays the same. She smiled up at me, delighted I was there, joyous in my arms, and then, when I told her I had lost the vote, she ducked out and ran. Beth liked me when I might become a prince, but now, not so much. Last night she said she'd be going home soon, as soon as she could book a flight. This morning I need to convince her that even if I'm not a prince, I still have something to offer. In the nearly two weeks she stayed here before, she never slept later than seven-thirty, even jet lagged.

She still hasn't left her room at eleven a.m.

I finally knock on her door. "Beth, you can't hide from me forever."

"Why not?" she asks.

I laugh. "Open the door."

When she finally does, I'm surprised to see that she's fully dressed, her bags packed, sitting on a fully made bed. "I have a car coming to get me in an hour."

"Cancel it," I say. "Please."

She rolls her eyes skyward. "I can't stay here."

"Why not?"

"That's the wrong question to ask."

I drag an over-embroidered chair closer to her and sit down. "I like you, Beth, a lot. I want to date you. I want to see you every day, and take you to dinner, and listen to you sing and play, and have you come cheer for me when I play football."

She lifts one eyebrow.

"I like you enough to call it soccer. Privately."

She snorts.

"I'm not a prince. I'm disappointed too, but it's not like I'm destitute. I have a great job in Antwerp that my buddy has been holding for me, and I kept my father's townhome there—it wasn't entailed. Plus, my dad has a few billion dollars, even without the entailed property and the shares that go with the crown. A lot of that will go to Holly and whatever children she has since it'll be split evenly among all heirs, but I bet I have nearly a billion dollars, between my trust and my share of Dad's estate."

She shakes her head.

"I'm not a prince, but I didn't realize that you would care so much."

Her eyes widen. "You think I care about money or titles?"

"Don't you?" I swallow. "You were happy to see me, until I told you that I lost."

She stands up, her hands clenched at her side. "I don't care about that at all, except that you're perfect for it and those people are too close-minded, selfish, and—" She splutters. "Too bigoted to see it."

"You didn't walk away from me because I'm not a prince."

She tilts her head sideways. "You're a prince in every action and word. That's the only kind of prince that matters."

I inhale sharply, my legs itching to cross the space still separating us, my arms aching to hold her again.

"But you gave up too easily." She bites her lip.

"There's nothing else to do," I say. "We can't hold another vote on the same thing—and even if we did, it wouldn't pass. It's not like it was even close. I do think that they might approve an amendment to the law that allows Holly to rule, but she's adamant that she wants nothing to do with the whole mess."

"She's a bull-headed idiot too," Beth says.

I'd argue with her, but Holly is pretty bull-headed. It's hard to argue with truth.

"This might be a stupid idea, and I'm not well educated or brilliant, but I was reading the Constitution online and I noticed—"

"Wait, you were reading the Constitution of *Liechtenstein?*"

She nods. "Yes, and I noticed something. I read up on how your dad got the amendment passed—you were only like seven years old at the time. Did you know that the dynasts were upset and the Landtag was against him?"

My mouth drops open.

"From what the records and articles say, he was brilliant. He went toe to toe with the entire parliament, and he told them that he would have a full veto power of everything, or he would quit and they could find a new prince."

I laugh. "That sounds exactly like Dad." Before his eyesight went. Before his heart problems. Before Noel.

"His son is every bit as phenomenal," Beth says. "And I think you should do the same thing."

I shake my head. "The people can't help with this. It's not up to them."

"Your people love you. The Prime Minister said that, and I've talked to some of them in my time at the Adler. You walk on water to them."

I try not to raise my voice. "It's adorable that you want to help, but our government is rather complex. Trust me when I tell you that there's nothing the people can do to reverse the House Law."

"You're not looking at it right," she says. "Your dad gave the people something, in exchange for them entrusting him with more power than any other monarch in Europe."

Huh?

"He gave them the right to vote him right out of power. They can, at any time, pull the escape hatch and terminate the principality, converting Liechtenstein to a democracy instead."

I knew that, but I still don't see how that would help us. "You want the people to fire my dad? Why? To spite Franz?"

"Do you know the biggest problem with showing up to a gunfight with a knife?"

Perhaps she's using an American phrase I don't know.

"You're outgunned, literally. You can't win a gunfight with a knife. You tried that, and the dynasts shot you down, brutally. It's not time to quit, though, it's time to rearm."

"With what?"

"Talk to your people, the ones who have watched you sell your family's art to set up educational programs for their kids, the ones who have watched you deliver Christmas presents."

My eyes widen.

"Paisley mentioned it," she says. "And I think that Distribution is about the most amazing thing I've ever heard."

"I don't get the credit for that. It's been around for a long time."

"But you kept it going," she says. "And you have signed treaty after treaty to open up new opportunities for your people. You learned to read and speak and write so that you could serve them, when others might have given up. You kept your country out of the EU to keep their taxes low. You take care of your parents."

"Not that I don't like the praise, but can you finish explaining what you mean about arming?"

She sighs like my primary school teacher used to, as though it's ridiculous I can't read what's right in front of me. "You ask the people to go to bat for you. They will vote the monarchy out if the dynasts won't change the law and allow you to step in for your dad."

That's not a gun to a gunfight—that's a gun held to the temple of every member of the Princely House. I'd literally be threatening them. They give me what I want, or I take their cake away forever. I have no idea whether it would work, but even if it would. . . I can't do it. "I don't deserve it."

Her shoulders fall. "Huh?"

"You don't know everything. If you did, you'd get that it was probably for the best that I'm not Prince. I'm sure in America they don't reward the person who has committed a crime."

"I feel like I'm on an Acme cartoon and someone just yanked the rug out of the way and knocked me down a hole."

I should have just told her I'd think about it. I shouldn't have said anything. I've been silent for a decade. Suddenly the truth claws at me, desperate to get out. "You remember my brother, Noel?"

She blinks. "I never met him, but yes, Paisley and I discussed him further. He passed away after a protracted fight with cancer."

"He stopped taking his medicine," Cole says. "And Mom and Dad blamed Holly—they thought she knew. They were sure Noel would have told her. They were two peas in the proverbial pod. He told her everything."

"Paisley mentioned that."

"Okay, so." I inhale and exhale. Can I really say it? "I knew."

"You knew what?"

"Mom took Noel his medicine morning and night. She stood and watched while he took it."

She frowns.

"He needed someone to help him with his plan. Some days he couldn't get out of bed. Mom would have seen if he hid the pills, no matter where he put them."

She closes her eyes.

"He told me he didn't want to do it again—he showed me the data. The rate of recurrence was very high. His odds of recovering again were never good, but the odds of relapse afterward were fairly close to 100%."

She reaches across the space between us and takes my hand.

Normally that would make me happy, but not right now. "You don't understand."

She picks up her phone and dials a number. "I need to cancel my car. Yes, that's alright. I'll pay the fee." She hangs up. "I think I get it. You let me know if I leave anything out."

I swallow.

"You watched as your little brother suffered. Chemo is basically poison. Doctors poison the patient and hope that the cancer dies before the person does."

I nod.

"And after enduring that, your entire family was elated. Noel might never have children thanks to the radiation and chemo, and he might be weaker and suffer other issues, but he was alive, he was *cured.*" She pauses and meets my eye.

"Yes."

"Then when he was sick again, you had just finished college. You came home, ready to start your life, with a job lined up, I imagine. Your family was too preoccupied to welcome you back because. . . Noel was sick again. You felt alone, left out, unwanted. Noel had always been closer to Paisley, and your parents obviously cared more about their sick child than you. You were easy, and you required no special care and attention."

"I wasn't upset about that."

She shrugs. "I would have been."

"Maybe a little," I say, "about the Noel and Holly thing."

She smiles. "Cole, when your brother Noel begged for your help, you heard him because you loved him. You didn't like watching him suffer. And you also felt special, because he asked you, not Paisley."

"Maybe a little bit," I admit.

"You did it because it was the right thing to do," she says softly. "Paisley told me that she sees that now, that his quality of life was unbearably bad, that he made his decision and she should have understood and forgiven him for it."

"They can't ever know," I say. "They'll hate me if they know." To my utter horror, I begin to cry like a distressed toddler, in front of Beth.

She kneels down and shuffles across the carpet toward me. This time, when she takes my hand, I let her. I pull her up and into my arms, but not like I wanted to earlier. This time she's salve on a stinging scrape, she's sunlight after a nightmare, she's warm wind in my face after a long winter.

"You hurt more because you kept it from them," she whispers. "Your family loves you, and they'll understand. You did what you did because you loved Noel. You were willing to be the bad guy to spare them the pain."

"What if I did it because I was jealous? He had everything I didn't."

She shakes her head. "No. I know you well enough to know that's not true. What you did was selfless, and I'm almost positive your parents will see that too. Paisley will, for sure."

Even the thought of telling them causes my hands to tremble. "I can't." I shake my head. "My dad would regret adopting me."

Beth sighs and stands up. "You know your own family better than I ever could, but I fear you're not giving them enough credit."

"You can see, though, why I can't force myself into the position Noel would have taken, right? I can't help him die and then, like a mob boss, force his family to give me his job."

Beth shrugs. "I'm American. I'll never understand, probably. We always take what we need, like mob bosses." She glances at her phone, and I wonder whether she's about to order the car again.

"Will you consider sticking around a while?" I ask. "Let me take you on a few dates. Talk to that agent, or if not him, another one." I pull out my phone and open the browser. "This is one of the videos. It has three hundred thousand views, and it's only been twelve hours."

"Is that a lot?" She lifts one eyebrow.

"It was in the newspaper today," I say. "You should check out the article. Downstairs. Maybe while eating some food."

She doesn't say no, and I know I've got her.

"Eggs," I say. "Toast."

"Waffles?" she asks. "Do you guys eat those here?"

"Absolutely, we do," I say. "Or, you know, we could always go over to Hotel Adler."

She giggles. "Maybe not right now."

"I'm kidding. Jostli would have a heart attack."

"Look, I'm not saying—"

Her phone rings. When she sees the number, she answers it immediately. "Rob?"

She's silent, listening intently.

"No, no. That's not—"

Silence again.

"I'm coming home."

A brief pause.

"I don't care about that. Believe me, it will be a relief. No, you can't change my mind."

Another pause.

"No, no one needs to pick me up. I have money. I'll get a cab. You're at Emory?"

She hangs up.

"What's wrong?" I ask.

"Brekka, my brother Rob's wife, isn't quite twenty-four weeks along." She shakes her head. "She hadn't felt the baby move in a while, so they went in to check things out, and her amniotic fluid is low. Way too low."

"Oh no," I say.

"I wonder if I can still get that car," she says.

"Take our jet. Mom and Dad won't care, I promise."

She gulps. "Are you sure?"

"Absolutely. Family is everything. I'm sure they need you there with them."

She smiles up at me. "Thank you."

I drive her to the airstrip where our jet is waiting. "I'll be praying for you and Brekka and Rob," I say. "I know it's not much, but if there's anything else I can do, please let me know."

"I'll miss you," she says. "But we both knew I had to go home eventually."

And I'm terribly afraid she's really telling me goodbye. Forever.

❧ 15 ❧

BETH

Songs have run through my head for as long as I can remember. Sometimes they were songs I heard somewhere, but often, they were songs that simply appeared. Notes, chords, words, strumming, buzzing, and chiming around in my brain. The busier I am, the more things I think about, the softer the background music becomes. When I'm studying for something, for instance, it drops to the barest hum. When I'm bored, or when I'm anxious, the music crashes over me, sounds, feelings, lyrics, all mixing together. Sometimes the experience calms me, sometimes it agitates me.

When Jostli expressed surprise that I was writing so many new songs, I nearly laughed. I don't write the songs: they tumble out of me, like carbon dioxide expelled from the body with every breath. Except when a good one emerges, it's the purest form of delight. As I sit here, alone and anxious in Cole's clean, sleek, and sophisticated jet, that familiar music should be bombarding me. It should distract me from my concern, my fear, my nervousness.

But no music runs through my head.

Ever since Rob said, "Beth, I'm scared for the baby," the music in my head evaporated.

My big brother is never afraid—not when he lost his best friend, or for a time, the use of his legs. Not when my dad's arthritis caused him to neglect the dealerships. No, Rob, who knew nothing of car sales, stepped in and turned those flailing dealerships around. Rob is as invincible as anyone I've ever met.

And he's afraid.

No one and nothing is ever really safe. Those words keep running through my head—no music, just a depressing realization that nothing lasts forever. Nothing is guaranteed. Knowing that, I still flew away from my family, chasing after a stupid dream of a mother who would 'get' me. To borrow Paisley's analogy, I threw a whole fistful of coins into the garbage, and I'll never get them back. Rob's afraid, and I'm not there. The music inside my head may have abandoned me forever as punishment.

But by golly, I won't leave their side now.

When the jet lands, my Uber is already waiting. Bless Cole for taking care of that for me. I like him a lot, far, far more than I ever should have. He said he liked me too, but I don't fit into his world. My home is here, in Atlanta, and it's so much easier to remember that when he's not smiling at me, not touching me, not talking to me in his low, low voice.

I breathe in the balmy, humid air. My blouse sticks to my skin after mere moments outside. Ah, July in Georgia. I've missed most of peach season. I wonder what else I've missed. When I reach the hospital, Brekka's asleep in a hospital bed, Rob by her side. His eyes are bloodshot, and his hair's sticking up in strange places. When he sees me, he leaps to his feet and hugs me for a little too long.

"You," I whisper. "Go. Shower, take a nap, recover. I won't leave her side, I swear it."

"You just flew international," he says. "You're jet lagged. You have no idea what you're saying."

"I smell a lot better than you." I lift one eyebrow. "Do you think you're exuding the sense of calm that you need to keep your baby safe and your wife happy?"

He gulps.

I glance at my watch. One-thirty a.m. "If you hurry, you could get in a quick nap and still get back before she wakes up."

Rob looks past me at his wife. Her face is pale, her frame so small, so delicate. I've never seen her asleep before. When she's awake and talking and analyzing everything you say, she's like five hundred pounds of dynamite in a ten-pound sack. No one notices the sack.

But now that she's asleep, my heart contracts. She looks so fragile. I used to long to be petite and tiny, like her. She's the kind of girl a guy wants to protect. At nearly five foot ten, no one ever thinks I need protection, but in many ways, that's a gift. I can carry my own luggage, and reach the dishes on the top shelf of the kitchen cabinets without a stool. I can run from here to my house. Okay, maybe not, since I never run anywhere. But theoretically, my body can do whatever I need. It's a blessing that I've selfishly taken for granted until this very moment.

"I'll keep her safe."

Rob blinks, and then he nods at me. He grabs a bag and ducks out the door.

The next few weeks pass in a blur. Mom and Dad come and go, but they have commitments, friends, and a schedule. Christine has work, and Jennifer has a job and kids and a husband. I put my life on hold before I left, and I haven't hit the play button. I have nothing but time, so we settle into a routine. I take nights, Rob takes days. Brekka's amniotic fluid never rises, but neither does it fall. The baby isn't growing fast, but she is growing. The doctors do ultrasounds every day, give her corticosteroids to help develop the baby's lungs just in case, and each day, they agree to wait one more day.

The day after thirty-one weeks, she goes into labor, and they give her magnesium sulfate.

"It's been shown in some studies to lower the risk of cerebral palsy." Dr. Stone rarely looks up from her clipboard, and she's not very personable, but I hear that's common for people who are on the spectrum. She's the best neo-natal doctor in Atlanta, so we don't care.

"Does that mean the baby is coming?" I ask.

She shrugs. "We'll know more in a few hours. I don't want to do any more pelvic exams than necessary."

"Me either," Brekka says, a half smile on her face.

She has stayed remarkably calm in all this.

Dr. Stone leaves, and Rob stands up. "I'm going to get dinner. Burgers? Anyone?"

I shrug. "Sure, but get extra fries."

"How are you not three hundred and fifty pounds?" Rob asks.

"Maybe I am," I say. "As long as I'm healthy, it's none of your business what I weigh."

He rolls his eyes and leaves.

"You don't look at your phone anymore," Brekka says.

I freeze.

"When you first came back, you looked at your phone a hundred times a day. Now, you never do. I haven't even seen it in days."

I turn around to face her.

"Why?" She places both hands on her belly. "I'm in labor, and I'm scared for the baby. You should distract me with the truth. What happened in Europe?"

I collapse into the hard, plasticky gray chair in the corner. We've talked about a lot of things. We've watched television shows. I've read to her and to the baby. I entertained her by trying to learn to knit, and then she and I ordered some things off Etsy together. But I never offered any information about the past few weeks, and she has never asked. Until now.

"It started out rough," I say.

"How so?"

I tell her about the tour delay and how Cole came and got me.

"You couldn't have looked that bad," she says.

I stare at her. "Do you know that character Hagrid, off Harry Potter?"

"Yes."

"He wouldn't have found me attractive."

She laughs, and then she grabs her belly.

"Oh no, is everything alright?"

She grimaces. "Try not to be so funny. Laughing hurts."

"Laughing leads to contractions. I hear you." I reach out and hold her hand.

She squeezes my fingers with her own, tiny hand, and then I tell her everything. How much fun I had in Liechtenstein, how much I like Cole. How we kissed. Rob jogs into the room then, with a bag in his hands.

Brekka shakes her head. "We need another half hour."

Rob's mouth drops open. "What?"

"Leave and come back in half an hour." Brekka blows him a kiss.

There's no way that my brother will—but then he does it. He pivots on his heel and walks out.

"You have him *really* well trained," I say. "That's amazing."

"That's a topic for another girl chat," she says. "But for now, continue."

I do. Right up until the time that he asks me to stay, and I hop on his private jet and fly here.

"And what does he say now?" she asks. "Has he asked you to come back?"

I shake my head.

"What does he say, then?"

I shrug. "Nothing. I haven't gotten a single text or a single call. I think he wanted me when he saw me as Henrietta Gauvón's daughter, a performer, a singer, famous, awe-inducing. I think he was attracted to that person—Elizabeth, I call her—but that's not me. I'm plain old Beth Graham. I like magnolias and sweet tea and porch swings."

Brekka whips out her phone and starts tapping away.

A jolt of adrenaline shoots through me. She has Paisley's number, and Paisley has Cole's. She could be texting him right now. "What are you doing?"

She flips her phone around. "This is you, no?"

I squint at the video. It's one of the songs I performed at Henrietta's concert. "Yes."

"Seven point three *million* views. Let me repeat that. Seven point three million views. Do you have any idea how many that is? And these other songs have millions, too. You're an idiot."

"You haven't contracted in a while," I say.

"Don't try to change the subject," Brekka says. Then she turns and looks at the monitor. "Hey, I haven't. In more than twenty minutes, actually."

When Rob comes back, we eat cold hamburgers, mushy french fries, and then I go and pick up some bundt cake.

"This is a celebration for you, little baby." I lift my forkful of cake in the air. "Since you stayed inside, you get chocolate cake, delivered by your mom, who loves you more than anything. Now just stay put a while longer."

After Rob finally kisses Brekka goodnight and leaves, she pivots on me like a used car salesman eyeing a new lead. "You will text him."

"It's the middle of the night there," I protest. "It would wake him up."

"Text him right now. If you don't, you'll chicken out."

I shake my head. "I stopped checking my phone because I realized that my message got through to him. I like Cole a lot, more than I've ever liked anyone, but we are like two puzzle pieces that just don't fit. My life is here, and his life is there, and it would never have worked, no matter how much I wanted things to be different."

She purses her lips. "Well, then, message that agent. You're still mooning over something and if it's not the guy, it's the songs."

My heart thaws, just a little. The singing and the guy are inextricably entwined to me. But maybe if I recorded an album there, just maybe my longing about Cole would diminish. Maybe I could stop thinking about him. Maybe I wouldn't have to hide my phone in my purse to keep from checking it a hundred times a day. "This is not a good time."

Brekka takes my hand in hers. "The second my baby is born, you will call that agent. Promise me."

"I promise."

Less than two weeks later, she goes into labor again, only this time, there's no bundt cake celebration.

"The labor has been steady for hours now," Dr. Stone says. "And I know that you wanted to try a natural delivery, but the baby is showing signs of distress. I'm going to recommend a delivery via cesarean section."

Brekka and Rob don't argue.

The nurse, Susan, puts a hand on Brekka's arm, carefully avoiding the IV. "You made it past thirty-three weeks," she says brightly. "You did good, really good. And she's a girl. They do better coming early."

"Is that true?" Brekka asks Dr. Stone.

"They typically spend less time in the NICU," Dr. Stone says, "so, yes."

A little color rises in Brekka's cheeks, and some of the tension in my shoulders eases. I follow them all the way to the door into the OR, but they stop me there. "Spouses only."

"You've seen her here, day in and day out for nearly ten weeks. Surely you can make an exception," Brekka snaps.

Dr. Stone looks down at her feet. "We're not supposed to—"

"It's fine," Susan says. "I won't document it."

I follow them inside, a little surprised that I'm allowed, and I watch in equal parts wonder and horror as they slice Brekka open and remove a tiny baby. She's purplish, covered with smears of white, and so, so small.

"She's not crying," I whisper to Rob.

When the nurses whisk the baby out of the room, Brekka shouts, "Go with her, Rob! Go!"

He shoots out of the room like a couponer on Black Friday, and I walk across the room to the operating table to hold Brekka's hand. Dr. Stone keeps working on her, sewing her up methodically, as if the baby wasn't just rushed from the room.

"Is she going to be alright?" I ask.

Dr. Stone says, "My expertise ends when the baby comes out of your belly, but she looked as healthy and strong as any thirty-three week old baby I've seen."

Rob returns half an hour later. "She's doing just fine. They put her on oxygen, but they don't think she'll need it long. She's just over four pounds, which is a very respectable weight for her age. They're going to try feeding her soon."

"Then get back in there," Brekka says. "Now." When he stares at her, gape mouthed, she glares. "Go—I'm fine."

I stay with Brekka until she recovers enough to sit up.

Then I wheel her over to see her baby, through the glass for now. She's wearing a white diaper and a tiny pink cap, and nothing else. Tubes connect to her tiny hand, and there's a tiny monitor on her foot. Itsy bitsy diodes attach to several places on her torso, but her skin is pink and her mouth and eyes are just perfect.

Brekka inhales sharply, tears rolling freely down her cheeks. "She's alright. Oh, Beth, she's perfect."

"She really is," I say.

Brekka places one hand against the glass, leaning as close as she can. "Rob and I have talked about it, and we want to name her Ruth."

"Are you sure?" My full name is Elizabeth Ruth Graham. Ruth, for the woman in the Bible who left her family and joined her mother-in-law. 'For your people will be my people.' My parents thought it fitting, since I was adopted, but I always felt like it was a giant bulls-eye, highlighting the fact that I wasn't originally a part of the family.

Brekka takes my hand with her free one. "Rob said that the family was missing something, a vital piece, something huge, until you came along. And then he just knew that it was perfect. As much as I love your brother, I've been afraid since long before I knew him that I would never hold a baby in my arms. I want that baby to be named after you, the missing piece in Rob's family—and the most beautiful addition to ours."

Five days later, when the nurse places Ruth into Brekka's arms and says she's ready to go home, I'm there, crying.

"You have to visit us all the time, because Baby Ruth already knows your voice." Brekka pins me with her patented stare. "But you didn't fulfill your promise to me, and now it's time."

"What?" I ask.

"You have someone to call."

For a split second, I think she means Cole and my heart

sprouts wings and takes flight. Then I remember she means the agent. "I don't want smoke and mirrors and enormous audiences of a million people."

"Tell him that," Brekka says. "You give him your terms and see if he'll agree. If not, at least you tried."

I hold Baby Ruth one last time, and then I walk them out to their car. "I'll call him, but you do this for me. If you two need help, you call me."

Brekka laughs. "My mom is flying into town to stay with us today. I can already tell you, I will need help." She drops her voice. "Help hiding a body." Her eyes widen with purpose.

"Far be it from me to tell you what to do, but I'd recommend against homicide this close in time to such a major surgery. It might make dragging someone difficult. And if you go to jail. . ."

"I suppose that for now, I'll wait," Brekka says.

I'm pretty sure Rob won't be able to fit everything into the trunk of Brekka's car. A metric ton of flowers, stuffed animals, baby clothing, and other gifts were delivered in the past week or so, and they were there so long that they accumulated quite a lot of stuff. But all those years playing Tetris as a kid paid off, and Rob actually squeezes the last box into the top corner and closes the back hatch.

Once Brekka and Ruth are loaded in the car, she rolls down the window. "Beth."

I walk closer.

"Thank you," she says softly. "For everything. You helped turn a dark time into one of my fondest memories. Other than Trig and Geo, I don't have any family that I really, truly love and enjoy. Now, I feel like I have a sister."

I hug her then. "Call me whenever you want."

She blows me a kiss.

And for the first time in a long time, I drive home. Brekka and Rob's house was close to the hospital, so I've been sleeping and showering there. Mom and Dad complained half-heartedly, but they understood. When I walk in the door, for the first time in months, it's the exact same as when I left.

But it's also different.

It hurts a little to admit this to myself, but it doesn't feel quite like home anymore. Mom hugs me, and Dad does too. They ask about Ruth and Brekka and Rob, and then they let me head for my room. Five minutes later, I whip out my phone.

No new messages.

I call Mr. Ferrars. He answers on the third ring. "Bonsoir," he says.

"This is Beth Graham," I say.

"Who?"

"Henrietta Gauvón's daughter."

"Oh!" I hear some kind of clanging and then he says, "I'm so happy you have called. Have you decided you want to make a record?"

"I have some terms," I say.

"What are they?"

I tell him. I want to do a record full of only my songs, my lyrics, my music. I don't want a lot of crazy production, extra sounds, and modulation. And if we do a tour to promote it, no huge venues, nothing over three thousand. No fancy lights, no back up band members, no gimmicks or dancers or smoke. Just me, my piano, and the audience.

"You have no idea how exhausting that will be," he says. "The dancers help you. They keep you from being so tired. They carry a lot of the show."

"I want to connect with the fans. I want to say something to them, and a conversation requires back and forth communication."

"It's different," he says. "But so is your music, so I think I can make it work."

"And I don't want anyone to know I'm Henrietta's daughter."

He tuts. "That I cannot do. Once the cat has escaped the Prada purse, it cannot be stuffed back inside."

Hm. "Well, fine. I guess I'm okay with that."

"I can't tell you how delighted I am that you will be coming on board," he says.

Surprisingly, I'm excited too.

❧ 16 ❧

COLE

When Noel died and Holly left shortly thereafter, I didn't have a smartphone. I hadn't wanted to be able to check my email everywhere. I prided myself on maintaining a healthy balance between tech and life. It took forever on my phone to compose a text to Holly, scrolling through the letters assigned to each number, painstakingly tapping out each letter of each thought. Even so, I managed to send her over four hundred text messages in the first month that she was gone.

I know, because we were charged for every one of them. International fees.

Mom and Dad certainly never noticed, and they wouldn't have faulted me for it if they had, but Mr. Heinrich handled all the day-to-day affairs of the household, and he certainly noticed. He waved the bill in my face.

"Mum won't mind," I said.

He crossed his arms and stared me down. "All these texts were outgoing. I looked it up on the itemized bill."

I jutted out my lip. "So."

"So it means she doesn't want to hear from you, and all

these messages are salt in a wound. Give her time and space."

That chastisement was the slap in the face that I needed. I thought, at the time, that Holly would come back to us on her own. I thought that once the wound had sealed over, she'd text me, she'd call me, or she'd fly home.

Of course, she never did.

I've learned, and I've grown from my youthful exuberance. This time, when my hand hovers over the phone, itching to text Beth, I set it down and walk away. I know Beth arrived safely, because our pilot told me so, but she didn't text or call to tell me herself. I'm sure she has a lot on her mind, so it's not that I'm offended by her lack of gratitude.

Before she left, I was very clear with her—I want to date her, I want to spend time with her, I want to be with her.

Three days later, still no word. Three days without a thirty second window to text me? Three days without the opportunity to say, "Thanks for lending me your jet. I miss you." I close my eyes and think this through. One text from me will turn into a hundred. I know myself. Every single day will be a struggle not to call her. I'll rationalize that one little message would be fine, casual, friendly, even. After all, if nothing else, Beth and I are friends. Right?

Wrong.

I can still see her in my mind, playing piano here, in my home. The music floating through the palace, Beth in her truest form, Beth blissful, unaware anyone else is even there, so in love with creating music. I want to worship her, I want to listen to her forever, I want to wrap her up in my arms and kiss her until she can't speak or stand, but I don't want to sit down and have a beer with her. I don't want to give her a ride from the airport to her boyfriend's house. I don't want to be her *friend*. It would kill me slowly. Chatting occasionally, hearing about her newest boyfriend, getting a wedding announcement with an image of her smiling face and some other bloke's arm around her.

I throw on my running clothes so I can go for a jog. Once I'm dressed, I check my phone again and that's when I remember my other option. I could delete her number so that it's not an everyday struggle. If I were an alcoholic, I'd clear the house of all liquor to remove the constant temptation. That's what I need to do here. I pick up my phone, my fingers shaking, and open my contacts, scrolling to her name.

Beth Graham.

I tap and tap and my finger hovers over the delete button. I should do it. I need to do it. I will do it. I do. It's gone.

Except our text chain is still on my messages. Now the number is there, splashed out in its international glory. With the swipe of my finger, that's gone too. I could always text Holly and ask for her to send it to me, but that would be too humiliating, even for me. I'd have to admit that I deleted it when I couldn't keep myself from messaging her, like an addict, like a lunatic.

Holly would know that I love Beth and that I'm pining for her. She would never let that go. Never.

So that seals it. I've removed the temptation and I won't be making the same mistake again. Beth has my number, and if she ever misses me, even the slightest amount, she can message me. Then I'd have her information and wouldn't need to feel bad about responding.

When she still hasn't called or texted two days later, I reluctantly call my friend Russ and take the job. I toss a suitcase in the back of my Range Rover and head for Antwerp. It's strange to live in a townhome alone. No family, no servants, no friends. In some ways, it's nice. I can walk around in my underwear, drink soda straight from a container, and watch TV in the living room all night. No one to complain, except for the neighbor who bangs on the wall the first, and apparently only, time I try it.

But I'm also lonely, as lonely as I've ever been, as lonely as I was after Noel died.

I spend more time thinking about my brother than ever before, and Beth's words haunt me. Did I do the right thing? Was I motivated by the right reasons? I think about the weeks and weeks that I spent with Noel, hiding his pills and disposing of them, watching as he grew weaker and weaker, and then the last day. His final words to me still haunt me, even now.

"Thank you, Cole." The bags under his eyes were pronounced. Worse than the day before? I couldn't tell.

"I think I did the wrong thing." I confessed to him self-ishly, like a greedy publican, hoping he'd put in a good word for me at the pearly gates. "I shouldn't have kept your secret. I should've told you what everyone else would have —that you need to fight. That you're just depressed and things will get better."

"I had cataract surgery at the age of twenty-one. Cataracts are what happens to eyes that have endured extreme age and exhaustion." Noel coughed. He closed his eyes, breathed in and out a few times, and then opened them again, as if moving his lids required a Herculean effort. "You did what no one else would. You understood me, and what I needed, and you—" That time, the cough wracked his entire body. He couldn't seem to stop.

I ran for the nurse.

He died thirty minutes later.

I selfishly stole his last words, his last minutes, whinging like a little baby, asking him to forgive me. He didn't get to tell Holly goodbye, he didn't get to hug our mother, and he didn't get a proper send-off. No, Beth may be terribly insightful most of the time, but in this instance, she's wrong. Dad would never forgive me, not for this. Not for being the reason he lost his real son, his perfect son, and everyone's favorite person—including mine.

My focus narrows to work. I show up before everyone else, and I leave after everyone is gone. When I'm home, I work out. I lift weights and run, then lift some more. Russ tells me he's never had an employee catch so many tiny details. He's never had an employee add so much value. He asks me if I'm gunning for his job.

I laugh.

I'm not gunning for anything. I'm just. . . lost. Adrift. I have a beautiful townhome, a paper that says I have a family, and yet I feel homeless. Without a place and without a purpose.

Weeks pass, each day the same as the last. Until one Sunday, the only day I'm stuck at home all day because the office is closed, there's a knock at my door. No one knows my address. Who could it be? My heart races. Could it be Beth? Could she have found my work profile or searched property records?

I answer the door, and Mom and Dad beam at me. "You never invited us out, so we thought we'd surprise you!" Mom holds up a basket—filled with all my favorite baked goods from Chef. I do not cry. Tears do not well up in my eyes, but only because I focus all my energy on not sobbing. If I hug them a little too tightly, well, they don't complain.

"Let's go to lunch," Mom says. "What's your favorite place?"

I'm embarrassed to admit that I haven't been anywhere. "The takeout from Little China is pretty good."

Mom frowns, but she doesn't comment.

After a quick search on my phone, I have a few suggestions. "French food," Mom says. "I bet it's good here."

It's not bad. I spend the entire meal discussing my work.

"But tell me about your friends," Mom says. "Have you met anyone new?" Her eyebrows wiggle and I realize she's asking about girls.

"Not really," I say. No one who can even come close to comparing to Beth, anyway. No one whose name I've bothered to remember. No one I have thought about more than once.

"What shall we do now?" Dad asks.

I rummage around in my brain for offhand comments, or suggestions co-workers have made. Most of the people I met when I first moved here had some kind of suggestion. Think, brain, think. "Uh, I've heard the Museum aan de Stroom is nice."

Dad frowns. "If that's what you want to do."

With his eyesight, anything indoors is hard. He can't see much unless it's very, very bright.

"I've heard they have a lovely zoo," Mom says. "And that the animals are very active, in beautiful enclosures."

"I love the zoo," I lie.

Mom smiles and Dad nods, and we head for the zoo. The entrance is vibrant, bright, energetic. Holly would love it. I wonder what Beth would say. We never spoke about animals. Would she hate that they're caged? Or maybe she would look on with glee as the seals bark and the baby elephants flap their enormous ears.

No one contests Mom's position as our unofficial tour director. We follow her around without contest, agreeing when she says something is cute, and heartily agreeing when she looks skeptical about whether our enthusiasm is genuine. Mom takes off to grab us some food, and Dad points at a bench. I follow over dutifully.

"What's going on with you, Cole? I promised your

mother that I wouldn't just spit it out, but I can't help it. It's who I am, and you know that."

I slump.

"Your mother thinks it's that your uncle is taking over. She says you took the loss hard, that you don't think you have a place with us. But I think you loved that girl, Beth."

Ah, Dad. He can't see, but he still understands. Too much, really.

"So which of us is right?"

"Those are my only two options?" I ask.

"Either that, or you're gay and you're afraid to tell us."

I laugh. "It's not that."

"Then it's Beth."

As he says the words, I realize that while I do love her, long for her, miss her with every breath, that's not it. That's not why I left. And I didn't leave because I don't want to see Franz at the capital, either. "Dad." I swallow hard. Beth's words bounce around in my head. I can't tell them, I know that. But the secret, now that I've spoken it aloud, is festering, in my mind and in my heart.

He puts a hand on my knee. "I love you, even if you have a boyfriend. You know that."

Even if. Well, he means well. I look heavenward. "Dad, Noel died because of me."

My dad flinches, his hand dropping from my knee. "Explain yourself."

"You blamed Holly all this time, and I let you. You thought she should have known, that Noel would have told her, but he didn't. Because he told me his plan, not her. He knew Mom would find his pills without someone to help him dispose of them every day. He gave them to me, and I flushed them for him."

My whole body is shaky, like I've drunk a gallon of espresso. Even the crisp fall air in Antwerp doesn't keep me from breaking out in a cold sweat. Will he understand, like

Beth swore he would? Will he forgive me? Or have I just shredded things beyond repair?

Dad doesn't meet my eye or say a word. He stands up and walks away. I'm not sure how he finds my mother, but she doesn't come back with food or looking for him. I sit at the bench for more than an hour, hoping that they're just talking, that they'll come back and hug me and tell me that they understand. I want them to forgive me, because I haven't ever been able to forgive myself.

My phone buzzes. I swivel the screen around slowly. YOUR FATHER'S NOT FEELING WELL. I'M TAKING HIM HOME.

That's it. My verbose mother never texts. She always calls.

They both know and sweet, kind, big-hearted Beth was wrong. They won't forgive me for it. I am the monster I always thought I was. I killed Noel, and I should have taken that secret to my grave. I walk around the zoo like an automaton. I don't call a cab to take me home. I walk the eleven miles that separate the zoo and my townhome one shuffling step at a time. I don't bother showering, either. I just flop into bed and close my eyes.

I'm nearly asleep when there's another knock at my door.

Probably the grim reaper, come to finish me off. I ignore it. Louder knocking ensues. I ignore it. But when the knocking continues, my neighbor starts banging on the wall.

"Fine!" I drag myself out of bed and stumble to the door.

Mom and Dad are standing there, no basket in their hands this time, but they have matching looks of concern on their faces.

"We handled this all wrong," Mom says. "I'm so sorry."

I can't move. I can't speak.

"It wasn't your fault," Dad says. "It just took me by surprise is all."

I step backward.

Mom and Dad take that as an invitation to come inside. Mom closes the door behind her. "Your neighbor is a rude sort, isn't he? We should buy that townhome from him and then we'd have a place to stay when we visit."

"I have a guest room." I blink. Is she really talking about buying a townhome in *Antwerp*? Even I don't want to be here.

"Can we sit?" Mom asks.

I nod, but I don't move.

Mom and Dad settle on the couch. Finally, I follow them over and sit on the edge of a chair.

"Why didn't you tell us before?" Mom asks. "That you helped Noel?"

"Helped?" My brain isn't processing words right. She must have meant to say killed.

"You said you killed him," Dad says. "I'm not making excuses for walking away, but I'm old, son. I—" He shakes his head. "Sometimes I take some time to figure out what I want on my toast these days. I had to sort through a lot of things with your mom to figure out exactly what must have happened."

"What?"

Mom leans toward me, her eyes kind. "Noel asked you for your help, didn't he?" Her entire face crumples. "Because." Her lip trembles. "Because we didn't listen to what he needed or what he was telling us about how miserable he really was." Mom's sobbing now, her face red, her eyes puffy. "I was torturing him because I couldn't accept that he was dying."

Dad wraps an arm around her shoulders. "We all were, but Noel knew that you loved him enough to *listen*."

It happens so fast, I'm not sure whether I move toward

them, or they move toward me, but suddenly we're a jumble of arms and legs and hugging and tears and murmurs and "I love yous," and before I realize what I've said, I offer to move back home.

"Oh, this is the best day ever," Mom says. "Just the best. Noel is up in heaven smiling down on us, I just know it."

Before Mom and Dad leave the next morning, over coffee, I decide to take Beth's other piece of advice. "Hey, Dad, strange thought."

He sips his coffee, but his eyebrows rise so I know he's listening.

"What if, and I know it's crazy, but what if we talked to the people. Do you think they'd prefer me to Uncle Franz? You haven't made him your regent yet, right?"

Dad shakes his head. "I haven't had the heart to do it. Your mother has been filling in during your absence."

I gulp and explain Beth's plan, sure that he'll hate it. After I finish, I watch his face like a pigeon watches a toddler eating a muffin.

"I'm ashamed," Dad says.

Ashamed? Ashamed of what?

"You say that sweet little friend of Holly's came up with this?"

"She did."

"It's *our* constitution, son, and those are our laws. A constitution I drafted, and yet, I'm embarrassed to admit that I never thought of that."

Mom claps her hands. "So we're back to fighting, then?"

Dad grins. "Back to fighting, yes." He stands up. "Only this time, we're going to knock Franz back on his rear."

BETH

"I have the best news!"

I drop the croissant I've been picking at while I waited for my agent to arrive for our breakfast meeting. Paris is making me fat—even the hotel restaurants have little cafes with food that is out of this world. The croissants, the crepes, the pastries. And I can't even think about the chocolate croissants. "I know, my album is climbing the charts."

He rolls his eyes and sits down, the purple suit he's wearing today not doing his complexion any favors. Even yellow was better than this. "No, that's a given. Please."

"Okay, then what?" I shove my plate away, taking out my irritation at him on an inanimate object. If he had been on time, I wouldn't be on my third croissant.

"Miguel Mandragoran *died.*"

My mouth drops. "I thought you said you had good news. That's awful."

He sighs, as though talking to me is like talking to a recalcitrant toddler. "Yes, of course that's terrible news." He leans closer, not even trying to fake sadness. "But he was going on tour next week."

"I don't understand."

"You need to grab the bull by the horns, dear, whenever life throws one your way."

"I hope no one is throwing bulls anywhere," I say.

He tosses his hands in the air. "He's with the same record label as you. They have to notify fans, and they would far prefer to offer them the option to transfer their ticket price to another performer. One of their performers, perhaps a new one, one about whom there is a lot of buzz would be the best of all. Someone whose shiny new record that we rushed through to capitalize on the current excitement is climbing the charts steadily." He lifts his eyebrows and beams.

"Miguel's music was beautiful," I say. "He played the most amazing ballads. Sweet, sad, thoughtful."

"Yes, yes, you've said, it's very sad. But if you spend all your time mourning singers who overdose, you'll never get anywhere."

I've always suspected Mr. Ferrars was the devil, but now I know. "Supposing the record label offers me the option."

His nostrils flare. "They are offering you this option. Why do you think I'm here? I don't set up meetings to giggle with my girlfriends, Elizabeth. I am here to offer you the spot, but you need to commit now, this morning. Otherwise, they pass it to the next new talent on their list."

Miguel had a solid following, but he wasn't huge. He's no Henrietta Gauvón, for instance. "The venues? They're mid-sized?"

Mr. Ferrars nods. "Yes, I knew this would be your question. One or two have more than five thousand seats, but not many."

"Do you have a list of the schedule?"

He whips one out so quickly that he must have known I'd ask. I scan the list. "Luxembourg?"

"Yes, as you see."

"But no Liechtenstein."

"Why would you want to go there? It's a small speck of a place, without culture or entertainment. No one goes there. If they want music, they travel to it."

I think about the people who came to see me play at Jostli's restaurant. If I hadn't had that experience, I never would have played my songs out loud. I'd never have had the guts to play when Beneficio canceled, and I wouldn't have this record deal. "I'll do it, but only if you add a stop in Liechtenstein. I'll give you the number of the person who will set the whole thing up. He's a local business owner there and a good friend of mine."

Mr. Ferrars stares at me, hoping I'll buckle. Beth Graham would have buckled, but as a singer, I'm not Beth Graham. I'm Elizabeth Gauvón, and I get what I want. Always.

"Fine—I think I can get them to agree, but it'll have to be tacked on the end and it won't have much of a budget." He stands up. "If I sit here another second, I'll eat that stupid croissant." He leans close. "Better cut back on those. You're about to be standing on a stage in front of thousands of people."

"Why me?" I ask.

He pauses. "Excuse me?"

"Why are they offering me this chance instead of the many, many other musicians they could be asking? Did you advocate for me?"

"Of course I did." He doesn't meet my eye.

"No, they came to you," I say. "And I want to know why."

He sighs. "They ran the budget numbers. Everyone else has entourage upon entourage. You just need a piano. It's cheap. Much cheaper. If they sell half full on the venues with you, they make all their money back and a small profit."

At least it's the truth. "Thanks."

After he leaves, I catch my waiter's eye and ask for the check. I've been working on my French while I've been here recording my album and meeting with the press to promote it. It's not great, but I can ask for food and communicate with the hotel staff.

"You visiting here?" the waiter asks in English. When he hands me my check, his sky blue eyes twinkle. Boyishly charming. At home in Atlanta, I'd be swooning right now.

"Uh, sort of," I say. "I'm working here right now, but it looks like I'll be traveling for work soon."

"You have plans for tonight?" he asks.

I shake my head and prepare to turn him down. I've been asked out a few times since taking up temporary residence here, but I always say no.

"I'd love to take you to dinner," he says. "Something. . ." His nose scrunches up. "I do not know word in English. Something easy?"

"Low key?" I ask. "Casual?"

"Yes," he says. "That, yes. You practice your French, and I can practice my English."

He's so earnest, like a puppy dog, and so non-threatening that I surprise myself by saying, "Yes. Okay."

"You're staying here at the hotel?"

He knows I am, since I paid by giving him a room number. I nod.

"I can come and meet you, and then we can walk together."

"Sure." I switch to French. If I'm supposed to be practicing, I better do it. "What time are you done with work?"

"Usually by six," he says.

"Great," I say. "So I'll see you then."

On my way back to my room, the news sinks in. I'll be on tour in a week. The remains of the croissants sit in my belly like a concrete lump. I head back to my room and change into workout clothes. My attempts to exercise here have been half-hearted at best, but today I'm motivated. I push hard and manage to jog almost five miles on the hotel's treadmill. I hope I can walk tomorrow.

I shower when I get back to my room, and a song idea strikes me. I hop out of the shower and turn on my keyboard. Time slips away while I work on it. Once I have it like I want it, I decide to work on a rough line in the song I thought of last week. Some of the lyrics that didn't work on this one might improve it. A knock on the door surprises me. I thought I put the 'no service' sign up, but maybe I forgot.

I walk across the room and open it, expecting Linda's kind face.

The waiter from this morning is holding his hand in the air, like he's going to knock again. His eyes widen and then look me over from head to toe. "Uh, I, um, you—"

Thanks to the inspiration of the song that struck as I emerged from the shower, my hair air-dried into a huge halo of frizz. I have no makeup on, and I'm wearing the sweat pants and a baggy t-shirt I threw on before I started transcribing. "I thought we were going to dinner at six," I say.

He nods.

I look at my watch. Five after six.

I swallow. "I am so sorry. I got caught up working and lost track of time. If you give me a minute, I can do my hair and change clothes."

"Or maybe another night would be better." He backs up a step.

"That's fine," I say.

He takes another step backward. "Great, another night." He forces a smile and then turns and walks down the hall, disappearing around the bend.

I realize that he may have been saying another night,

but he doesn't even have my cell number. Clearly he was just trying to escape. One look at my hair in all its untamed glory, paired with my lounge around clothes and Mr. Boyishly Charming bails? And here I am, alone again. The solo act—the cheapest option in life just as I am the cheapest option professionally, because I'm always alone. I fling myself onto my bed and shove my face into a pillow and cry. Maybe I should have ignored Brekka and stayed home.

I'd be alone there too, but at least I'd have Mom and Dad to keep me company.

After a few moments, I realize what a brat I'm being. I'm here because I'm pursuing my dreams. I have no band because I wanted a small show, an intimate feeling. I've chosen this, and I caught a huge break today. Who cares if some waiter I haven't spoken fifty words to thinks I look unattractive? Not me.

But it does remind me of another guy who saw me looking far worse than this—streaked dress, makeup running down my face, hair every bit as awful as this—and he didn't care. He never looked at me like the waiter did tonight. He never made me feel small—quite the opposite in fact. His lip didn't curl, his eyes didn't widen. In fact, if anything, he looked at me with empathy, with concern, and with care. He couldn't have been attracted to me then, we'd barely met and I looked my absolute worst, but he didn't miss a beat at lending me aid.

Ah, Cole.

No waiter I meet, no accountant, no artist, no one will ever compare to you. If only you had called me, or texted.

Brekka made *me* call Mr. Ferrars.

The thought strikes my brain like lightning. She made me take that first step. Cole told me how he felt, and I never said a word about my feelings. Then I ran to his jet and disappeared. Is it possible he thinks he's being a gentleman? Does he think that he put himself out there, and I shot him down? Could he be missing me too?

Or is he glad, now that I'm not constantly underfoot, that he's rid of me? I may never know—unless I take steps to discover the truth.

My heart hammers frenetically inside my chest as I pull out my phone. I MISS YOU, I type.

That's pathetic. I delete it.

I'M IN PARIS. Nope. That's too. . . click-baity. I'm practically begging him to ask me why. Plus, it's a loaded location. The last time he kissed me, it was here, in this very city. No, I'm not ready to tell him where I am, because if he doesn't ask, if he doesn't come. . . then it's over. Dead. Done.

I realize that I've been holding out hope this entire time. If only I make it big enough, if I gather enough fans, if word of me spreads, I'll be good enough for Cole. Maybe once I'm the star who wowed him the last time we were here, he'll like me again. Maybe he'll come to one of my performances. Maybe he'll barge backstage and tell me that he loves me like I love him. I lean back against the headboard. Do I love him? Do I know him well enough to love him? Two weeks together in Liechtenstein, a few weeks of texts, a handful of phone calls, a night in Paris.

It's crazy.

But I feel something for him, something stronger than a crush. I've felt it for a while.

HEY STRANGER, I text. I hit send before I can think about it.

Now that I've sent him a text, my fingers fly over my phone screen, tapping, tapping, the words flowing almost like when I'm writing a song. YOU KNOW HOW, WHEN TOO MUCH TIME HAS PASSED, YOU HAVE NO IDEA WHAT TO SAY? SO YOU SAY NOTHING.

THEN THERE'S NO WAY TO RECOVER FROM THAT. . .

He still hasn't replied.

WELL, THAT'S WHAT HAPPENED, AND NOW I HAVE NO IDEA WHAT TO SAY, SO I THOUGHT MAYBE YOU'D BE A GENTLEMAN AND LET ME SKIP ALL THAT AND PRETEND THAT WE'VE BEEN IN TOUCH ALL ALONG.

Nothing.

No dots. No reply. Nothing at all. I stare at my phone for far, far too long. It's embarrassing, really.

I finally force myself to do my hair and put on real clothes and leave my hotel room for a sandwich so I don't stare obsessively at my phone. My hotel isn't far from the Eiffel Tower, which I've discovered a lot of residents think is tacky and touristy and awful. I mean, it was intended as a temporary structure, and when you get up close, it's just a bunch of ugly metal blocks all screwed together. It's not really a work of art when you focus on the details. Even from a few hundred feet away the rust is apparent, and the bolts and the construction lines.

But I'm a tourist, and I love it unabashedly.

So I grab a caprese panini and sit on a bench and watch people walk past until the lights on the Eiffel Tower click on. Only after the air begins to chill enough that goose bumps rise on the backs of my hands and run up my arms do I head back to the hotel. When I reach my room, I can't help myself. I race for my phone. When I see that I've received a text, my heart soars.

I'M GAME, BUT YOU NEED TO CATCH ME UP ON A FEW THINGS SO I CAN PLAY ALONG.

Butterflies chase each other around my stomach. SURE. SHOOT.

HOW IS BREKKA? HOW'S THE BABY?

DIDN'T PAISLEY TELL YOU THAT?

SHE TOLD ME THAT BREKKA HAD THE BABY AND SHE WAS IN THE NICU. HAVEN'T HEARD AN UPDATE SINCE.

I send him a photo of me holding Baby Ruth the day I left for Paris to record my album.

BEST PHOTO I'VE SEEN THIS MONTH.

ANY OTHER QUESTIONS? I ask.

ARE YOU HAPPY?

In this moment? Deliriously happy. I AM. ARE YOU?

TODAY? BETTER THAN EVER, he says.

I almost ask whether he's in Antwerp, but I worry that he'll ask me where I am. I'm not ready to go there yet. It makes everything too real, and I need to float on a cloud for a while.

When my phone starts ringing, I nearly drop it. It's Cole. I wobble back and forth for a moment, but just before it goes to voicemail, I click talk. "Hello?"

"Hello," he says. "How was your day?"

"I've had better." Right up until right now, anyway.

"Uh oh, what happened?" he asks. "Your favorite European flat iron won't work in America?"

I giggle. "I hope I would have gotten that problem resolved a long time ago—if I hadn't, I'd be wandering around frightening who knows how many people for months."

"I thought we were acting like we hadn't missed any time at all."

"No, we're just pretending that we've been talking every day."

"Ah. Well, now that I have my marching orders," Cole says, "why don't you tell me what made today lousy."

"It didn't start out so bad. I met a friend for breakfast, and after he left, the waiter asked me to dinner."

"Wow, two guys in one day. Impressive."

"For the record, the breakfast was most definitely not a

date. My friend is gay and has a very good-looking husband. Actually, I have no idea why his husband stays with him, because my friend is pretty much ridiculous—and high-strung—and sort of awful. Did I say he was my friend? I meant that we work together."

"Noted. But how did getting asked out turn bad? Did he follow you home? Stalk you?"

"He came early to pick me up," I say, editing a few details, "and I wasn't ready. He took one look at my hair and my non-made-up face and ran the other direction."

"I don't believe you."

"God's honest truth, I swear."

"Why would you accept a date with someone that stupid?" Cole asks.

"I must have been mesmerized by his dreamy blue eyes."

"A sucker for the blue eyes," he says. "I'll have to remember that."

"I like green eyes better," I say. "But those are exceptionally rare. Actually, I looked it up. They're the most uncommon color."

"You don't say."

"It's hard to find a good guy whom my hair won't scare away who also happens to have green eyes."

"I can imagine," Cole says. "Especially when you're restricting your search to Atlanta."

I want to tell him that I'm not in Atlanta. I'm in Europe, probably not far from where he's working in Antwerp. In exactly three weeks, I'll be performing there. Suddenly it hits me—he will have to see that. He may not immediately put together that Elizabeth Gauvón is Beth Graham, but if he sees posters, they feature my face.

"True," I say. "Just not enough green-eyed men in Atlanta. And it's even harder because I'm so tall. I basically need a green-eyed giraffe. Maybe I should try the zoo."

He laughs. "Probably a good idea."

"Or I could lower my standards, I suppose."

"No, don't do that." His voice is deep, serious. "Never do that. You deserve exactly what you want in life."

Mr. Ferrars calls in on the other line. I ignore him. "You do, too."

"I didn't think so for a long time," he says.

Mr. Ferrars calls again. "But now you do?"

"Do you have a call on the other line?" Cole asks.

"Yes, and I'm afraid they're going to call back over and over until I answer."

"You better take that, then," he says. "But maybe if you text me tomorrow, we won't have as much catching up to do next time."

"You didn't text me either," I say.

"You're right."

"Well, I guess now you know."

"What do I know?" he asked, his voice puzzled.

"You know that it takes me about a month to recover from wounded pride."

"We haven't talked in nearly four months." He's keeping track of how long it's been.

My heart flip-flops inside my chest. "But for most of that time, I was living in a hospital with my brother and sister-in-law."

"That's the kind of person you are," he says. "But you had a phone, I assume."

"You're saying that time still counts?"

"I might give you a pass this time," he says. "But next time, toss the pride out the window and text me."

Mr. Ferrars calls again. "Alright," I say.

"You better take that call before they come and bang your door down."

"Yeah. Okay. Good to hear your voice."

"You too," Cole says.

When I click over to see what my agent needs, a smile is plastered across my face.

"Good news," Mr. Ferrars says.

"Oh, no. Who died now?"

He huffs. "You aren't very funny."

"Really? I always thought I was at least somewhat funny. That sounds like bad news to me."

"Miss Gauvón, please pay attention. The label has agreed to add a stop in Liechtenstein, however the pay for that location will be scaled back dramatically due to limited venue size."

"Agreed," I say. "Actually, I'll be donating my share of the proceeds for that location to a local charity for kids with dyslexia."

Mr. Ferrars grumbles about the extra paperwork involved, but we finally square up the details. I go to sleep alone like always, but for the first time in many months, I'm not lonely.

⚜ 18 ⚜
COLE

"**A**re you ready?" Dad asks.

I nod my head. "As ready as I'm ever going to be."

"You can do this," Dad says.

I hope he's right. I shut off my phone—can't risk any distractions, not today. Dad and I walk toward the podium at the front of the temporary stage we built so that our people could see and hear us. We initially planned to make our plea in the government building, but far, far more citizens expressed an interest in attending than we expected.

"Thank you for coming today," Dad says into the microphone, surveying the crowd as much as he's able with his failing eyesight. "You all know that it has been my life's greatest joy to serve as your prince, with the support of my wife and children, of course."

Thousands and thousands of citizens stand shoulder to shoulder, spreading across the entire pedestrian mall and spilling into the streets. Many of them wave flags. I can't tell what's printed on them, but they're waving them with gusto.

"You may be wondering why we've asked you here

today," Dad says. "I know we merely told you that my son and I wanted to address you personally. Most of you have met me—and many of you who live locally have waved to me every day for years when I went for my morning runs. Unlike the huge monarchies spread across Europe, Liechtenstein has always been small. It wasn't until the rule of my grandfather, Francis Joseph the second, that my family moved here, but ever since then, we have been an active presence in not only the government, but also the lifestyle and everyday affairs of this fine nation."

Dad pauses until the cheering fades.

"As you all know, I married my son Cole's mother three years after he was born." He shrugs. "It was bad timing, I know."

Laughter.

"Of course, she had given birth to Cole before I met her, while she was yet married to her first husband. It was quite the scandal at the time. You may not remember, but I was quite the rascal in my youth, marrying a *widow*."

Even I laugh this time. The image of a white haired, half-blind old man as a rascal because he married my very respectable mother and adopted her child—it's ridiculous.

"I soon realized that as wonderful as my wife was, and still is, her son was every bit as amazing. It didn't take long before I felt he was *my* son. I never formally adopted him since he would not be able to take, legally speaking, much from my estate, and his own father had left him a hefty inheritance in several places across Europe."

People nod and murmur.

"That was one of the biggest mistakes I made," Dad says. "I should have adopted this boy as my son the year after I married his mother, when he first began to call me Dad." He puts a hand on my arm and squeezes. "But I am human, and I do make mistakes. More than I wish I made, but there we are."

More murmurs.

"You also know of the tragedy that struck our family ten years ago when my second son, Noel, passed away." Dad closes his eyes for a moment.

Many of the gathered citizens do the same, and nearly everyone in the crowd crosses themselves.

"I knew when he passed that no child of mine would inherit this responsibility that I have treasured, the job of ruling over you fine people. Two years after my son's death, the Landtag proposed a measure that would strip both me and any future rulers of the right to veto referenda. You all voted that down, and I felt your support and faith in me when you did. But after my son's death and my own subsequent illness, it became harder and harder for me to complete the tasks with which I had been entrusted. I tried, but I failed."

Heads shake all over.

"I didn't run past your homes and businesses anymore. I couldn't see well enough to review treaties or proposed legislation. I prepared to step down and pass the mantle of leadership to my brother Franz. You didn't know him well, as he had been living in New York at that time, but he would have done a suitable job. I still believe that he would make a capable ruler. However, my son Cole knew that stepping away from all of you would pain me, and to spare me as much pain as possible, he took over every time something overwhelmed me. You have witnessed his tireless efforts yourselves. At first he merely did as I directed, but he has grown in the past ten years, and in the past few years, he has begun changing things, for the better. He passed new education initiatives, a program for single parents to help them care for and support their children, and measures to create new roads. He has hammered out agreements with the European Union and other governing bodies, as well as other trade agreements that don't sacrifice our rights or hike our taxes to pay for their programs."

Everyone cheers again, which is promising.

"Today, I have a favor to ask of all of you. It's a large one. I only ask it because of what I believe to be a grave injustice that I need your aid to rectify. You will all recall the new constitution I created, expanding my own power relative to the Landtag. But in the same amendments, I built in a failsafe for all of you, to ensure that ultimately the power here always rests with the citizens of Liechtenstein. I'm going to ask Cole to take over from here, but I hope you'll listen to his words knowing that he has my full support. What he asks of you all today is also what I ask of you."

I step up to the podium and look over the gathered faces. Young and old, male and female, well-dressed and roughly clothed. But all of them are watching me, listening intently to learn what favor I'm here to request of them. "Hello, many of you know already that I'm Cole. A few months ago, in spite of the financial loss it caused, my dad proceeded to finalize my adoption. I am the very same person now as I was before, but for the first time in my life, I'm legally one of you—a Liechtenstein citizen."

Cheers. That's promising.

"Just as you knew my father before me, you know me. You've seen me play football alongside your brothers, friends, sons, or even for a few of you smaller audience members, your fathers. I want to talk for just a moment about the importance of legacy. My great grandfather, Francis Joseph the second, decided to relocate his family from an impressive palace in Vienna because he felt it was important that he live among the people he governed. I think the reason that he was able to make such a wise decision is that he wasn't raised with the belief that he would rule. In fact, it took two great uncles dying without children and a father who declined to accept the position before the task fell to him. But he proved more than up to doing it, which is good, because he took over when things were dire for us indeed. He transformed the economy, which was in a free fall after not one but two world wars. He brought new commerce here, and then once he found success there, he didn't stop. He chose to bring liberty to each of you as well. He was in power when the referendum was brought that finally granted women the right to vote."

Loud cheers.

"His son, Hans Adam the second, followed the path set by his father. If you knew my grandfather, you knew he was passionate in the defense of what he believed. A heart attack stole him from us too soon, but he weathered storms with grace, with strength, and with bravery. He taught my father to do the same." I clear my throat. "And my father has taught me in words and by his example to follow in their footsteps. I may not have been born to my dad, but he chose me, and I chose him. I know it may not be a popular belief, but I think that the family we choose is even more powerful than the family we are given. My dad owed me nothing, but he *chose* to take care of me. That has meaning. Every single one of you chooses your children when you turn off your phone and take them outside to kick a ball. You choose them when you put your money aside into an education fund instead of buying the latest technological gadget. You are just as familiar as I am with the power in choosing something purposefully—in sacrificing for it."

Silence. I better get to the point.

"Many of you know that I don't like to speak in public. I had trouble in my early years with learning languages, even my native Dutch. I didn't write a speech today, because reading is still a chore, and I'm likely to fumble over my words. I apologize for my failings, but that isn't the reason I was nervous to ask you for a favor. My dad told me, when he adopted me, that he wanted me to take over for him as his regent."

They're still silent, but many of them look at one another, assessing their feelings on the information.

I grab the podium so my hands won't visibly tremble. "You may have been aware that we requested the dynasts of the Princely House to consider an amendment to their House Law to allow a legally adopted child to be added to the line of succession." I swallow. "You can guess how that vote went. They told me that even if I was suitable, other adopted children might not be. Ultimately, they were uncomfortable entrusting the important position of prince to someone who was not born into the family." I close my eyes, and then reopen them. The citizens are silent, but they're listening. I can't tell whether they're upset, supportive, or dismissive. I wish I knew. "I threw in the towel then, and you may know that I took a job working for Argenta in Antwerp."

Murmurs, small ones, but murmurs. No one is scowling, and no one is booing. I'll take it as a positive sign.

"While I lived there, I discovered that I longed for home. I missed my parents, my room, my friends, the restaurants that I loved. . . and all of you. I may not be my father's biological son, but you'll never meet someone who loves Liechtenstein more than I do. Today I'm here to ask you, selfishly, to do something for me. My father and I would like to fix two glaring errors in the House Law, but we don't have the power to do it. Only you have that power."

Conversations explode all around me.

I hold up my hands. "I can see that you're confused. Let me explain. My father gave you the power—when he granted you the ability to dissolve the monarchy. I'm asking you to sign a petition that tells the Princely Family that if they don't agree to modify the law on two points, that you'll vote to dissolve the monarchy. For this to work, I need the signatures of a *lot* of you. The two points I hope you'll demand are, first that the law be amended to allow adoptive children to be included in the line of succession as though they were natural heirs. The second is even more overdue. Article thirty-one, subsection two of our Constitution grants equal rights to women, but currently they're not allowed to rule. It's wrong. For my sister, for your daughters, for every citizen here, this needs to be changed."

The applause when I finish is deafening. By the time I finish visiting with people, thanking them for their support, it's late. Much later than I expected.

"Over seven thousand signatures already," Mom says. "That's more than twice what we hoped to obtain tonight."

"We need many, many more," I say. "But it's a good start."

"Most of them are taking petitions home for their neighbors and friends to sign. I imagine in the next few days, we'll have the numbers we need."

"What if the family still refuses?" I ask. "What if they call our bluff?"

Dad shrugs. "That's up to you. You could be the first Prime Minister of a new government. They love you—that much is clear."

I swallow. "I don't think I'd pull that trigger."

"We can deal with that roadblock if it crops up," Mom says. "For now, we should get you food and some sleep."

On the short drive home, I finally turn my phone on again. An unknown number, an international number, has texted me. HEY STRANGER.

It has to be Beth. It has to be. But why is she texting me now? Could she have heard about what's going on? Is she interested because I might finally be prince again? No. That's crazy. She's in Atlanta. She can't possibly know.

Before I can even think of something to say, two more texts come through.

YOU KNOW HOW, WHEN TOO MUCH TIME HAS PASSED, YOU HAVE NO IDEA WHAT TO SAY? SO YOU SAY NOTHING. THEN THERE'S NO WAY TO RECOVER FROM THAT...

WELL, THAT'S WHAT HAPPENED, AND NOW I HAVE NO IDEA WHAT TO SAY, SO I THOUGHT MAYBE YOU'D BE A GENTLEMAN AND LET ME SKIP ALL THAT AND PRETEND THAT WE'VE BEEN IN TOUCH ALL ALONG.

Definitely Beth. I gulp.

"Cole, are you alright?" Mom asks.

I shake my head. "No, I mean yes. I'm fine."

"You look ill," she says.

I tap out a reply, determined not to overthink it. I'M GAME, BUT YOU NEED TO CATCH ME UP ON A FEW THINGS SO I CAN PLAY ALONG.

She doesn't reply immediately, and no little dots appear either. I set the phone down. "I'm fine, honestly."

"You probably need food," Dad says. "That was a very long day."

They won't give up, so I finally capitulate. I'm wiping the soup off the corners of my mouth when my phone buzzes in my pocket. "I think maybe I should head up to bed," I say. "Maybe I do feel a little bit sick."

"Can I do anything?" Mom stands up.

I wave her off. "Just a headache. I'll be fine once I've slept it off."

"If you're sure," she says.

I race up the stairs.

The text says, SURE. SHOOT.

I want to ask her everything. Is she safe? Is she happy? Has she missed me? Has she missed performing? Does she miss Europe? Liechtenstein? Did she hear that I'm fighting back, using her advice? Would Holly have told her? But I can't lead with any of that. I need to keep this casual, calm. I finally settle for asking something to which I already know the answer, thanks to Holly. HOW IS BREKKA? HOW'S THE BABY?

DIDN'T PAISLEY TELL YOU THAT?

Well, crap. Hm. SHE TOLD ME THAT BREKKA HAD THE BABY AND SHE WAS IN THE NICU. HAVEN'T HEARD AN UPDATE SINCE.

I expect the normal. *She's so cute,* or *doing great,* or maybe *I love her so much!* Instead, a photo comes through. In the past few months, one of my biggest regrets was not taking a single photo of Beth. I've closed my eyes and imagined her, standing on the stairs, playing at the Adler, sitting in front of the piano in Paris, but I haven't once seen her eyes, her hair, or her smile. And now, she casually sends me one of the most stunning photos I've ever seen. The only thing more beautiful than Beth playing piano is Beth with a tiny baby in her arms. I've never particularly thought about having a baby, but I want one now. With her. BEST PHOTO I'VE SEEN THIS MONTH.

ANY OTHER QUESTIONS?

So many. Too many. How much can I ask without scaring her away again? I wish I knew whether she was dating someone. I finally text, ARE YOU HAPPY? Maybe she'll mention a guy, or her romantic status.

I AM. ARE YOU?

After the most miserable months of my life, I'm fighting for what I want, and then Beth reaches out again, out of the blue. TODAY? I text, BETTER THAN EVER.

An overwhelming desire to hear her mellifluous voice grips me. If she's texting, why not talk? Isn't it easier? I can pick up clues from her tone, from her pauses. And I want to hear her voice again, desperately.

"Hello?"

She answered. My smile is so wide it nearly hurts my mouth. "Hello, how was your day?" Because mine was amazing. I want to tell her all about it, but I pace myself.

"I've had better."

"Uh oh, what happened?" I think about the last time she had a truly lousy day. At least, the last one I knew about. "Your favorite European flat iron won't work in America?"

Her giggle is the cutest sound I've ever heard. "I hope I would have gotten that problem resolved a long time ago."

I lean back on my bed and close my eyes. I can almost imagine she's here, next to me, in Liechtenstein instead of Atlanta. "I thought we were acting like we hadn't missed any time at all."

"No, we're just pretending that we've been talking every day."

"Ah. Well, now that I have my marching orders, why don't you tell me what made today lousy."

"It didn't start out so bad. I met a friend for breakfast, and after he left, the waiter asked me to dinner." A friend who is a guy, *and* a date.

Relief rolls over me that she doesn't have a boyfriend, but I can't quite leave the waiter and friend thing alone like I know I should. "Wow, two guys in one day. Impressive."

"For the record, the breakfast was most definitely not a date. My friend is gay and has a very good-looking husband. Actually, I have no idea why his husband stays with him, because my friend is pretty much ridiculous—and high-strung—and sort of awful. Did I say he was my friend? I meant that we work together."

So that's one down. Now for details about the waiter. "Noted. But how did getting asked out turn bad? Did he follow you home? Stalk you?"

"He came early to pick me up, and I wasn't ready. He

took one look at my hair and my non-made-up face and ran the other direction."

The man is an utter moron. "I don't believe you."

"God's honest truth, I swear."

I wish I could buy that idiot a drink. I mean, I'm sorry that Beth feels bad, but if he's too dim-witted to realize that Beth is so much more than shiny hair and startlingly large eyes, that's a win for me. "Why would you accept a date with someone that stupid?"

"I must have been mesmerized by his dreamy blue eyes."

Gross. "A sucker for the blue eyes. I'll have to remember that."

"I like green eyes better, but those are exceptionally rare. Actually, I looked it up. They're the most uncommon color."

Green eyes, like mine? Is she flirting? *Please* be flirting. "You don't say."

"It's hard to find a good guy whom my hair won't scare away who also happens to have green eyes."

She *is* flirting. She must be. "I can imagine, especially when you're restricting your search to Atlanta." Hint, hint. Atlanta sucks. Come here instead.

"True. Just not enough green-eyed men in Atlanta. And it's even harder because I'm so tall. I basically need a green-eyed giraffe. Maybe I should try the zoo."

A giraffe? I've been compared to worse things. "Probably a good idea."

"Or I could lower my standards, I suppose."

Do not accept any imposters. Do not. Hold out for me. Tell me that you want the real deal, the original green-eyed giraffe. "No, don't do that. Never do that. You deserve exactly what you want in life."

"You do, too."

"I didn't think so for a long time." I should keep things

light, but I want to tell her that I confessed to my parents. I want to tell her that she was right.

"But now you do?" She sounds distracted, and that sounded like a click.

"Do you have a call on the other line?"

"Yes, and I'm afraid they're going to call back over and over until I answer."

Probably smarter for me not to dump the heavy stuff the very first time she texts me. That would be a typical Cole mistake. "You better take that, then." I try to stop talking there, but more words just spring out. "But maybe if you text me tomorrow, we won't have as much catching up to do next time." Oh, no. That sounded attacky. Bad, Cole.

"You didn't text me either."

Because I'm a coward. "You're right."

"Well, I guess now you know."

Huh? "What do I know?"

"You know that it takes me about a month to recover from wounded pride."

A month? Did she message me and I missed it? Did it not come through? "We haven't talked in nearly four months."

"But for most of that time, I was living in a hospital with my brother and sister-in-law."

"That's the kind of person you are." And now I look like the guy who has been creepily marking the days on a calendar since we last spoke. Which is kind of true, but not very flattering. I need to make this into a joke. Light and maybe a little sarcastic. "But you had a phone, I assume."

"You're saying that time still counts?"

"I might give you a pass this time." Or anytime, about anything, forever. I swallow. Breezy, Cole. Breezy. "But next time, toss the pride out the window and text me."

"Alright," she says. Another click.

"You better take that call before they come and bang your door down."

"Yeah. Okay. Good to hear your voice."

"You too," I say.

When she hangs up, I pull up the photo she sent immediately and set it as my wallpaper. She's so beautiful. My heart aches from a mixture of joy and longing.

I cannot screw this up. Not this time.

❧ 19 ❧

BETH

Cole texts me every day, and calls me most nights. I don't confess that I'm in Europe, much less about to go on tour. He either doesn't know or he does an excellent job pretending that he doesn't know.

I can't keep any food down on the day of my first concert. "How many tickets sold?" I ask my manager, Jonathan.

He smiles. "I told you. Three thousand, two hundred. Seven hundred people requested refunds after the initial cancellation, but eight hundred and fifty more sold when we announced you would be taking the spot."

I gulp. "That means twenty-five hundred of the people here didn't really want to see me. At least, not when they bought the tickets. I straighten my blouse—er—my blousy, backless, blinged handkerchief shirt. I have no idea what to call it. "Are you sure I shouldn't wear the black dress?"

Jonathan's tone is flat. "You looked like a teacher in that. This is young and hip, and if you're sticking with the 'I perform alone to connect with each of you' gimmick, you need something to draw their attention."

"I don't really wear sequins."

Jonathan's eyes bug a little.

"But it's fine. I'm sure I'll get used to it." I lower my voice as I walk toward the backstage prepping area. "Probably."

"Good luck," he says. "I really hope this goes well."

He doesn't tell me that if I screw up, they'll replace me. But they haven't officially announced that I'll be taking the entire tour, and I can guess why not. They gave me the first two concerts to make sure I can handle it. Which means tonight is half concert—half audition. The fact that I've only really been assigned two concerts so far may also be why Cole hasn't figured out that I'm in Europe. Two performances, the first in Barcelona, the second in Madrid, isn't exactly something that would make the European papers.

"Tonight will be your hardest audience," Jonathan says, "since this is Miguel's hometown. If it doesn't go smoothly, chin up. After tonight, it'll get easier."

I didn't need the reminder. And if I truly botch this, I won't have much of a chance to do better. Ugh.

When I walk out on stage, a handful of people cheer—a few hundred, maybe. At least as many people boo. I tune it out and pretend that I'm playing at the Hotel Adler. I pick up the mic. "I'm so sorry, but I don't speak Spanish." An interpreter translates for me.

More boos. Hooray.

"I know that usually a performer, like Miguel, would start the concert with one of their huge hits. Since I don't have any of those, I thought I'd do something a little different. I was absolutely gutted when I learned that he had passed, as I'm sure many of you are right now. I'd like to thank you for coming out anyway, and for giving me a chance. I'm going to play some of my music, a lot of it actually, but I also prepared my favorite two songs of his. I'd like to begin and end with them. I can't always understand the reason why bad things happen in this world, but when

237

we lose someone like Miguel, the world is a dimmer place for it."

As the translator finishes, the boos taper off.

Now I need to do his song justice in front of his original and biggest fans. I sit at the piano bench and close my eyes. I ask for God's help in honoring Miguel and his purpose in singing. So many of his songs were about dependency, which is also what took him in the end. I play the opening notes, usually played on a guitar, to his saddest song. He talks of his childhood, his lowest lows. In his version, it's the wailing of a raw guitar, light on bass, and light on drums.

I add a new line of depth, hopeful notes, but they're subtle. When the song ends, on his fear that he won't be able to overcome his addiction, the audience stands up. They don't clap. They don't cheer or boo, they just stand up and put their hands over their hearts.

"I haven't experienced the same type of pain in my life as Miguel," I say, "but I think we've all experienced loss, fear, doubt, and frustration. I wrote this song just after I graduated high school—the week I discovered that I hadn't been accepted to Juilliard. I had failed to achieve my life-long dream. I carried around this pain for a long time, but recently I've discovered that there are many paths we can take in our climb up the mountain, many different ways to reach the top. Sometimes we don't take the path we planned, but the journey is more beautiful because of it. I'd like to thank all of you for being here, on what is a huge step for me along my path—my first solo concert."

There aren't any more boos, and when I close the concert with my final song from Miguel, one about the joy and peace he found—clearly written when he was clean—the audience stands again. This time, they clap, and clap, and clap. A standing ovation at my first concert. I breathe a sigh of relief and sit down. "It didn't occur to me that you might be such a supportive audience," I say. "I didn't prepare anything else—as you know I'm relatively new. But I did write a little song a week or so ago about second chances. It's pretty rough, but I'd be happy to play it for you guys—yours would be the very first ears to hear it, if you'd be interested?"

When I finish, they give me a second standing ovation. "I'm really out of songs this time," I say. "How about I play "Piano Man," and you can all sing along?"

They love it. I have even more fun tonight than I had at the Adler, or in Paris, and without any drama from my bio mom. Thankfully, it's more than enough to keep my label from replacing me for the tour.

Over the next few weeks, I develop a routine. I wake up, work out, text Cole, or sometimes talk to him on the phone, shower, get ready, practice or work on new songs, and then prepare for my performance. Every day a part of me hopes he'll realize that I'm Elizabeth Gauvón, and that I'm geographically close.

But he never does.

I tell myself that he's probably waiting to do some grand gesture. He's probably figured it out, and he's going to surprise me again, like he did in Paris. The week leading up to my show in Antwerp is one of the longest of my life. I read and reread every text he sends, trying to figure out whether he's coming. But he doesn't come, and I cry for an hour afterward. I don't answer the phone when he calls me the next day. Which is why, when he calls me again two hours later, while I'm on the road to Luxembourg, I answer.

I usually don't answer when I'm not alone in my room, but if I screen his call twice, he might worry that I'm upset. I am, but not for any reason that's fair. "Hey," I say.

"You have the day off?" he asks.

"What?"

"Aren't you usually busy cutting and dyeing hair right now?"

Dangit. "Why did you call if you thought I was busy?"

"I had some good news," he says. "I figured I'd leave you a message asking you to call me back, since you didn't answer earlier."

"What's your good news?" I ask, just as my merchandising manager asks me in German, "Did Jonathan order more shirts? We're nearly out. If his contact can't get them done fast enough, I have a guy. He'd give us a good price."

"What was that?" Cole asks.

"What was what?" I wave my merchandising manager off.

But it's too late. "Shirts? Ordering shirts?"

Up until now, I have never lied to him. To get out of this, I'll have to lie. "It's a long story." I wince. "I better go. I'll call you tomorrow for sure. Okay?"

"Sure," he says.

After he hangs up, I think of four or five decent explanations. Maybe I've been practicing my German with someone at the salon, and one of those people was asking about salon shirts. Or maybe I'm at a store, and maybe one of the employees was speaking in German. But all of them sound pretty flimsy. Which means I might have just given him the key to figuring out my secret. And if he does figure it out and I didn't tell him, then what? Will he be mad? Will he think I've been lying to him? After all, a lie of omission is still a lie.

Why have I been lying?

Because I wanted him to pursue me. I wanted him to demand to know where I am, or offer to fly out to Atlanta, or, I don't know. Do something. . . big. I'm a bigger diva than I realized. And I wanted him to want me before he found out that I'm becoming successful.

At the end of the day, I didn't tell him because I want him to want *Beth*, not Elizabeth.

Oh, well. No way to stop him if he decides to investigate why he heard someone speaking German in the background. The tour has been wildly successful so far, which is a huge blessing, but it also means it's at the top of most Google searches for anyone who makes half an effort. I walk to the front of the bus. "Hey, Jonathan, Harris wants to know if you ordered the shirts."

He rolls his eyes. "I'm good at my job. Of course I did."

"Just checking. Hey, what's the tart thing you said is amazing in Luxembourg? I'm going to need about three of those tonight."

"Rough day already?" he asks.

I shrug. "Not my best."

"They only make quetschentaart in the fall, when plums are in season. It's made with damson plums, and the top has a crunchy sugar." He closes his eyes. "No matter what happened, two of these will fix it."

The more I think about it, the more I worry that I blew it. Maybe I should call Cole and explain. Maybe I should text an explanation, so he has to at least read it. How mad will he be? Especially when he realizes I was actually *in* Antwerp and never even told him. . . Although, I guess I don't *know* that he took that job his buddy was holding. He never said that, specifically. He just talks about being busy with work a lot.

Jonathan stops the tour bus at his favorite bakery and buys a whole box of the plum tarts, and he's right. They are almost enough to calm me down. But by the time we reach the hotel, I'm antsy again. I don't want to sit around, obsessing over my phone. Since we have the night off—my concert here isn't until tomorrow—I decide to go for a walk. I grab a jacket I picked up in Rome, my very favorite jacket ever, and head out to get a look around Luxembourg.

Since I have nothing else to do, I walk for a long time. I figure I have two plum tarts to work off.

When a song pops up in my head, a good one maybe, about secrets, I decide to head back. When I don't write them down quickly, sometimes I lose them. I'm so preoccupied that I walk past the lobby of my hotel and have to circle back. Embarrassing. I almost have the entire melodic line hammered down by the time I reach the elevators. They bing and I step in, thinking of ideas for the second verse. I wait and wait—which I've become accustomed to by now. Some European elevators are slower than taking the stairs. Even if I crawled up them on my hands and knees. Finally the doors ding and open. I step forward and nearly run into someone who was clearly waiting to enter. I throw my hands out to keep from falling and strong hands catch me.

When I look up, my gaze locks on the most gorgeous green eyes I've ever seen. The color of freshly cut St. Augustine grass. The color of the purest emeralds ever mined. "I was worried you could see me from the peephole on your room and weren't answering." Cole beams at me.

"What—what are you doing here?" I swallow, but my throat still feels like I blow-dried it with a round brush.

"I think that's a question I could be asking you." Cole hasn't released my forearms, and the heat in his hands radiates up my arms, even through the sleeves of my leather jacket.

"I'm on tour," I say.

"You never mentioned that to me," he says.

"I thought you might come, when I performed in Antwerp." My voice is soft, almost apologetic. I shouldn't have to apologize. Anger pulses through me. He never even asked. He just assumed I was still in Atlanta. "But you never asked me—and I never lied." I lift my chin.

"I love when you get feisty."

I can't breathe. I can't blink. I can't move, or this dream will shatter. I'll go back to always being alone.

"Last time I tried this, your mother screwed it up."

Henrietta is not my mother, but I don't interrupt him, not right now.

His head lowers toward mine slowly, and his arms finally release their hold on me to wrap around my waist. "You have no idea how good this feels, to be near you again." His lips find mine then, firm, insistent, unyielding.

Every single thing I remembered.

And so much more.

He kisses me until I forget what I'm wearing. He kisses me until I forget why I'm here. I forget where we are at all.

Until the elevator bings. "Oh, excuse me," a man says.

A familiar voice.

"Elizabeth?"

I stiffen in Cole's arms. He stands up straight, his arms loosening enough that I can spin around. "Hey, Jonathan." I meet Cole's eyes. "Jonathan is my tour manager, and Jonathan, this is Cole." Uh. Cole with nine names that I can't remember. "Of Liechtenstein."

"Beth's boyfriend." Cole's voice rumbles behind me, deep and possessive, like he's claiming his territory.

I love it. I smile and say, "Yes, my boyfriend."

"You were upset earlier." Jonathan is a pretty big guy, and he doesn't back down at Cole's clear demarcation of our relationship. "Didn't have anything to do with this guy, did it?"

I laugh. "I thought he wasn't going to be here this weekend. But he surprised me."

Jonathan nods. "Alright then. You know where to reach me if you need anything." He heads down the hall and ducks into his room.

"My boyfriend?" I arch one eyebrow.

"I'm sorry," Cole says. "I don't know why I said that. He

seemed so. . . proprietary when he looked at you. Is that the right word?"

"You and I talk every day," I say. "And you're a green-eyed, gorgeous giraffe."

The smile steals across his face slowly. "That I am."

"I might be okay with being your girlfriend. I mean, how much would really change from how we already interact?"

"Well." His voice is low again, rough. "I can think of a few things." His eyes move to my mouth.

My heart hammers in my chest.

"How would you feel about discussing details over dinner?"

"This would be our first date?" I ask.

"I guess it would." His head dips toward mine.

"Would there be kissing on this date?"

His eyes smolder. "Oh, I hope so."

I go up on my tiptoes until our lips are nearly touching. "Alright."

We find some decent fish stew, and then we find a bakery and I introduce him to the plum tarts. And there is definitely more kissing. All in all, a perfect first date. Cole walks me back to my room and when I open the door, he braces his arm against the frame. "I should go. You have a show tomorrow and you need your sleep."

"I do," I say. "But I don't want you to leave yet."

He touches my nose with his index finger. "Then that means I did this right."

"I'm sorry I didn't tell you," I say softly.

"You didn't want to see me?"

"I wanted you to figure out that I was in Europe," I say. "And I wanted you not to figure it out."

His eyebrows draw together. "I speak three languages, but I don't imagine that what you said would make more sense in German or Dutch than it does in English."

I laugh. "Pretty sure the language I'm speaking right now is 'girl.' I have a hard enough time making sense of it most days, but I think I wanted you to *do* something, to make an effort. That's the part of me that hoped you'd figure it out."

"I tried," he protests. "I asked you to stay, I practically begged you to date me."

"But I didn't have a chance to agree to that," I say. "And months later, when I was finally free to do as I chose again, you hadn't texted or called me in months."

"I was trying to give you space," he says.

"I thought maybe you didn't want me unless I was *somebody*," I whisper. "And I desperately wanted you to want Beth Graham, not Elizabeth Gauvón. That's the part of me that didn't want you to figure it out."

He steps inside the door and wraps both arms around me. He pulls me tightly and whispers against my ear. "I've been starstruck by you since the first time I heard you play, but you've been *someone to me* a lot longer than that. You could walk away from your career in music today and I wouldn't mind, as long as that decision made you happy. I've seen you on stage, and you're alive in a different way than when you're eating dinner with friends. I thought you needed that in your life and were turning away from fear."

"I was never afraid I'd fail," I say.

Cole leans back to meet my eye. "I know that, silly."

"What fear, then?"

"Fear that you'd turn into your mother."

I inhale sharply. I never even realized that was my fear, not until this very moment, but somehow he knew. That is what held me back.

"You never needed to worry about that," he says.

"How can you possibly know that?"

"Your mother might have turned out better if she had better parents. She may have endured tough breaks, or hard

245

relationships, I don't know. But I know that there's no world in which your mother would have chosen *not* to go to Juilliard because her family needed her."

He might be right. "I've learned since then that there are a multitude of ways to reach for your dreams, and if a roadblock arises, you should simply locate another path."

Cole beams at me. "You're nothing like Henrietta. You're so much better. You inspired me too, honestly."

I lift my eyebrows. "How?"

"I talked to my dad and mom." He releases me and steps backward, leaning against the doorframe again. "You were right. They forgave me for helping Noel."

A weight I didn't realize I was carrying lifts from my heart. "I'm so relieved. I wondered whether that was bad advice. I knew what my parents would do, but I don't know yours very well."

"Yet." Cole's sideways grin gets me every time. "And that wasn't even the only good advice you gave me," he says. "I also decided to fight for my country."

I swallow. "You didn't."

He nods. "We've had a few rallies, and collected nearly thirty thousand signatures from the citizens, which is close to eighty-five percent of the adults."

"I'm so proud of you."

"We have no idea whether it will work, mind you," he says. "But at least I didn't give up without trying every single thing that I could."

"When will you know?"

"The family is gathering to vote again on Monday morning."

"And you'll tell them that if they don't sign, the people will vote to dissolve the monarchy?"

He nods. "Even so."

"Will you really do it?"

Cole leans his head against the doorframe, his face

pained. "I want to—I'm almost angry enough. But I think that Franz would be a decent ruler, and there's more consistency in a monarch than there is with a democracy where the leadership is always changing. I believe that's one of the reasons that tiny little Liechtenstein has done so well. So, no. If it comes to that, I won't. But the family needs to believe that I will."

"I'm off for two days—Monday and Tuesday. I could come, if you want me there."

Cole straightens and takes my hand in his. "Actually, I wanted to ask. I have an idea of a way that you might be able to help. But first, I need to know something."

"What?"

"This vote matters to me," he says. "A lot. I've always wished this could be my future and never thought it was even an option. But the more I think about it, even with as close as I am to finally getting what I've longed for, something has bothered me."

"Okay," I say.

"You."

"What?" Me? What do I have to do with this?

"You matter more to me than ruling Liechtenstein. My entire life, I've always thought that the palace didn't feel *quite* like home because I wasn't Dad's son. When he adopted me, I expected that to go away. I've been thinking about this a lot, and I've realized that for me, home is where I feel safe. It's where I feel heard. It's where I know that the person I'm with is looking out for my best interests, and I've only felt that in one place in my entire life. Only once have I ever felt completely at home."

"Where?" I ask.

"It's not really a where," he says. "It's more of a 'with whom.'"

"It is?"

He nods slowly. "When I'm texting you, when I'm

talking to you, and especially when I'm with you, I'm finally home. So I need to know, would you ever consider living in Liechtenstein?"

"I—"

"I'm not proposing. I'm aware this is our first real date. But if you don't think you could ever leave Atlanta for more than a tour, then I'm going to shred the petitions. I'll look for a job in the USA, and I promise you that I'll never blame you for it. Because more important than being prince, more important than being in the place where I grew up, is being with the woman I love."

My breath catches in my throat. My entire body tingles. "I love you too, Cole. And I don't care where we live. When I went back to Atlanta, it didn't feel like home to me either, not anymore. I think maybe my compass reset, because my new true North is you, too."

When he kisses me this time, I never want to let him go.

20

COLE

When Beth walks down the curved staircase in the palace, she takes my breath away. After she reaches my side, once my brain starts to work again, I realize she's wearing a suit that she could have borrowed from my mother.

"I promise not to ever provide input on what you wear, ever again," I say. "But this one time, can I ask you to change into something else?"

She lifts one eyebrow.

"Remember my plan?" I ask.

She nods.

"It might be more. . . effective if you dressed for the part."

"What exactly would that look like?"

"Well, that handkerchief sparkle thing you wore to the concert sends a clear message."

"The one that's backless?" she asks. "The one I pair with leather pants? That one?"

I shrug. "You could wear normal jeans with it."

She laughs. "It's your event. I'm happy to wear whatever your serene highness needs."

"Say that again." I yank her closer and kiss her firmly. This thing between us is new enough that I still marvel every time she leans in for a kiss. My life felt imbalanced until I met her. It's new and exciting, and it's familiar and comfortable all at once.

"I'll go change," she says.

By the time Mom and Dad are ready, Beth's coming down the stairs again in tight, dark jeans and the American flag sequin handkerchief shirt. When I saw her wearing that in Luxembourg, I nearly lost the ability to think straight. Mom's mouth drops open when she sees her, and when I glance back at Dad, even he's squinting.

"Is your shirt lighting up?" he asks.

Beth laughs. "Your son told me to wear this. It's one of the tops I wear for concerts. You can take up any objections you may have with him."

Mom turns toward me. "Why—"

"You'll see," I say.

To my surprise, neither Mom nor Dad argue. They simply load up in my Range Rover. "Your sister is going to have her baby any day," Mom says. "So while I hope this goes well, either way, I'm headed for America. Soon."

"I understand, Mom. And if it goes badly, I might be following you over."

Beth reaches across the dash and puts her hand on my leg. "I doubt it."

This time I don't arrive early. I don't schmooze anyone. I walk through the door, Beth at my side, and march to the front of the room. I tap the microphone. "I'd like to thank you all for coming to Vaduz a second time. I know that none of you want to be here, so I'll get right to the point. I asked nicely the last time you were here, for you to get on board and fix two of the injustices in the House Law. You refused."

I glance back at Beth, who's standing just behind me. She shoots me a thumbs up.

"I'm here today with the support of over thirty thousand of the Liechtenstein citizens, all of whom have promised to dissolve the monarchy if you refuse to make these changes. Should they do that, your responsibility for governing them will be removed from your hands. And if you want to challenge me on this, go ahead. I'll dissolve the monarchy and serve as Prime Minister for as long as the people will have me. And as soon as they won't, well. My sister already lives in Atlanta, and my girlfriend is from there. I have a wealth of options yawning before me, as you can see, but you'll all have to figure out how to move in society without the prince in front of your names."

I step backward and take Beth's hand in mine.

"So I'm the wild American girl who has stolen your heart?" She cocks one eyebrow.

"It's true enough," I say.

"I'm pretty sure you delivered that heart to me of your own accord," she says. "And it certainly had nothing to do with my wild, rock star ways."

"I meant it, you know."

"You'll really move to Atlanta," she says. "I know you would, but I don't think it'll come to that."

"You sound disappointed." I glance down at her face.

"Well." Her voice is wistful. "I will miss baseball games and hotdogs."

I laugh. "Private jet. There's no reason for you to miss anything for very long, if you agree to live over here near me."

More quickly than I think is possible, it's time for my dad to count the votes. Adrian, the Prime Minister, steps in to help, since Dad can't really see.

"For someone who doesn't care what happens, you're sure holding my hand tightly," Beth says.

I scowl at her, because she's right.

"We've tallied all the votes," Adrian says. "And I'm pleased to announce that all but two dynasts have voted to amend the House Law."

I swing Beth around in a circle and kiss her on her gorgeous mouth. A press conference and a lot of mingling and congratulations later, we finally climb back into my Range Rover.

"Strange question," Beth says.

"Anything," I say.

"I haven't noticed any salons in town. Do you know how stiff the competiton here is?"

I laugh. I like her line of thought. "I have a barber. I can ask him."

"Why is that so funny?"

"You've been performing for audiences of thousands and you want to know whether you can find a job here cutting hair."

She quirks one eyebrow. "Who said anything about a job? I've got money now, sir. I'm thinking about what my future with you will look like," she says. "And there might be some performing, *and* a salon, or a chain of salons, in it."

"Well, when you put it like that. . ." I pull over on the side of the road, glad that Roger took my parents home, and kiss her until she has a few other ideas of what our future will entail. Because thanks to her, everything I always hoped for is coming true. "I think that whatever future you envision is probably within your grasp. Just make sure that I'm a part of it."

Because a future with her is the only future I want.

21

BETH

The tour is so much harder to endure now, because it means not being with Cole every day. That wasn't an option before, but now that it is, I yearn for it. He comes to as many performances as he can, but he can't make it to all of them. Besides, it's not quite the same to know he's sitting in the midst of a few thousand other people as it is to have dinner and talk to the person I love most in all the world.

Even so, I love meeting new fans. I love singing. I love connecting with them and conveying my emotions through the keys of a piano. I'm constantly surprised by how many fans have traveled to see me perform again, on the same tour in a new place.

I'm still glad when the tour bus pulls into our very last stop—Vaduz. Jonathan gets out and stretches. "Your one stipulation for this tour was that we play here?" His nose scrunches and his eyes reflect disbelief.

"Um, my boyfriend is the Regent—a hereditary prince of Liechtenstein."

"Yeah, yeah, the ruler of all the sheep we passed, and almost fifty people, too."

I swat his arm. Making fun of Cole is one of his favorite pastimes, mostly because Cole intimidates him. "Go start working out the details. We don't have much time."

When I turn, Jostli's sprinting across the pedestrian mall toward me. "Beth Graham!" he shouts. He barely avoids running me over, and I'm genuinely worried for a few seconds that he'll crush me with his broad shoulders and beefy arms, but it's nice to be welcomed. It's nice to belong somewhere.

"I'm happy to be back," I say.

"Today is the last day of your tour?" He lifts his eyebrows.

"Don't even ask me about playing anything or anywhere else right now," I say. "I'm exhausted."

"You didn't say not to ask you next week," he says. "I hope you'll still be here."

I chuckle. "Me too."

"Our prince is a very wise man. He will not let you go."

The next few hours fly past, and too soon, it's time for me to change clothes. After performing for a few thousand people a night, I assume the eighteen hundred that have purchased tickets here will feel small. When I walk up onto the stage they've built for me, I'm surprised to see an instrument I recognize.

I turn back and look down the stairs to where Cole is waiting in a makeshift backstage area.

"That's your Grand Fazioli Brunei! You moved it out here just for this?"

"It's a concert piano that's never been used for a concert. It seemed an obvious call."

I glance up at the open sky. "What if it rains?"

He laughs. "It was either that, or Jostli's piano from the Adler."

"Oh, fine." I walk across the stage to the microphone and pick it up. "I can't tell you how honored I am to be here, in Vaduz, the first place I ever played my own songs in front of anyone other than my mom's cat. I haven't been here long, but I have a deep and abiding love of the people of Liechtenstein."

I have to pause until the applause dies down.

"As you all know, the funds from this tour will go to pay for my boyfriend's dyslexia program. I want to thank you all sincerely for making that possible as well."

More cheers.

"I'm inspired in my music by so many things, but I wanted to start tonight with a song I wrote right here, about the beauty of the Alps, the majesty of your town, and the welcoming smiles of the townsfolk." I sit down and set the microphone in the stand. My fingers settle over the keys and I begin to play.

But instead of the mellow sounds that should emerge from the Fazioli, it plinks. Plink. Plink. Plonk.

My eyes widen with horror, and I lean toward the microphone stand. "Small technical issue." I stand up and look back over my shoulder, hoping one of my useless crew members will come up and try to help me. After all, I can't communicate with the fans if I'm digging around inside the piano case.

Not a single soul moves toward me. I'm totally alone up here, looking like a total amateur. I duck under the cover and look around. It's immediately obvious what's causing the problem. I grab the mic and then reach for the box that's jammed inside. "I think during transit, somehow, something was stuck. Once I remove it, hopefully. . ."

The box is small, really small, but even so, the piano technician should have noticed it was there. What kind of idiot— When I straighten up, Cole is on stage, down on one knee.

The audience goes wild.

"I know that technically I'm cutting into your time

here," he says into a second microphone, clearly addressing the audience. "But I was hoping you could help me with something."

More cheering.

"This beautiful woman in front of me captivated me from the very first day I laid eyes on her."

I shake my head, my eyes welling with tears. "He's a liar —I looked absolutely hideous."

"Do you believe a single word of that?" he asks the audience.

Shouts and screams of 'no' and 'no way' make my boyfriend smile. "It's total nonsense. She's always been a stunner. When we met, she had just gotten some bad news. But Beth, she just keeps on going in the face of setbacks, disappointments, and even emergencies that would knock the rest of us down. I've seen her find the good in every situation time after time, and it was her idea that I come to you to help me convince the family to amend the House Law."

So much cheering. A few audience members scream, "We love you, Cole!"

He rolls his eyes. "But Beth has been a little hard to pin down. As you're about to discover, she's a mega star. She may not think I'm quite good enough for her. So when I ask her a special question, I need you to help me convince her to say yes."

The audience cheers and he shakes his head and shushes them. "Did you hear me?" he whispers into the mic. "I need your help. . . when I say! Not right now."

They all laugh.

He finally turns toward me. "I was told I had to do this on one knee, you know, from Holly. She says that's what they do in America." He stands up. "But I also heard that you're looking for a man who is really tall." He steps toward me. "And if I'm kneeling, how will you know whether I qualify?"

I laugh. "A fair point."

"And also, I don't want to kneel before you, and I don't want you to kneel before me. I want to walk through this world for as many days as I'm lucky enough to have, with you by my side. Elizabeth Ruth Graham, please tell me that you'll marry me."

Silence.

Cole turns toward the audience and waves his hands. They go wild.

Once they finally quiet down, I lift my microphone. "Don't I get a look at the ring first?"

So much laugher.

He yanks the box out of my hand and opens it. "It's a family heirloom."

"So you're saying you didn't even pick this out yourself?" I scrunch up my nose. "It's a hand-me-down?"

"She's so American." Cole turns toward the audience again. "Maybe I should rethink this."

"Marry me, Cole!" a lady on the third row shouts.

I laugh. "I can't change where I was born."

"But you can choose where to live now that you're all grown up," Cole says. "Pick here. Pick me. Pick us." He waves his hand at the audience again and they cheer even louder.

I sigh. "You know, we Americans *do* recycle, so I guess this is okay."

I pull the simple solitaire from the box. It's the biggest diamond I've ever seen in my entire life. I slide it on my finger smoothly—a perfect fit. Now it's my turn to tease the audience. "If I can't play well tonight, you should blame him. This ridiculously large old rock is going to weigh my hand down something fierce."

More laughter.

"So that's a yes?" Cole reaches for my hand.

"Well, you didn't pick me something new, and the stone is criminally large, but I love you so much, your serene highness, that I'll marry you anyway."

I kiss him then, and he dips me. "You don't really hate the ring, do you?" he whispers against my ear.

"I love it," I say. "Almost as much as I love you."

He beams at me.

This part, I stage whisper into the microphone. "Now get off my stage so I can put on a show for these amazing people."

The second he does, I miss him. But that's okay—I'll have a lifetime to stand by his side.

22

COLE

I've been in awe of Beth's talent since the very first time I heard her play, but watching my people singing her songs, swaying along with her, my heart is full. Nothing can bring Noel back, but the hole carved out of my heart when he passed away doesn't ache as much anymore. In some ways, I feel like maybe he sent me this gift of healing—a woman with the same talents that he possessed to fill in the broken parts of our family.

After the concert finally ends, Beth signs posters and shirts and scraps of paper for what feels like hours. Even with all of today's excitement, my eyes keep drifting closed, but not Beth. She's still smiling, chatting, and signing. And smiling, chatting, and signing. The stage has been broken down and the chairs and other decorations stowed away by the time the last fan steps toward her. I exhale softly, delighted that this wonderful night is finally almost over.

After all, it's not like I've been able to celebrate with my fiancée properly.

My phone buzzes in my pocket. Who in the world would message me at one-thirty in the morning? I blink to clear my bleary eyes.

MOM'S NOT ANSWERING, BUT MY WATER JUST BROKE.

My heart accelerates. Holly isn't due to have her baby for nine more days. Mom and Dad were planning to fly to the United States for their first ever trip to visit Holly and James in Atlanta three days from now.

I'M HEADING HOME—BETH HAD A CONCERT HERE IN VADUZ. I PROPOSED, AND SHE SAID YES.

BIG DAY FOR OUR FAMILY!

MOM AND DAD AND I WILL GET ON A JET RIGHT NOW.

Heart eye emojis.

BE SAFE. AND IF POSSIBLE, HOLD THAT BABY IN FOR A FEW EXTRA HOURS. DO. NOT. PUSH.

ARE YOU KIDDING?

NOT REALLY! DON'T YOU WANT YOUR MOM AND BROTHER THERE?

I WANT THIS BABY OUT, she texts. AND I WANT TO KNOW WHETHER IT'S A BOY OR GIRL. WAITING WAS STUPID. IF WE EVER HAVE ANOTHER ONE, I AM NOT LETTING JAMES TALK ME INTO THIS.

"I'm so sorry that took so long." Beth's arms reach around my waist, and her head tucks up against my chest.

My heart swells. "I would wait a lot longer than that for you." I slide my phone into my pocket. "But as it happens, it's good that you kept me up this late."

"It is?" She yawns.

I yawn too, of course. "Holly just sent me a message."

Beth's eyes widen and her arms drop. She blinks. "And?"

"I'm about to be an uncle."

The smile rolls over her entire face. She claps her hands. "Oh my goodness! Are we leaving right now? Will we get

260

there in time? You have no idea, I know, but can we go? This is so exciting!"

I can't help laughing. "We better hurry back to the palace and wake Mom and Dad. I am guessing they'll want to come with us."

"Tell them to throw their stuff in a bag, like, right now!"

I jog toward my Range Rover. "That's the idea."

My mom is just as excited as Beth, but my parents move quite a bit slower. Beth falls asleep in the front seat of the car, waiting for my parents. We don't wake her up, so she gets a forty-minute nap on the way to our jet.

"How long is this flight?" she asks.

"You tell us," my mom says. "You've made it the most recently, I think."

Beth yawns again, setting off another chain reaction. "Oh, right. I was so worried the last time, I didn't even notice how long it was."

I take Beth's hand and squeeze. "It's just over nine hours, which means you can get a pretty decent nap on the way."

Even though she's been on the jet once before, it's still a delight to watch her face when we board our family's jet. She oohs and ahhs over every little thing. The seats, the size, the view, the snacks, the upholstery on the chairs.

"It's a pretty standard private jet," I say. "The Grand Duke of Luxembourg spent far more than we did."

"Ah, well, if it's more modest than the Grand Duke's," Beth says. "Then I'll stop being impressed immediately. Is he single, did you mention?"

I roll my eyes.

After downing two Shirley Temples and a cheese plate, Beth finally conks out. Once she's asleep, I fall asleep too. I wake up as we're preparing to land and shake Beth gently. It's sunrise in Atlanta, and Beth twines her fingers between mine while we watch it together.

"If you told me last year that I'd find my mom, and be engaged to the man of my dreams, and move to Europe, all in less than nine months, I would never have believed it."

I scrunch my nose up. "I'm glad you're fine with moving, and I'm delighted to hear that I'm the man of your dreams, but I thought you said that Henrietta isn't your mom."

She shakes her head. "She's not. But the strange thing about being adopted is that I never really considered my mom to *be* my mom. Not a hundred percent, anyway. I always figured that somewhere, someone was the exact same as me, and she had to give me up, but she was longing to know me."

"Really?"

She smiles. "The combination of watching Brekka and Rob and sweet Baby Ruth, and meeting my own bio mother has taught me that being a mother doesn't mean that your child is just like you. It doesn't mean you'll always agree either, but it does mean that you'll always stand with or behind them, as they need, and that you'll give your entire life to shape them into the person they need to become. My mom has always done that, so in a way, this trip has helped me to *find my mom*, because it helped me appreciate what I already had."

"So maybe the biggest threat to our own joy is unrealistic expectations," I say.

"Yes, but I also think it's a lack of gratitude. If we're content with what we have, we don't have to always be longing for something else."

My fiancée is so smart.

The second the jet lands, we climb off, and luckily, there's a car waiting for us. We rush to the hospital, the sleek black sedan pulling around the front just as my phone bings. And Mom's phone bings. And Dad's.

"Oh no," Mom says. "We're too late."

I shift my phone so that Beth can see. "Holly and James had a little girl. They're naming her Greta."

"We're not too late," I say. "We're right on time. With family, what matters is that you do the best that you can, and you make time for them. That's what Holly and Greta will always remember."

When the nurses let us back to Holly's room, Mom immediately claims baby Greta, sighing with contentment.

"James and Paisley," Beth says. "She is just absolutely gorgeous! I am so happy for both of you!"

"And I hear that congratulations are in order for you too," Holly says.

"Today is your day," Beth says. "We can talk about us later."

"Oh, pish," Holly says. "I want details. Where and when and what colors will you use?" Only Holly would move on to planning a wedding three seconds after bringing new life into the world.

She and Beth start discussing details and by the time we head for Beth's house to drop her at her parents, they've worked out most of the big issues. Spring wedding, in Liechtenstein, and between Trig's, Brekka's, James', and our family's private jets, everyone Beth cares about should able to come to the ceremony without worrying about cost.

"And for the primary color," Beth says, "I was thinking a bright, grassy green."

"That won't be easy." Mom frowns. "No flowers are green."

"Lots of big, shiny green foliage—that's all green. And maybe coral and white accents," Beth says. "But bright green has always been my favorite."

"What were you thinking about the dress?" my mom asks.

After being deprived of having Holly's dress custom made, she's sure to pressure Beth. "Mom, that's for Beth and her mom to figure out," I say.

"I have no idea," Beth says. "I'm sure I'd love your input —but keep in mind that I'll be on a much tighter budget than you might be accustomed to following."

My mom's eyes light up. "We would just *love* to contribute to the wedding in any way we can. Perhaps the gown could be part of our engagement present. There's a designer in Florence whom I simply adore—"

"Mom." I shake my head.

Beth rests her hand on my hand. "I would be delighted to meet with a designer. Can my mom come along?"

That's the last time I try to insert myself into any part of the planning. Mostly, I just express my support and excitement that it's all coming together. But Mom, she has the time of her life. She and Beth and Beth's mother make a weekend of it in Florence. They're still gushing about the majesty of the David when they return.

"I had no idea it would be so tall," Beth's mom says. "I mean, the base alone was taller than me."

"It's quite an experience," Mom agrees. "And I'm so happy that we found the perfect dress."

"Oh." Beth spins around. "So am I."

I grab Beth and pull her close. "Welcome home." I kiss her squarely on the mouth. "What does it look like?" I murmur.

Her mother throws a kitchen towel at me. I expect my mother to be horrified, but she only laughs. "You can't ask about the dress," my mom says. "It's supposed to be a surprise."

It feels like it takes years before the wedding day finally arrives, but eventually, a year to the day after I first met Beth, it's time. Mom has outdone herself with the wedding bower, which features every white and coral flower grown within a hundred miles of us, and an abundance of ivy and shiny green leaves all woven together. I'm standing just under the bower, my hands clasped in front of me, but I can't quite keep from tapping my foot.

Even now that we're finally here, I'm impatient to be married to the woman of my dreams.

But, after what seems like a million years, the wedding march begins on the family's Fazioli behind the bower. I eagerly eye the aisle. Holly walks down first in a bright green sheath dress with a little pillbox cap on her head. Beth's sisters, Jennifer and Christine, follow behind her, wearing the same dress and hat as Holly. Beth's friends Kate and Lauren walk behind the sisters, wearing the exact same dress and hat, but in coral. And finally, Brekka wheels her way down the aisle in the same exact dress and hat, but in white. Geo follows behind her, also in white.

But where is Beth? My eyes scan the seated crowd, a little nervous.

I'm about to ask the priest if he has any idea what's going on when Rob begins his way down the aisle, pushing a stroller in front of him. What in the world? The music finally stops. Has Beth had second thoughts?

Someone taps my shoulder, and I spin around.

Just behind the bower was the piano, and I didn't even think to turn around and see who was playing. Of course it's my Beth. She's wearing a silk gown that hugs her every curve from shoulder to hip in the brightest white, but at the top, running down from the bodice all the way around, are deep black streaks. They start out large and taper downward, inconsistent in size and width, as though they were painted on the silk. I've never seen anything quite like it.

Beth reaches out and takes the microphone that's

waiting for the priest. "Could you translate into German for me?" she whispers in my ear.

I nod and grab the other microphone from the stand meant for us to make our vows.

"This might not be common for a wedding, but we're not a normal match." She glances from one side to the next. "A prince marrying a hair dresser." Her laughter rings out like the most harmonious bells. "Talk about a fairy tale, but it didn't start out that way. Both Cole and I had a bumpier start in life. He lost his father when he was very young, and I never had parents who were willing to sacrifice in the ways necessary to raise a child."

Beth looks from my parents on the right to hers on the left as I translate.

"But both of us were lucky enough to have a mother and father who loved us deeply," she continues, "parents who were devoted to our education, our development, and our future. Even so, as I grew, I always wondered about where I came from. So when I had the chance to learn more about my biological mother, I took it. It was a mistake for me to hope and dream about someone else when I had such a wonderful family, but it was that foolishness that led me here. I like to think that maybe God knew what he was doing."

Chuckles.

"If my biological mother hadn't been such a selfish flake, I wouldn't have been stranded in Frankfurt that fateful day—a day on which I felt cursed. And if my flat iron hadn't melted from the European current, I might not have had a breakdown, necessitating Cole stepping in to save me. I also might have looked nice—instead of having mascara running down my face and staining the top of my dress—and a halo of frizzy hair that nearly reached the ceiling."

I translate, but this time I add my own commentary. "I should insert here that, in spite of the unfortunate circumstances leading up to our meeting, Beth captivated me from that very first day."

She blushes. "But that's because Cole is less worried about appearances and more worried about the hearts of the people around him. I knew it then, and it has been confirmed to me every day since. And so, to honor the way in which we came together, I want to be married in a gown that represents the beauty in things going wrong. These dark streaks represent the day we met, and how our past has brought us to where we are. Our missteps, our rabbit holes, our mistaken or misguided purpose, they have all helped to write the story of Cole and Beth, a story that I cherish with all my heart."

The priest steps toward me.

"And now I'll relinquish this to you, gladly." She hands him the microphone.

The rest of the ceremony is fairly standard, except the translation moves the other way around, into English from German. "Do you, Elizabeth Ruth Graham, take this man, Cole Michael Alois of Liechtenstein, to be your wedded husband, as long as you both shall live?"

"I do," Beth says. "Always and forever."

"And do you, Cole Michael Alois of Liechtenstein, take this woman, Elizabeth Ruth Graham, to be your wife, as long as you both shall live?"

"With joy, I do," I say.

"Then I now pronounce you man and wife," the priest says.

"Don't you mean *prince* and wife?" Beth asks.

The English speakers laugh.

"Do I get a kiss now?" I ask.

"Yes," Beth says. "Take it already!"

But I don't just lean down and kiss her. No, nothing so boring will do for my vivacious bride. I yank her against me, pivot and dip her, and only then do I press my mouth to hers. Her eyes are wide open when we kiss, as are mine. We may not be perfect, and we may be as different as can be, but we're also alike in every way that matters, and we're going into this marriage knowing exactly what we're getting into.

When we stand back up and turn to face our American and Liechtensteiner guests, they're all equally joyful. "Well, Mrs. Cole Michael Alois of Liechtenstein, how do you feel?" I ask.

Her eyes shimmer with tears. "Like I'm glad that I used waterproof mascara this morning, your serene highness."

I snort.

"And like I'm very glad to be home next to you at last."

***

I've decided (thanks to many many emails and posts on my fb page) to continue the series with at least one more book. Finding Peace, Ethan's story, will be out no later than March 15, 2021. I am really hoping to get it out this fall, but I have no idea what the next few months will look like. Since I don't want to overbook, I'm putting it on preorder for March 2021, and I'll try and aim for much earlier. If you don't want to miss it, you can preorder it now here.

If you'd like a FREE book to read in the meantime, you can sign up for my newsletter on my website at www. BridgetEBakerwrites.com! I'll send you an ebook copy of Already Gone, a standalone YA romantic suspense.

I am also including the first chapter of my YA post

apocalyptic novel, Marked. It features a prevalent romantic subplot! Read on to check it out.

Finally, if you enjoyed reading *Finding Home,* please, please, please leave me a review on Amazon!!!! It makes a tremendous difference when you do. Thanks in advance!

23

BONUS: SAMPLE CHAPTER OF
MARKED

I'm a big fat coward.

I've known this about myself definitively since one month before my sixth birthday. The night I lost my dad.

Case in point: I'm just shy of seventeen. I've been in love with the same guy for almost three years. Even though I see Wesley a few times a week, I haven't said a word. But tonight I have the perfect opportunity to do what I've always feared to try. Tonight, to celebrate our upcoming Path selections, all the teens in Port Gibson play a stupid, risky game.

Spin the Bottle.

I glance around as I walk toward the campfire in front of me. Only thirty-five kids turned seventeen in the past year, so of course I know them all. My best girl friend, Gemette, waves me over. I try to squash my disappointment at not seeing Wesley. When I played this scene in my brain earlier, I was sitting by him.

"You gonna scowl at the fire all night, Ruby?" Gemette pats a gloved hand on the slab of granite underneath her.

"You couldn't have saved us one of those seats?" I point

at the smooth, flat stumps on the other side of the fire. I sit down and shift around, trying to find a flat spot.

"I think what you meant to say was, 'Thanks, Gemette. You're the best.'"

Her straight black hair reflects the campfire flames when she tosses it back over her shoulder. It's against the Council's rules for hair to cover your forehead. Gotta make it easy to see anyone who might be Marked. Except tonight, no one's following the rules. Everyone's wearing their hair down, and Gemette's silky locks frame her face beautifully. I envy her sleek hair almost as much as I covet her curves.

"My bum's already hurting on this," I mutter.

"If you weighed more than eighty-five pounds soaking wet, it wouldn't bother you so much."

Instead of curves, I've got twig arms and a non-existent backside. I shift on the huge slab, trying to find a position that doesn't hurt. I arch one eyebrow, not that she can see it in the dark. "I weigh ninety-two pounds, thank you very much."

Gemette snorts. "That proves my point, you bony butt."

She leans toward the fire and picks up the glass bottle lying on its side. She tosses it a few inches up into the air before catching it again.

"Be careful with that." That bottle's the only reason I'm sitting here, sour-faced, stomach churning.

Slowly the remaining seats around the fire fill up. Wesley shows up last. There aren't any seats left, but before I can convince Gemette to squish over, he grabs a bucket. He turns it upside down and takes a seat a few feet away from everyone else. I guess that's fitting. His dad's the Mayor of Port Gibson and a Counsellor on the Centi-Council, so Wesley's in charge by default tonight. He'll probably take over for his dad one day, which isn't as glamorous as it sounds since less than two thousand people live here.

He looks around the fire, and his gaze stops on me. He bobs his head in my direction, and I shoot him a smile. I'm glad he can't hear the thundering of my heart.

Although we're all huddled around a campfire, and I've known most of the kids here for years, we maintain carefully measured space between us. Tercera dictates our habits even when we're rebelling. Which we're only doing because it's a tradition.

Maybe Tercera's made cowards of us all.

"Are we starting?" Tom's sitting to my left. His parents are both in Agriculture and he's Pathing there, too. He has broad shoulders and tan skin from working outside most of the day. Gemette likes him, and it's easy to see why. Of course, he's nothing to Wesley.

I glance across the fire in time to see Wesley stand up. He straightens the collar of his coat slowly and methodically, like his dad always does before a town hall meeting. Wesley loves doing impressions, and he's usually convincingly good at them.

"I'd like to take this opportunity to welcome you all to the Last Supper." His voice mimics his father's, and he touches his chin with his right hand in the same way his dad always rubs his beard. Wesley himself is tall and lean with long black hair that he's wearing down, for once. It falls in his eyes in a way I've never seen before, and I feel a little rush. I want to touch it.

Wesley smirks. "I know you may be less than impressed with the culinary offerings for our gathering, but as I always say, Tradition has Value." He cracks a grin then, and everyone laughs. "Seriously though." He drops the impression and returns to his normal voice, which I like way better anyway. "I know the food sucks, but this whole thing started with a bunch of teenagers who were sick of rules and ready to throw caution to the wind for a night."

I look down at the three or four-dozen nondescript metal cans with the tops peeled back, resting on coals. Another few dozen are open but sitting away from the fire. Presumably they contain fruit or something else we won't want to eat hot.

Wesley leans over and snags the first can, his gloves keeping him safe from the heat. "I hope you'll all forgive me, but this was what we could find."

"This is a pretty crummy tradition." Lina reaches down and grabs a can with mittened hands. Her dark brown hair falls in a long, thick braid down her back, like it has every single time I've seen her.

"Traditions matter, even the silly ones. They help pull us together as a community, which is valuable when fear of Tercera yanks communities apart. We're stronger when we aren't alone. Thinking every man should look out for himself hurts all of us." Wesley takes his first bite right before Lina. I grab a can of baked beans.

The food really is as bad as it looks, but at least it's not spoiled.

Wesley talks while we eat.

"As you already know, we come from a variety of backgrounds. Before the Marking, Port Gibson housed approximately the same number of people, but not a single person who lived here before the Marking survived. We cleaned out the homes, burned some to the ground and rebuilt, circled the city with a wall, and made it our own. The Unmarked who live here are Christian, Muslim, atheist, black, white, Hispanic, Russian, German and Japanese. I could keep going, but I don't need to. Before the Marking, these differences divided humanity. Now, we know that what truly matters is what we all share. We embrace the traditions that bring us all together, because we're more alike than we are unalike."

I swallow the last spoonful of baked beans from my can and set it down on the ground by my feet. I'm almost the last one to finish eating, but several half-full cans are scattered around the campfire. A few people grab a can of fruit. I prefer the stuff my Aunt and I process and can ourselves, so I don't bother.

I rub my hands together briskly. Even in mittens, my fingers feel stiff. It's usually not too cold in Mississippi, even in January, but a late freeze has everyone bundled up. The Last Supper's supposed to be a chance to rebel, but I'm grateful that everyone's as covered as possible. It means I won't look as cowardly for keeping my mittens on. My aunt is Port Gibson's head of the Science Path, so I know all about how Tercera congregates first in the skin cells, even before the Mark has shown up on the forehead in some cases.

The wind moans as it blows through the trees, and we all huddle around the meager fire. Even though the flames have died down to coals in most places, it burns hot. My face roasts while my back freezes. The bottle lies stationary on the weathered flagstones by the fire where Gemette set it, light glinting off of the dingy glass at strange angles.

The quiet conversations die off and the nervous laughter ends. Eyes dart to and fro among the thirty something teenagers gathered.

"So." Evan's voice cracks, and he clears his throat. "Who goes first?"

"Thanks for volunteering," Wesley says.

I suspect no one else asked for just this reason. All eyes turn toward poor, gangly, redheaded Evan.

Evan gawks momentarily. Even though he and I work in Sanitation together, I don't know him well. I haven't been there long enough to guess whether he feels lucky or put upon. He sighs, and then leans forward and tweaks the bottle. It twists sharp and fast and skitters to the right, spinning furiously.

I really hope the bottle doesn't stop on me, and I doubt I'm alone in that thought. Evan's funny in a self-deprecating way, but he isn't smart, and he definitely isn't hot. I bite my lip, worried about what I'll do if it does stop on me.

It slows quickly and finally stops pointing to my left. I sigh in relief, which I belatedly hope no one heard.

Tom gasps, and then in a raspy voice says, "No way. I mean, you're nice and all Evan, but I'm not . . . I don't . . ."

"Yeah, me either. Chill, man." Evan laughs. "So, does it pass to the next person over?" Evan raises his eyebrows and glances at me.

I want to protest, but my throat closes off and I look down at my feet instead.

Evan stands up. "So Ruby . . ."

He may not have saved me a seat, but Wesley jumps in to save me now, thank goodness. "That's not how it works. If you get someone of the same gender, and neither of you . . . well, then your turn passes to him or her. Which means you sit down Evan, and you spin next, Tom."

"Who made these rules?" Evan grumbles as he sits.

Gemette smiles. "They make sense, Evan. I mean, it's not spin the bottle and pick best out of three. Your way, you'd basically pick someone in the circle who's close and kiss whoever you want."

Evan shrugs and glances at me again with a smile. "Sounds pretty okay, actually."

Tom snorts. "I don't hear Ruby complaining about Wesley's rules. I'd say that's your answer, man."

I look back down at my shoes, but not before I see Tom's wink. Jerk. Evan must feel idiotic, and I definitely want to sink into the ground.

I bite my lip again, this time a little harder. Tom's an

obviously good-looking guy, but I have no interest in kissing him. I hope his wink was a joke about Evan and not some kind of message.

Cold air blows past me as Tom leans forward to spin the bottle, his body no longer blocking the wind. One thing jumps out at me as he reaches for the glass bottle. In spite of the cold, Tom isn't wearing gloves. He must've taken them off at some point. He's either a daredevil or an idiot. I'm not sure which.

Tom spins the bottle less forcefully than Evan and rocks back and forth as the bottle circles round and round. His eyes focus intently on the spinning glass as if he can somehow control where it stops. I wonder who he's hoping for and look around the circle for clues. Andrea seems particularly bright-eyed. My eyes continue to wander. One gorgeous, deep blue pair of eyes in the circle stares right back at me. Wesley. I've looked at him a lot over the past few years, but this feels different somehow. A spark zooms through me, and I quickly stare at my feet.

No luck for Andrea tonight, or Gemette. The bottle comes to rest on Andrea's best friend, Annelise, instead. She and I were in Science together a long time ago. Her dark brown hair hangs loose, framing high cheekbones and expressive chocolate eyes. She frowns. Tonight doesn't seem to be going right for anyone so far.

"Now what?" Annelise's voice shakes. "We just kiss, right here in front of everyone?"

"No, of course not," Gemette snaps.

"Who made you the boss?" Evan frowns. Judging by his sulky tone, he's still mad about losing his turn earlier.

"Unfortunately, I'm the boss," Wesley says, "and she's right." He points to a dilapidated shed at the top of the hill. "You two go up there."

"Romantic." Tom rolls his eyes as he stands up. He rubs his bare palms on his pants. Gross. At least I know I'm not the only nervous one here. Tom and Annelise trudge a path through clumps of frozen brown grass toward the rundown tool shed.

What a special memory for their first kiss.

Gemette sighs and I pat her gloved hand with my own. I'd feel worse for her, but Gemette likes every decent looking guy in town, including a few boys a year younger than us. She'll recover from missing out on a special moment with Tom.

I glance again toward Andrea, an acquaintance from my time in Agriculture. She and Tom trained together for years. She may have liked him as long as I've liked Wesley. She looks into the fire while her foot digs a messy hole in the soil. I wonder how I'll feel if Wesley spins and gets Andrea. Or worse, Gemette. I'll have to sit here and twiddle my thumbs while I know he's in there kissing a friend. My stomach lurches. Coming tonight was a stupid idea. I clearly didn't think this through.

No one speaks to distract me from my anxiety. The shed isn't far. We could easily eavesdrop on them if the wind would shriek a little less.

"How long does this take?" Evan asks.

"Who the heck knows?" Gemette points at the bottle. "Impatient for another crack at it?"

Kids around us chuckle.

After another few awkward moments, Gemette grabs the bottle and gives it a twist. "No reason we have to wait on them."

"Sure," Wesley says. "Whoever it lands on can go next."

"Wait," Evan asks, "whoever it lands on goes next as in it's their turn to spin? Or goes next as in Gemette's going to kiss them?"

The bottle stops before anyone can respond, pointing directly at Wesley. His perfectly shaped brows draw together under disheveled black hair. Gorgeous hair. His lips form a perfect "o". His bright blue eyes meet mine again.

My heart races and the baked beans sit like a lump in my belly. I shouldn't have come. Of course Wesley will want to kiss her. Gemette's gorgeous, curvy, and smart. Ugh. Am I going to have to sit here while my best friend kisses the guy I like twenty feet away? This is all my fault. If I'd only told Gemette, she'd beg off.

I bite down a little harder on my lip and taste blood this time. I really need to kick this particular habit, especially with kissing in my future. Maybe. Hopefully. I'm such an idiot.

Wesley clears his throat. "I think I'm going to sit this game out. I'm more of a moderator than a participant."

"No," I blurt out. "You can't. You're here, you're seventeen, you have to participate." What am I doing? Why am I shoving him at my friend? But if I don't make him play, I'm flushing my chance to kiss him down the toilet. I want to cry.

"Well, then I guess it's my turn to spin." His deep voice sounds completely different than any of the other kids here tonight. My stomach ties in knots when I hear him speak, which is ridiculous because I've heard his voice a million times.

I glance at Gemette. She looks disappointed and I want to cry with relief, but I don't blame her. He could've kissed her but didn't pursue it. I imagine most any girl here would be disappointed. He glances up and his eyes lock with mine again. Caught. I start to shiver and try to stop it. This look is different somehow from any before, like something shifted. Wesley clears his throat, looks down at the bottle, gracefully reaches over, and snaps it between his fingers.

It spins evenly, not moving to the right or the left. It spins on and on, and I wonder if it'll ever stop. It slows, whirling a little less with each rotation, the butterflies in my stomach swooping and swirling with each pass.

Until it finally stops. On me.

My eyes snap up reflexively, wide with shock. Wesley doesn't even seem surprised. He simply stands and inclines his head toward the shed.

"Isn't it still..." I clear my throat. "Umm, occupied?"

"We can wait over there." He gestures at the hill to the right of the shed. One side of his mouth lifts in a smile and I feel an answering grin form on my lips. Which makes me think about what we're about to do with our lips.

Swarms and swarms of butterflies flutter in my chest.

"Sure," I say.

I stand up and without even thinking, I wipe my palms on my jeans. They aren't even sweaty and what's more, I'm wearing mittens! I really hope no one noticed. Okay, more specifically, I hope Wesley didn't notice. Gemette holds something out to me when I stand. I can't tell what it is from feel alone thanks to my thick mittens, and in the dark I have to squint to make it out at all. A tube of something. "What—"

"Lip gloss," she whispers. "A gift from my mom. I was going to use it, but looks like you need it more, you lucky, lip-biting brat." She winks.

I'm glad Wesley's still across the fire from me and that it's dark. Maybe he somehow miraculously missed both the palm wipe and her wink.

I walk as slowly as I can toward the old shed, partially to avoid tripping, but also so I won't look overeager. I try to hide my face while I apply the fruit-scented lip-gloss so that Wesley won't notice. It's dark, but I don't want him to be put off by dry, scratchy lips, or worse, dried blood. Gemette's a good friend. I feel guilty for overreacting earlier when I thought she might kiss Wesley. Not super guilty, but you know, a little.

Neither of us speaks a word, but I feel the eyes of the other teens follow us toward the shed. We're only a few crunching steps away when the swinging door flies open and Tom and Annelise barrel out. I jump when it bangs shut behind them.

Tom looks as ruffled as I feel, his eyes darting back and forth. He ducks his head and reaches down to take Annelise's hand. They walk out and away from the fire and the rest of Port Gibson's teens. I can't tell where they're headed, but somewhere far away from here.

"Did you know almost a third of the couples in town trace their start to the Last Supper?" Wesley asks.

"No way."

He shrugs. "We've only been an Unmarked town for seven years, so it's even more impressive. Not all of them are matched up from a bottle spin, but I think the game helps people realize how they feel."

A thrill rushes through me. Does Wesley feel the same as me?

My hand reaches for the door handle and collides en route with his. I'm wearing mittens, of course, and he's wearing shiny, brown gloves, but a thrill runs through me when we touch, even through layers. He doesn't move his hand away, but instead draws my hand in his and pushes the door handle back in one fluid movement. My heart skips a beat and time stops. When the door's completely open, he slowly releases my hand. I lower my eyes and step over the threshold into the rundown little building.

Although there's clearly no power, and consequently neither heat nor an overhead light, the walls at least cut the wind. It's at once both warmer and quieter. Two tall candles burn softly on a pile of rusted metal boxes in the corner. Someone prepared this dump, I realize. I wonder whether it was Wesley. The flames provide enough light that I can see his face. His dark brows are an even more startling contrast to his dark blue eyes than usual, accentuated by his hair falling in his face.

"So," I say. "Here we are."

Wesley looks at me from less than a foot away. The shed's small and crammed full of moldering farm implements. The air around us practically hums, but that isn't new. It's always like the moments right before a lightning storm when he's near. Supercharged almost, like the electrons around my body might fly off at his slightest touch. The difference is that here, away from the town's work projects, away from my family and his, it feels like anything really could happen.

Wesley's so close I can smell him, the same citrusy, woodsy smell I've secretly savored for years. It's even stronger tonight, like he put on more of whatever it is he usually wears. I breathe deep, and all the memories of him re-imprint on my brain. Scrubbing, sanding, painting, digging, cleaning, hammering. Projects his dad made him attend, but I suffered through to be near him. When I'm with him, I belong somewhere for the first time in a decade.

When we become adults next week, Wesley's mandatory attendance at work projects ends. Wesley steps into his role as an administrator, and I'll become part of Port Gibson's janitorial crew. It's now or never if I want to make any kind of permanent place with Wesley.

I never thought I'd be close to him like this, and I know I may never be again. I lean toward him and tilt my face upward, eyes closed, ready for what comes next. Maybe I'm even a touch impatient. I have waited for this for years.

Except I keep waiting, and then I wait some more.

Not a single thing happens. The trouble with being ridiculously small is that Wesley, who's on the tall side anyway, towers over me. Even with my face angled up, his lips are pretty far away. I can barely make out his expression, but it looks guarded.

Maybe he doesn't know how to do it?

No way. Wesley must know. I mean, it's not hard, right? You just push your lips onto the other person's mouth. Why isn't he doing anything? This is the moment. THE moment!

Until it passes. And then another moment falls on top of it, and another. All passing. Even the butterflies in my stomach get bored and go look for flowers elsewhere.

I'm not sure exactly how much time has elapsed, but the seconds drag, heavy with my growing frustration. Soon, someone will bang on the door. "You've been in there forever," they'll say. "Make room for the next couple."

I want to smack them in their eager faces.

I know I don't have much time, and I want to say something, anything. I need to tell him how I feel, say the words, take a gamble. But like it always does, my tongue shuts down. My throat closes off. The words stick inside my throat. Why am I such a coward? Our perfect moment withers and dies. Tears well up in my eyes, and I can't breathe.

Wesley isn't similarly affected. He steps back and says, "We don't have to do this, Ruby. It's not safe at all. I don't know why my dad even lets these dinners happen."

"Why'd you spin the bottle in the first place?" I hear the desperation in my voice, but the words pour out in spite of myself. "I know you, and you know me. How's it dangerous for us?"

He takes another step back, his expression registering surprise. "People get Marked, Ruby. It still happens. Every few weeks, in fact. Maybe I'm Marked. You don't know. It happens, even here, even with all our rules. It may take years to die once you're Marked, but it's inevitable."

I roll my eyes. "Well I'm not Marked, if that's what you're worried about." I point at my forehead. "See? Clear."

"We shouldn't be taking these risks." Wesley scowls. "Not now, not right before our real lives begin. This whole thing's supposed to be a time to say goodbye to being a kid, not act like an idiotic five-year-old, breaking rules for no reason."

Our real lives? Maybe he never thought it felt right, the time we spent, the way we are together. Maybe I never belonged with him at all. "Why'd you even come, then? Why follow me in here if you're not going to kiss me?"

Was he hoping for someone else? Was he stuck with me and looking for any excuse to bolt? Am I Evan in this scenario?

I look up, but I'm too close. The hair cascading over his face obscures my view. I want to touch his hair; I want to kiss him; I want to tell him I love him, and that I always have. My fingers and toes and everything connecting them zings in spite of the bitter cold, in spite of the indifference of his words. Energy spins round and round in my body, a closed circuit with nowhere to go.

"Look, Ruby, I don't know what to say . . . but the thing is . . ." He sounds torn, confused.

Suddenly, I don't want to hear "the thing," whatever it is. I've been talking to Wesley for years, talking and talking, and working alongside him, but I don't want to talk to him anymore. I know what I want and I'll never have a better chance to play things off as part of a game, if he feels like I now suspect he does. The notion of an excuse appeals to my cowardly heart. I can't speak the words, but I won't stand here and do nothing, not anymore, because he's the real life I've longed for.

I stop thinking and step toward him instead. He tries to step back and slams up against the back wall. I quickly take one more step and use my gloved hand to pull his head down to mine. I push my lips against his. In my haste, I push too hard and pull a little too fast. Our teeth smack into each other and my tooth knocks against my own lip, splitting it wide open again.

It's the opposite of magical.

I look up at Wesley instinctively. He has blood on his mouth, but whether it's his, or mine, I can't tell. And if it's not awful enough already, Wesley stiffens from head to toe like I mauled him, like I forced him into something torturous.

A tear rolls down my cheek and I inhale deeply. I won't cry over this. I can't, because there's no way I can play it all off as a game if I bawl my eyes out. I turn away from him. If I can't stop the tears, at least he doesn't need to see them. When did this go so wrong? I should be calm, cool, in control. I need to laugh it all off and tell him friends can't be expected to kiss well. Whoops.

Except my heart won't listen to the screaming from my head. I'm not calm. I'm the opposite of cool. I've lost all control.

He grabs my shoulder and tugs me around. I turn, but my eyes stay glued to the ground, too ashamed to meet his gaze.

"Ruby, look at me."

He puts two gloved fingers under my chin and lifts. His head comes down then, but slowly, too slowly. My heart stops pumping and I worry it might never beat again. His lips brush mine gently, then with more pressure. I ignore the discomfort of my torn lip and lean into him, connected to him in a way I can't explain. I need more air, but I want less, because that means more space between us. If this never ends, maybe it'll erase the moments that preceded it.

Suddenly, he lets me go and steps back. Emptiness fills the space where he stood. I reel again, sucking air in and blowing my breath back out to steady myself.

When I raise my eyes, our gazes lock. All my sorrow from before is gone, replaced with a feeling like I'm flying, soaring, floating on top of the world. His sapphire blue eyes reflect candlelight back at me. He's breathing as deeply as I am; he's as affected as me. I can't look away from his strong, almost hawkish nose, his square jaw, his flashing eyes and thick black lashes. I continue to stare as Wesley reaches up and brushes his unkempt hair away from his eyes.

I almost faint.

Such a simple movement. Small in the grand scheme of things, but also vast, earth shattering, all encompassing. My dreams crumble. My world spins out of control. He moves his hair off his forehead, and suddenly things make sense. His reticence to touch me, his skittishness, but also his quick recovery. Once he knew it was too late, he didn't hesitate to kiss me.

Because we'd already touched.

A tiny rash mars his otherwise perfect forehead. Before the world died, it wouldn't have mattered. Before the Marking, no one would have cared about a few bumps. It would be harmless: acne, a bug bite, or a reaction to hair product. It shouldn't matter that his forehead has a blemish. It shouldn't terrify me, but it does. Because that small rash means Wesley is Marked, and in under three years, he's going to die terribly.

And now, so am I.

G rab the full ebook of Marked here!

ACKNOWLEDGMENTS

First and foremost, as always, I have to thank my husband. He has been unfailingly supportive from the very beginning, and he continues to be exactly the same. (Or possibly, honestly, MORE supportive.)

My kids are right behind him in their excitement and genuine desire to help. And my parents have been extremely helpful on this book (and all of them, really) to lend a hand or have the kids come visit so that I can get the words down on the screen! All my love to my family.

I would like to take this opportunity NOT to thank my horses, as they definitely split my focus between writing and riding... :P

And my fans—you guys are EVERYTHING to me. Your kind comments on fb ads, your emails, your reviews, they make my day, my week, and sometimes even my month.

My advance team readers—you guys are THE BEST. I love you so much!!

My editor Carrie Harris—you are the hyphen queen. Thank you for making me look smarter than I really am.

ABOUT THE AUTHOR

Bridget loves her husband (every day) and all five of her kids (most days). She's a lawyer, but does as little legal work as possible. She has two goofy horses, two scrappy cats, and one bouncy dog. She hates Oxford commas, but she uses them to try and keep fans from complaining. She makes cookies waaaaay too often and believes they should be their own food group. To keep from blowing up like a puffer fish, she kick boxes every day. So if you don't like her books, her kids, her pets, or her cookies, maybe don't tell her in person.

Made in the USA
Columbia, SC
26 June 2020

11659747R00178